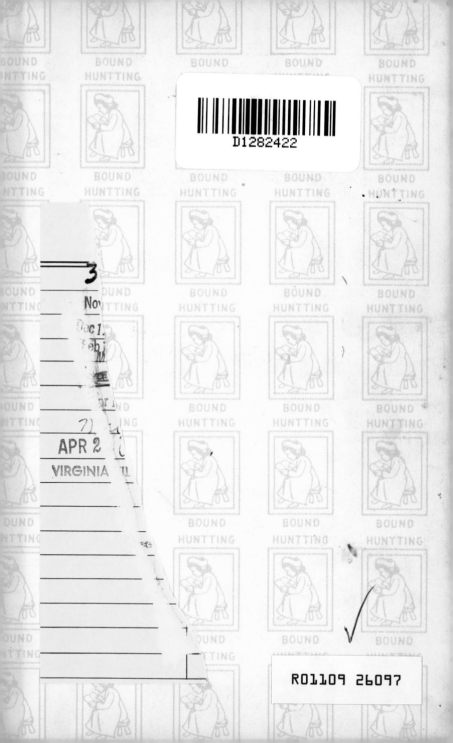

FORT CARIBOU

LAKE CARIBOU

MUSKEG

PORTAGE
TRAIL

RAPIDS

SPRUCE
SWAMP

WOLF JAW
RIVER

PE-TAH-BO'S CAMP

BLA

ISLAND

N

ADVENTURE NORTH

ADVENTURE NORTH

Books by Kathrene Pinkerton

WILDERNESS WIFE
THREE'S A CREW
ADVENTURE NORTH
TWO ENDS TO OUR SHOESTRING
FOX ISLAND

ADVENTURE NORTH

BY KATHRENE PINKERTON

**ILLUSTRATED BY
STEPHEN J. VOORHIES**

HARCOURT, BRACE & CO., NEW YORK

jp653ad

Designed by Hilda Scott

PRINTED IN THE UNITED STATES OF AMERICA

CONTENTS

CONTENTS

ADVENTURE NORTH

1 FAR LAKE

Ann wakened early. She knew it was very early because birds had begun their dawn twittering and daylight shone dully through the tent. It was cold, too, and she pulled the blankets to her ears and squirmed into the hollow her body had made in the thick bed of balsam boughs.

She was dropping off to sleep when the noise which must have awakened her was repeated. It sounded as though someone had poured a bucket of water into the lake. She sat up and could not see anyone. The lake was only a few yards down the slope, but the noise came from behind a clump of willows.

Ann had more courage than most girls of four-teen. In this, her first week in the Ontario wilder-ness, she had not been frightened by the great empty stretches of forest and the remoteness of Far Lake. But now, despite an effort to keep calm, the prickles started up her spine and she could feel her heart thump.

Philip, her younger brother who shared the tent, was curled up in his blankets. Philip was eleven and he slept like a puppy or a kitten. Ann always said that if he had a tail he'd curl it over his face. He'd be no help in danger. Mr. and Mrs. Jackman slept in another tent across the campfire, but they had not awakened.

Ann believed the intruder was an Indian because no one except Indians lived in the country. Their only white neighbor, Alan Gillespie, manager of the Hudson's Bay post, was many miles away. Ann had never seen him nor had she seen an Indian. In the week in which the Jackmans had camped beside Far Lake they had not seen anyone.

Now the emptiness of the land made an early morning prowler the more terrifying and Ann was sure he could only intend harm. She remembered

too that their canoe was beached behind that same
clump of willows and she feared an Indian might be
stealing it. Already she knew the importance of a
canoe in the northern wilderness where all travel
must be on lakes and rivers. There were no roads
and without a craft the Jackmans would be helpless.

Her father should be wakened at once. Ann
threw back the blankets, reached for her shoepacs
and pulled on one. The oil-tanned leather was stiff
and cold and she looked for her woolen socks. But
Ann's whirlwind fashion of undressing had left her
clothes scattered, and suddenly a new sound came
from behind the willows.

This time it was a heavy splashing. Ripples
circled into view. Ann heard a grunt and a long
sigh. No man had made such a sound. Only a large
animal could have breath enough, and then Ann
thought of bears.

While the Jackmans had been making preparations to live in the north woods, Ann and Philip
had talked endlessly about the strange new life in
store for them. They had eagerly demanded just
how soon they could see their first bear and their
first Indian. Now Ann didn't want to see either, at
least not in early morning while her family was

asleep. She wasn't even sure she cared to leave the shelter of the tent and call her father.

At this moment an enormous pair of antlers appeared in the water beyond the willows. From the antlers trailed long streamers of grass and roots and beneath was a long black head. The nose was something like that of a horse but much longer. Ann knew instantly that it was not a bear for bears don't have antlers. The head turned shoreward and she saw a second head beside it.

The two beasts swam to shallow water and began to wade. Then Ann saw high-humped shoulders and knew they were moose. She'd seen pictures of them, but she had thought of moose as land creatures. Now she remembered her father had told her that in summer they dived for lily pad roots and did the greater part of their feeding in lakes. Their enormously long legs and short necks made it impossible for them to get their heads to the ground to crop grass.

The two moose came toward her like a pair of harnessed horses. As they emerged from the lake, water dripping from their bodies left the hair black and shining. They were the largest animals Ann had ever seen. Although the lake was down a slope, when the moose stood on shore their heads were higher than Ann's where she crouched in her blankets.

They were not aware of the camp and walked straight toward her. As Ann watched these huge creatures, she had the feeling they could walk right through the tent and over Philip and herself and never know they had done so.

A cry came from Ann's lips. It wasn't loud, but it was all she could manage. One moose must have heard it, for he stopped and moved his head, searching for the sound. The other took a few more steps toward Ann. She drew in her breath for a scream, but the moose halted, thrust out his long black nose and sniffed. She could see an uneasy look in his eyes and remembered her father had said forest creatures were much more afraid of people than the people were of them.

It seemed impossible that this great animal could be frightened by a girl of fourteen. The moose's shoulders were far taller than a man. The lifted head was still higher. The antlers were broad and flat and branched into many small sharp prongs.

As the moose stood, tense and sniffing, Ann began to believe he was frightened. The thought made her suddenly feel very brave. She even dared to peer out and study the creature.

Evidently he got a whiff of something he didn't

like for he turned back to the lake. He and his companion didn't hurry. Their slow walk was almost dignified, but they didn't stop or look back when they disappeared past the willows.

Ann sank back and pulled the blankets to her chin. She admitted to herself that she had been frightened, but now that the moose were gone she thought of the thrilling story she'd have to tell her family.

But when the family wakened a little later, no one would believe Ann. Her father listened, and then laughed. Philip laughed too, although he'd been all ears before.

"Huh!" he jeered. "If any moose'd come that near, I'd have heard 'em."

Ann knew Philip's remark was pure envy because she'd been the first to see a moose. Philip even hated to admit she was three years older.

Mrs. Jackman heard the laughter and called from her tent to ask what had happened.

"Ann's been seeing things again," her father said.

Ann's stories of things she saw and heard were a family joke.

"But, Mother!" Ann protested. "I really saw two moose. One stood near that tree and looked at the camp."

14

"Sure you weren't dreaming?" Mrs. Jackman asked.

"I don't care if you people won't believe me," Ann retorted. "Dad says there are moose in this country. Why couldn't I see two of them?"

"You'll have to be careful of your stories in the woods, Ann," her father said. "It's too easy to prove you're wrong."

Mr. Jackman had started the breakfast fire, and as he carried kettles to the lake, Ann wondered what he meant. She hoped he would see the moose at the head of the bay. Then Philip Jackman would have to stop his snickering.

Her father returned and set down the kettles.

"Come here, Philip," he said. "You too, Mary," he added to his wife. "Got something to show you."

He led the way to the lake. Halfway down the slope he pointed to imprints in the soft earth.

"Biggest moose tracks I ever saw," he said. "And look!"

He walked to the birch tree where, Ann had said, the larger of the two bulls was standing. Deep hoofprints proved her story.

In the past Ann had sometimes stretched facts a bit. She liked to make a story sound exciting. This morning she had been tempted to say the

15

moose had come right up to the tent. Now she was glad she had not added any dramatic details.

"Fifteen feet from camp," Mr. Jackman said. "And not half an hour ago."

Philip had stopped jeering. He was finding the early morning visit of the moose exciting even though he had not been awake to see them. But Mr. Jackman's face was grave.

"That moose was too close," he said.

"Was Ann in danger?" Mrs. Jackman asked quickly.

"Not any more than the rest of us," he said. "Everyone tells stories, but I've never heard proof. Old woodsmen won't camp on a moose trail in the fall. I'm sure a moose wouldn't attack. But if he were frightened, or lost his head, or started through a camp for any reason, it would be a good deal like being run over by a steam engine."

Mrs. Jackman turned a little pale and impulsively threw an arm around Ann's shoulders. Philip gave up his attempt to measure the tracks with a handspread. Ann began to feel a little like a heroine until her father added:

"I don't want to frighten you, and I don't want you to have a false sense of safety. A wounded or frightened moose could be dangerous. Hardly a chance that Ann or Philip will find themselves so

16

close to one again. But if they did, I'd like them to know enough to shout or wave something—let the moose know they were there while he could still run away without getting into a panic."

"Gee!" Philip said. "And Ann just sat and looked at him!"

"Which was rather brave of Ann," her father said. "A bull moose is something to see. Seven or more feet high at the shoulders, with that powerful body and great spread of antlers! Wasn't it fine, Ann, that you could see two of the grand old boys so close?"

2 OJIBWA HOUSEKEEPING

The Jackmans had been in camp at Far Lake only a week when Ann saw the moose, and everything about the wilderness was still new and strange. Ann and Philip had spent their lives in the small town of Bradford, where the family lived while Mr. Jackman was in the Forest Service.

Their father had talked a great deal of the north woods, which he called the "bush." He had promised that some day he would take Ann and Philip camping, but they had never gone. In summer vacation he was always away on long patrol trips, for that was the time of greatest danger from forest fires. Often he was gone for weeks. They knew he hated to leave his family, yet his eyes glowed as he got his camping outfit ready, slung his packsack on his shoulders and went whistling down the walk.

"Some day we'll all live in the bush," he would tell them when he said good-by. "Time my family learned a small town isn't the whole world."

Mrs. Jackman would laugh and remind him a small town was her world. She liked Bradford where everyone knew her. She had taught in the same building where Ann and Philip went to school, and one year when a teacher was ill, Mrs. Jackman had taken her place. Then Philip and Ann and her mother had set out for school together each morning. This world of their mother's was always close at hand and familiar.

Ann knew their mother understood their father's world, too, for they often spoke of the summer when they'd gone camping. When Ann was small she'd resented their having had good times without her, but later she'd asked for stories of how her mother learned to paddle and had been frightened when she saw her first black bear.

These stories made her father's world seem more real.

But despite them, the north woods remained only a vague place where one met adventure and even danger. Ann had no idea what a primitive forest was like. It was impossible to imagine a vast land with no towns, no farms, no roads, a land inhabited only by Indians.

So she was the more startled when she had learned that the family was moving to the Canadian wilderness. Her mother had told her this one morning. When she'd called Ann into the bedroom Ann had expected news of import, for ordinary events were usually discussed by all four at the dinner table. She had dreaded what she might hear and hoped it wouldn't be as bad as the winter when her mother had told her before she told Philip that there could be no Christmas presents.

To Ann's relief, Mrs. Jackman had been brisk and cheerful as she said their father was leaving the Forest Service and they were going to live near a Hudson's Bay post in Ontario. Mr. Jackman would become a trapper.

Her mother pointed to Far Lake on a map. Then, for the first time in her life, Ann saw her mother troubled and uncertain.

"Oh, my dear!" she said as she drew Ann close. "I hope we've decided wisely."

Ann stared. It was almost as though her mother were asking for Ann's opinion. But almost immediately Mrs. Jackman was her energetic self.

"Your great-grandmother crossed the plains in a covered wagon," she said.

Ann had heard many stories of those early days. She'd seen a picture of her great-grandmother and thought how much her mother looked like her. "The Sherwood chin," they'd called it. But crossing the plains in a covered wagon didn't have anything to do with the Canadian woods.

"But your grandmother was a pioneer," Ann protested.

"And we will be too," her mother said. "We're going into a new and unsettled country so that your father can make a better living for his family. That's why pioneers went westward. Only we are going north. For a long time your father has wanted to become a trapper but I've advised against it."

"Don't you want to go?" Ann asked.

"More than I can tell you," her mother said. "It means independence and building a business, for your father plans to start a fur farm. And no matter how hard he may have to work, at least he can be home with his family. But I've worried about you children. No schools, no young companions. That's why I've told you first for it will make more difference to you than to Philip. You're older, and a girl."

At supper that night they talked about the new adventure. Nothing so exciting had ever happened in the Jackman family. Ann planned how she'd tell the girls at school. A Hudson's Bay post and a log cabin sounded much more thrilling than the West, and when the Jordans had moved to Montana the seventh grade had given a party for Bessie Jordan. All Bradford had been deeply stirred by the Jordans' departure.

The school principal had read a speech in which he had repeated, "Go West, young man, go West," and Bessie Jordan had cried when she said good-by. But Ann wouldn't feel like crying. She was much too excited.

Philip asked if he'd wear skin clothing like Daniel Boone, and his father said he could if he'd tan the pelts. But the fact which impressed Philip most was that his father would be home to help with chores.

"It takes two men to keep Mother's wood-box full on baking days," he said.

"But there won't be any farmer to bring us a

load of wood, son," his father said. "You and I will have to cut down the trees and haul them in."

"And there'll be no store to run to when we need sugar or a loaf of bread," their mother added.

Life with no stores, no farms, even no neighbors except Indians, had sounded exciting. In Bradford a purchase at the grocery meant a ten minute errand. Farmers had delivered barrels of apples and sacks of vegetables and cords of wood. These had appeared as regularly as the autumn.

But now in camp on Far Lake even food was an adventure. The first thing Mr. Jackman did was to clear a garden. Mrs. Jackman cut potatoes and warned Ann and Philip not to be prodigal in the planting.

"Four pieces to a hole," she said. "One sack must grow into enough for a year."

"If moose and deer don't trample them down," Mr. Jackman said.

"We ought to have a dog," Philip said. "He'd drive 'em away."

Wild strawberries grew in an open place and Ann and Philip picked enough for a shortcake supper. They walked along the shore and found a *brule*, or place where a forest fire had swept through. Raspberries had grown thickly and the new fruit was forming.

"Good," their father said when they'd rushed back to camp to tell of the discovery. "We'll have jam all winter."

The most exciting event of the day was "going to fish market." Mr. Jackman had stretched a net in the bay and assigned its care to Ann and Philip. Ann saw her mother start to speak and then close her lips firmly. Ann knew what that meant. Her mother didn't want them to go alone in the canoe, but she wasn't going to say anything about it.

"This is a job, not a game," Mr. Jackman said. "No monkeyshines. A canoe's our team and wagon in the bush. Treat it that way."

"I'll be the driver," Philip said.

Mr. Jackman smiled, and then he saw his wife's face.

"You're only crew," he said to Philip. "Every ship's got to have a captain. Even a canoe. Ann is skipper of the Peterborough till you prove you're as good as she is."

They had trouble with the big canoe at first. It wouldn't go where they wanted it to, and without a load it seemed very tippy. But Ann loved the water, was a good swimmer, and she soon learned how to paddle in the stern. She and Philip went out every forenoon, caught one end of the net and pulled the canoe along until they felt a whitefish

24

struggle. Then they lifted net and fish aboard and slipped it gills from the webbing. They always got enough for dinner.

To Ann, the canoe was the most exciting thing in her new world. She wished Philip didn't always want to go with her because she'd remember Pocahontas and the Hiawatha poem and would picture herself drifting idly along the shore, trailing her paddle and staring at the sunset. Later, when the moon was full, she decided, she'd sneak down to the shore some evening and paddle away by herself, alone in the golden quiet night. She couldn't think of anything more romantic.

Ann didn't have much time for canoeing in those first days. Mr. Jackman began at once to build a log cabin and that left camp-making to Ann and her mother. They slept in the two tents and cooked over an open fire in the space between.

"This was all right while we traveled," Mrs. Jackman said, "but I don't like squatting on the ground like an Indian woman when I'm at home. We ought to have a table and cupboards."

"Dad can make anything with an ax," Ann said. "And he's busy building our cabin."

Ann thought of that when she and Philip walked along the shore looking for strawberries. They didn't find any and on the way back they stopped at the big birch tree where Philip had carved his initials in the white bark. Above that, someone had stripped all the bark from the tree in one big sheet. They had found the knife marks and decided it was Indians.

"I can cut off as big a piece as that," Philip said.

He went to another large birch and began cutting the bark. When he pulled it back it came off in shreds.

"You have to cut deeper," Ann said. "This way."

They spoiled the bark on that tree learning how, but on another they loosened a strip two feet wide. When it was all off and spread on the ground they were amazed by its size.

"We can make a wigwam," Philip said.

"Or a table!" Ann cried.

They cut off more strips, spoiling some but getting several large pieces.

"We can build anything!" Ann cried excitedly as they gathered the rolls under their arms.

They dashed into camp and laid the birchbark before Mrs. Jackman.

"That's enough kindling for a month," she said.

"Mother!" Ann said. "Be a pioneer. Look!"

Ann spread out the biggest sheet. It was much bigger than a card table.

26

"Ann," her mother said, "you're a genius. And that's waterproof!"

"Sure," Ann said. "It'll make cupboards to keep food in."

That noon they asked Mr. Jackman to cut stakes and poles for a table frame and Ann and her mother laid the largest sheet of bark over the poles and fastened it with string.

"Now let's make a pantry to match our table," Ann said.

They built a framework by tying poles to saplings and then fastened sheets of bark to the poles to form shelves. The largest sheet was saved for back and roof, and a smaller one for a hanging door. Ann was no more excited than her mother when they had completed a rainproof kitchen cupboard.

"But think of all the trees that have lost their bark to give us a kitchen," Mrs. Jackman said that night at supper.

"Every one of them will make fine stovewood this winter," Mr. Jackman said. "And Indians have been building canoes and wigwams of bark for a thousand years, but birch trees still die of old age in this country."

When Ann went to bed that night she noticed the confusion of the tent. In town she hadn't been very orderly, and tidying bureau drawers Saturday mornings wasn't exciting. But here, with shirts, socks and sweaters mixed up in the blankets, there was a reason for neatness. The next morning she and Philip cut more bark and by noon Ann had built shelves in the tent and a dressing table outside to hold combs and brushes. A mirror hung above it on a tree.

Philip need only run his fingers through his short dark hair. Ann's was blond and wavy and when in order it framed her face. But when she forgot to comb it or grew excited, it stood out from her head like a golden bush, and she hadn't paid much attention to it since her arrival at Far Lake.

Now she stood before the mirror and experimented with her hair. A ribbon band had seemed only a convenient method of keeping short wavy locks from dangling in her eyes, but suddenly Ann realized that she had been overlooking natural assets. The ribbon could also serve to hold her wave in place and she pulled her hair forward and allowed it to curl softly on her temples. The effect pleased her. Not only did it look well with shirts and breeches but it made her seem years older.

As proof of this new maturity she piled Philip's and her clothes neatly on the shelves before she called the family to see the birchbark furniture.

"First time I've known Ann to have a sense of order," her mother said.

Mr. Jackman smiled as he looked in the tent.

"Ojibwa housekeeping," he said. "Female nature, red or white, is the same. Give an Indian woman enough birchbark and she'll make and furnish a home, even down to cooking pots. Give Ann some bark and she fits up a room. Now I'll show her a trick."

He walked out of the clearing and returned with a poplar sapling. From this he cut the branches so that they formed pegs and then drove the sapling into the ground between Ann's and Philip's beds.

"And that's how the first hall clothes tree happened," he said.

The trimmed sapling did look like the pole with coat hooks in their hall at Bradford. And it was more fun to use. Even Philip hung his clothes on it at night, although in town he'd merely thrown his cap at the hall tree as he passed.

But birchbark furniture was only temporary. The real interest of the family was centered in the log cabin that was to be their home. Mr. Jackman worked on it from breakfast until dark. He had already felled the trees and had hewed planks for doors and furniture. Ann and Philip had never seen boards with ax marks on them and ran their hands over the satin-like surface. They were astonished that they found no splinters.

"Only kind of lumber the pioneers had," Mr. Jackman said. "Boards don't grow. Have to be made with an ax or in a sawmill."

Ann had never even wondered how boards were made. Philip brought his new ax and tried to hew a short stick of poplar.

"Stop him, Dave!" Mrs. Jackman cried. "He'll hurt himself."

"I was no older when I owned my first ax," her husband said. "How else is Philip going to learn?"

Owning an ax placed Philip in the male world and he spent hours chopping while his father put up the lower tiers of logs. There were three rooms. The largest would be kitchen, dining and living room; the two smaller would be bedrooms, one for Ann and Philip. Even partitions between the rooms were of logs.

In Bradford, Ann and Philip had seen workmen finish the framework of a small house in a day. Now the building of a log cabin seemed slow. The corners were notched carefully so that the logs would fit in snug and solid fashion. The children had expected to see their father pile logs as one would build a square with matches. Instead he worked hours making each tier tight. Even partitions had to be dovetailed into the outer wall.

Philip watched his father and then began to build a small cabin with three-foot sticks.

"We might need a dog house," he explained.

"But we want a bigger dog than that," Ann protested. "Let's make a big one."

What Ann really wanted was to use Philip's ax, for now that the birchbark furniture was finished, she was out of a job. But Philip refused and continued to hack away as joyfully as though no one had ever owned an ax before. Ann went to her father.

"Can't I help?" she asked.

Her father always understood Ann's need of action.

"Sure," he said. "Want to start chinking?"

The spaces between the logs must be filled with moss to make the cabin warm in winter, and the moss could be gathered in quantity only in a big spruce swamp far across the ridge.

"Can Philip and I go get the moss?" Ann asked.

Her father didn't say anything for a moment as he looked down at her from the logs.

"You and Philip will have to start finding your way around in the bush sometime," he said at last.

"You're not going to let them go to the swamp!" Mrs. Jackman protested as she came around the corner of the cabin, where she had been gathering clean dry chips for a baking fire. "That swamp extends for miles! They could get lost and wander for days."

"No need for them to go into the swamp," their father said. "Plenty of moss along the edge. I'll show them the trail. They can fill the sacks and come home by themselves. We can't keep them on a leash forever."

3 SPRUCE SWAMP

The three started at once, Philip striding ahead and swinging his arms as if he had spent his life in the woods. Ann had not thought they'd been on a leash, for they had explored the bay and climbed beside the creek which tumbled off the rocks into the lake. She recalled, however, that they had never been out of sight of water. The forest was open and even from the crest of the ridge they could see the lake through the trees.

Now they were going to cross the ridge and

enter unfamiliar country. At first they followed a trail they knew. Ann and Philip had used it to reach their best strawberry patch. When they left the patch behind them, Ann began to wonder where the trail went. All trails had to end somewhere.

"It's a portage," her father said. "Indians have used it a long time, judging by the way it's beaten down. Leads to waterways north of here."

The trail turned to the left, keeping on the crest of a spur of the ridge. The forest was open in places where great shields of rock prevented growth of trees. Mr. Jackman turned aside in one of these places and led them to the edge of a steep slope.

"There's the spruce swamp," he said.

They saw a vast stretch of green. It was level and smooth, unbroken for miles. Ann had not thought there could be so many trees or that they could grow so thickly.

"How many million do you suppose there are?" Philip asked.

"Hate to have to count them," Mr. Jackman chuckled. "You can see why that swamp's a good place to keep out of. One acre of it is just like all the other thousands of acres."

SPRUCE SWAMP

Ann saw almost treeless country off to the right and caught glimpses of water in it.

"Muskeg," her father said. "Open swamp. And that creek twisting and turning out there is the stream that flows into our bay near camp. Runs around the end of the ridge."

They went back to the portage and followed it along the ridge until it finally turned down a slope. The growth was more dense now and the trail was damp, even muddy in places. It twisted and turned until suddenly it came out in an open place. Across this was the spruce swamp.

Ann and Philip stared curiously. Trees grew so thickly their branches met, and beneath them it was dark and cool and eerie. Long streamers of grayish-green moss festooned the trees and here and there slender shafts of sunlight filtered through the matted greenery overhead.

Mr. Jackman tore a bunch of moss from a tree. Ann felt of it, found it dry and brittle, so light she could crumple a huge handful into a small ball.

"Caribou moss," her father said.

Philip walked boldly into the swamp beneath the trees.

"Want to get lost in there?" his father asked.

"But I see paths," Philip said.

"Moose trails," his father said. "They branch

and twist and never get anywhere. Only make it easier to get lost."

Ann and Philip began to cram moss into the bags.

"Don't fill them too full," their father warned. "It's a long way to carry them home."

"Suppose we can make two trips this afternoon?" Ann asked.

"Shouldn't wonder, at the rate you're going. I'm leaving you on your own now."

They watched him disappear on the trail. Philip climbed a tree and began to throw down great armsful of moss. Ann worked beneath, stuffing it into a sack.

"I bet we wouldn't get lost on a moose trail," Philip said.

Ann didn't answer. She had been thinking the same thing.

"We could walk in on a trail, turn around and come back on it, couldn't we?" Philip demanded.

Ann had thought of that too, but she hadn't expected Philip to figure it out. In Bradford, Ann had played with girls and Philip had been just a younger brother. But since coming to Far Lake she had made surprising discoveries about Philip. He was as daring as she, only he didn't act so quickly. Once she had thought Philip was slow because he didn't do things on swift impulse, as she did. He always had to have a reason for doing anything while she often acted first and thought about it afterward; especially if she had to think herself out of trouble.

Ann wanted as much as did Philip to prove they could explore the swamp. So she didn't answer but went to a tree she could climb. It was fun to tear dry moss from the branches. Each tendril was fastened by a small round cup and as these were pulled off it sounded like the whisper of torn cloth. She threw down more than a sackful, then sat and stared at the world beneath her.

She could see the creek through an opening. It looked cool and inviting and she was glad her father had not said anything about swimming. They'd need a bath after the hot work of gathering moss.

She slid down the tree to ask Philip, but, though she found a half-filled sack of moss, he was not in sight. She called, but didn't get an answer. A moose trail led among the spruce trees, and in the mud at the edge of the swamp she saw the faint print of Philip's shoepacs. Ann stared along the trail, calling his name.

Once she thought she heard him.

"Philip Jackman, you'd better come out of this swamp," she said.

Then she heard the noise again, and knew it was made by two branches rubbing together. It had a mournful sound. As she went on, the trail deepened until it was waist high, like a ditch. Hundreds of moose must have traveled there to make that depression in the thick moss for her own weight hardly left an imprint on the springy growth. It was like walking on a mattress.

The swamp was cool and dark and very pleasant. The ground moss was shot through with small stiff grasses and flowerets so tiny she had to examine them closely to make sure they were flowers. They seemed only to dust the moss with specks of color. She saw vivid scarlet and purple mushrooms. A broad-leafed plant held a great white waxen flower that had never known the sun.

Ann wandered on with a clear conscience, her ears and her eyes drinking in the strangeness. After all, she had to search for Philip. Her extra three years made her responsible for his safety. But Ann thought that never before had she known what the word "wilderness" really meant. A sense of remoteness made her tingle with excitement.

Then, at a bend in the trail, she saw Philip coming toward her.

"I knew I wouldn't get lost," he began at once. "It's easy if you just come back on the same trail."

Philip always offered proof of wisdom when he knew he'd disobeyed. Ann, too, didn't see how anyone could get lost. The deep moose paths crossed and recrossed almost like streets. Anyone would know if he'd turned a corner. But nevertheless Ann's manner was decidedly disapproving, and Philip was silent and serious as he started back behind her.

Their shoepacs sank softly into the deep moss and made no sound. The trail turned sharply around a tree and almost doubled back, and they looked up to see an enormous bull moose coming toward them. His antlers brushed the branches of the trees and the long black tassel, or "bell," at his throat was nearly a foot long.

The moose stopped a few yards away. He sniffed but the slight breeze was toward Ann and Philip and brought no scent. He had no way to determine the nature of these strange objects in his path.

Baffled, the moose lowered his great antlers to a position of defense. This forest trail belonged to him.

Ann and Philip were so terrified their hearts crowded into their throats. Then with a cry of panic, Ann turned so swiftly she knocked Philip down. She stopped long enough to drag him to his feet and then both turned and sped along the trail. They didn't even glance back to see if the moose were following, but ran until they could run no longer. Their breath was coming in great gasps when they halted.

The moose was not in sight.

"Now see what happened because you didn't mind Dad!" Ann cried.

Philip didn't deny that.

"Was the moose you saw in camp as big as this one?" he demanded.

"Bigger," Ann said, although secretly she doubted it. She had found the encounter in the swamp much more terrifying. "What do we do now?"

"We'd better hide until the moose gets past," Philip said.

They saw a tangle of fallen tree trunks near the trail and crouched behind it.

"Will the moose smell us when he goes by?" Philip asked.

Ann had been wondering about that. Their father had told of the moose's keen nose. They waited with pounding hearts for the great creature to appear. He'd seemed determined to keep that

40

trail. But although they hid for what seemed hours, the moose did not come.

The afternoon was slipping by. Long pencils of sunlight slanted in among the trees. Their father must have come to the edge of the swamp in search of them hours before. Ann stood up. She tried to sound very brave and confident.

"We've got to go back on that trail," she said. "We can't wait here any longer."

They walked slowly, watching apprehensively, dreading every turn. When a twig snapped they jumped in terror.

The sun was almost down and they had walked much farther than they had run from the moose. Yet there was not the slightest indication they were coming to the edge of the swamp. In every direction spruce grew thickly and the forest appeared the same.

"I bet we took the wrong turn back a ways," Philip said.

Two deep moose trails had crossed each other. They returned to the intersection and followed the other trail, but even streamers of moss hanging from branches looked the same. Another trail turned off and both were sure it led in the right direction. They followed it for some distance, but like the others it kept turning one way and then the other.

They stopped. There was no use in pretending any longer. They admitted they were lost. They were tired and more frightened than they had ever been. They started on, walking even faster, soon were leaving one moose trail for another, and abandoning that for still another, all without reason. But always it seemed important that they hurry.

When the sun set they were running, heedless of direction. Neither wanted dark to overtake them in the swamp. Ann, ahead, thought the forest was not so dense, and then she caught the glint of water. A moment later they stopped beside a creek. The trail ended in a trampled place where many moose had drunk.

"Philip!" Ann cried. "If this is our creek, we can follow it to the lake."

"Yeah, but which way?" Philip demanded as he stared at the calm water.

Not a ripple showed. Ann knelt and bathed her hot face. There must be some way, she thought, to make the apparently motionless water give up the secret of its course. She dipped her hand deep but could not feel a current.

A leaf would float, she thought, but when she

dropped one in the water a zephyr carried it in circles. Farther along the bank she saw a dead sapling, and when she had broken off a piece she tossed it in. It began to move slowly to the right.

"That's the way to Far Lake," she said. "Come on."

Following a creek wasn't as easy as she thought. The stream flowed through thick alders under which they had to crawl. It turned into an open marsh and they fell off grassy hummocks into mud-holes. Philip lost a shoepac and they had to dig it out of the mire. The creek kept turning and twisting more often than had the moose trails. And all the time the long northern twilight was fading.

The low banks of the stream became higher and more solid, but now in places they had been cut steeply by the current. Often the top was blocked by fallen tree trunks and they clambered over jackpots and fought through brush. Yet, no matter how hard the going, they didn't dare turn aside for fear they would lose sight of the stream.

It grew darker and they stumbled often. At last both went headlong as they slipped on a moss covered rock.

"It's no use," Ann admitted. "We can't walk any farther."

"We can't stay here all night," Philip said.

43

The fear in his voice helped Ann to fight back her own. Now she must be stout-hearted for both.

"Sure we can," she said. "And when it's daylight, and we're rested, we can walk home much faster."

They were in a small open glade where the darkness was not so black. They found a tree and sat with their backs against the trunk. Thick moss covered the roots and made a soft bed for resting. The open space around them gave a sense of protection.

Ann put an arm around Philip and he didn't shrug away. It was cold, and they snuggled. Ann was wondering how long it took for a person to starve to death when Philip spoke.

"What do you suppose they had for supper?" he asked.

"As though Dad and Mother stayed home and ate while are are lost!" Ann said.

"You know what I bet," and Philip sat up abruptly. "I bet they're hunting for us right now."

That thought was comforting until Philip spoiled it by asking the question Ann had been asking herself.

"What if this creek doesn't come out in Far Lake?"

Ann didn't answer. At that moment she would

44

have found it hard to pretend confidence. She was wishing she hadn't been so positive about where the creek led. Perhaps they had been going in the wrong direction. If they had, she wondered whether their father would ever find them.

4 NIGHT AND THE FOREST

The forest was not quiet as it had been in the afternoon. Ann and Philip could hear soft rustlings and scurryings as small animals went about their nightly business. Twigs snapped. Once they heard the crash of brush across the creek.

"That's a moose," Philip whispered, and drew closer.

They scarcely breathed as they waited. Nothing but a moose could be so noisy. But the next crash sounded farther off and the third was not so loud.

When finally the crashing died away they felt easier.

The moon rose and that seemed to help until a sudden call from near by cut the silence. It was startling but mournful, a loud "hoo-hoo" that seemed a part of the night and the forest. Almost at once it was answered by the same call from down the creek. Then back and forth the calls went, "Hoo-hoo! Hoo-hoo!"

Ann giggled in relief. "Remember Granddad's farm when the owls hooted at night?"

"Owls!" Philip said. "I thought it was Indians."

Ann had too at first, but she didn't mention that. Instead she tried to remember what their father had told of the big snowy owls of the north. She repeated this to Philip. It wasn't a cheerful conversation, but it was better than not to talk at all. She recalled these owls were almost as large as eagles, and Philip added that they could fly off with a snowshoe rabbit. Philip guessed that they might be able to carry off a baby. His school reader had a picture of an eagle doing that.

At this moment a great owl flew down the creek. As it crossed their open space they saw it clearly in the moonlight. His great wingspread made a shadow. Philip jumped to run. The owl

47

saw him and swerved up and away. After that the forest was quiet.

" 'Bout all that's left to scare us is a bear," Philip said. "Think one will come?"

Ann didn't answer. She'd thought of bears but hadn't wanted to frighten Philip. She listened for every movement and soon found her senses were attuned to forest noises. The rustle of a mouse in leaves had startled her at first, and now she scarcely heard it as she strained for other sounds.

She heard one at last, far away and low and rumbling. Ann even thought she heard an echo. After a while it was repeated.

"That sounds like shooting," she said.

"Who'd be shooting?" Philip asked.

"Dad. To show us the way home."

Philip sat up and listened. When the faint sound came again he too thought it might be a rifle, but they couldn't decide on the direction. They waited a long while until they heard it again, but it seemed to come from one direction, then from another. While they argued they heard a sudden crashing of brush upstream.

"What's that?" Philip whispered, and Ann felt his body stiffen.

The crashing came nearer and they jumped to their feet. Then they heard a shout.

48

"Ann! Philip! Heigh-o!"

"Dad!" they shouted together. "Here we are! Here we are! Dad! Dad!"

Philip went to the creek and called. His voice was full and unafraid now.

"Stay where you are!" their father shouted. "I'm coming."

They could hear him plainly, threshing through brush, but it seemed a long while before he finally came into the opening. They ran to him and threw their arms around him and felt his arms hold them tight.

Mr. Jackman didn't say anything for a few moments, just held them close. Suddenly he let them go.

"We've got to get to camp," he said. "Your mother'll be worrying. She thinks you're lost."

"But we were lost!" Philip cried. "Good and lost!"

"Didn't you hear the rifle?"

"Yes," Ann said, "but we couldn't tell which way."

"I should have taken your mother onto the ridge to fire signals," Mr. Jackman said. "But let's get going. It's a long hike."

He started at once, away from the creek and up a slope. Brush was thick but soon they came out

49

on top of a ridge where walking was much easier and the moonlight brighter. Mr. Jackman kept ahead, looking back occasionally to see that they followed. He never hesitated, though there was no trail. Ann and Philip had hard work keeping up with him. When he got too far ahead he stopped to let them rest.

"How do you know where you're going?" Philip panted.

"That's easy," his father said. "Keep the moon over your left shoulder and stay on top of the ridge."

"But, Dad!" Ann began, and then she didn't say any more.

The excitement of being rescued was past and she was beginning to think. She'd known enough to learn which way the creek flowed, and now she remembered how she had watched the moon come up each night. She knew the direction of the swamp from camp and where the creek came out in the bay. Suddenly she started on.

"Where to?" her father asked.

"Home," Ann said. "And I know the way."

Mr. Jackman chuckled as he arose and followed, but before he could speak they heard the report of a rifle. It seemed very close. Mr. Jackman

50

shouted and Ann and Philip called as loud as they could.

At once there was another shot, and then a second and third close together.

"Mother's wasting ammunition," Mr. Jackman said. "But it's in a good cause. Take us home, Ann."

She went along the ridge, looking back occasionally at the moon until she found she could tell where it was by the shadows of the trees. In a few minutes she came to an open space and stopped. It seemed strangely familiar. She felt smooth hard earth beneath her feet.

"The portage trail over the ridge!" she cried, and started running.

She ran swiftly down the slope among the jack pines and the birches, she sped around the old black stump and out into the clearing. She did not even pause at the cabin but rushed on toward the lake and into her mother's arms.

Mrs. Jackman said only, "Ann!" and then held her tightly. Ann's mother seldom talked of things she felt deeply. She said nothing now. It wasn't necessary. Her voice and her embrace had told everything.

She released Ann only to kiss Philip and then her husband, and for a few moments everyone talked at once and no one listened. Ann thought she'd never seen anything so cheerful as the leaping flames of the campfire when her father heaped on more wood and her mother moved a kettle out of the blaze.

Her mother's dark wavy hair was loosened, her cheeks were reddened by the fire and her eyes were shining. Ann thought her mother didn't have to talk. Her face showed so clearly how she felt. No one could look more beautiful than her mother when she was happy. And she was happy now.

She set two steaming bowls of soup on the camp table and Ann and Philip began to eat. The soup was the kind they liked best, thick with scraps of vegetables and meat, and they made it thicker with crumbled pilot biscuit.

"Smells good," their father said.

Mrs. Jackman filled two more bowls. Her hands trembled, but she smiled at her husband.

"Isn't it wonderful for you and me to feel hungry again, Dave?" she said.

It was strange, sitting at a table lighted by a campfire and eating supper in the middle of the night. Ann thought she'd never eaten better soup. Philip scraped his bowl and asked for a second helping.

Mrs. Jackman looked inquiringly at their father.

"Shouldn't I be careful about their first meal?" she
began.

"First!" Mr. Jackman laughed. "They haven't
really missed one yet. To hear you talk you'd
think they'd starved. Give 'em what they want."

They topped off with jam on pilot biscuit. Ann
doubted that she could ever eat again and Philip
was actually swollen in the middle. He patted the
bulge tenderly.

"Now we'll hear what happened," Mr. Jackman said.

"Not tonight, Dave!" their mother protested.
"Let them explain tomorrow."

"Rather get it over with?" their father asked.

Philip nodded unhappily. Then he looked up at
his father.

"I went into the swamp first," he said. "Ann
came in to find me."

"But I was glad Philip went," Ann added. "I'd
wanted to go. At least I was glad till we saw the
moose."

"Moose!" their mother cried. "How—"

"Let them tell it," Mr. Jackman said.

When the story was finished, Mrs. Jackman
looked at her husband.

"Don't you see what might have happened?"
she said. "If they hadn't found the creek—"

"Or if Ann hadn't sense enough to use it," her husband said, and he grinned at Ann.

"But, Dave! This is serious. If we can't trust them to—"

"Don't blame them, Mary," Mr. Jackman said. "It's my fault. Listen, you two. We scared the everlasting daylights out of your mother and ourselves. Know why?"

"Because we went in the swamp when you told us not to," Ann said.

"Partly. But we haven't gone at this right, you or me. If I'd told you how dangerous the swamp is, how you might wander in it till you starved to death, you wouldn't have gone in. And now you know, so I needn't tell you."

Ann looked quickly at her father. He wasn't scolding. He was talking to them as he talked to their mother.

"You had luck," he said, "coming out on the creek. I saw your tracks there, just at dark, and thought you were trying to get home that way. I felt pretty good, knowing you'd used your heads. But you can't expect luck all the time. So do you know what we've got to do?"

"Stay in the clearing," Philip said.

Ann didn't think so. She felt that her father

54

wasn't going to make strict rules, that he had something else in mind.

"And make a couple of softies of you?" Mr. Jackman said. "Your mother doesn't want that. She'd rather feel you can take care of yourselves. She'd like to know you're trying your darnedest to help us make a go of it here so we can all be together and be happy. If I make a success of trapping and your mother feels we're getting somewhere, no matter how hard we have to work, we still can't stay if you two don't do your share. If you do foolish things and scare her again, we'll go back to Bradford."

Ann started. She'd known that getting lost was serious and she'd expected to be warned of consequences or even scolded. But her father was saying something new. When they'd disobeyed in Bradford, it had been only disobedience, but anything she and Philip did here was important. They might spoil everything for all of them. This had never occurred to Ann before. She looked at Philip. His face was as serious as her own.

"Dad!" she cried. "We'll remember to be good. Honest!"

Her father smiled, and Ann knew he believed her. His trust strengthened her resolution.

"You will do the wrong thing, and the dangerous thing, if you don't know any better," he said. "That's where I'm to blame. I've been so busy I haven't shown you the bush. That's going to be changed."

"I'm partly to blame, Dave," their mother added. "I never explained how much Far Lake meant to all of us. I didn't want to spoil their fun."

"It's a lot more fun to know we're all doing a job together," their father said. "That's the way it has to be in the bush."

He stood up then, began to prepare kindling for the breakfast fire. Ann knew suddenly that the matter was settled, without scolding or punishment. And then she wondered if her father had read her thoughts.

"It's this way," he said. "If you break bush rules, no one has to punish you. The bush takes care of that. It'll starve you, or freeze you, or drown you, or maybe it will only drive us out because you can't learn to live safely. Understand?"

Ann nodded and turned to help her mother clear the table. Philip and his father piled up the morning wood. Then all four walked to Ann and Philip's tent.

"You'll have to hurry to get to sleep before daylight," Mrs. Jackman said as she kissed them good night.

"And if you see a moose coming at you, poke your middle finger in his right eye," their father added.

"But he'll jab you with his antlers," Philip giggled.

"A bull moose can't move his antlers if you use the middle finger of your left hand," his father said.

He started toward the campfire, and then halted.

"Good night, Ann, and 'night, son," he said.

Ann felt warmed and somehow comforted by a tone in her father's voice. Never had she had a greater sense of all four standing together. They made a family. She lay awake thinking about it. From her bed she could see her father push the burning embers of the campfire apart, and it was like turning off the lights in a room, except for a small one in a corner. The tent lost its whiteness and the forest rushed in closer.

She heard Philip stirring and whispered his name.

"What you want?" he demanded.

"Listen, Philip!" And in her earnestness Ann sat up in bed. "You and I are going to learn how to live in the bush."

"I suppose even Dad had to learn," Philip said.

"Weren't we dumb!" Ann said. "We never

57

even stopped to think we could spoil everything for Dad and Mother. Did you see Mother's hands tremble when she poured the soup?"

Philip didn't answer. Ann thought he had dropped off to sleep. Boys weren't much help in dramatic moments of self-accusation. But when he spoke she knew why he'd been so silent. He couldn't keep the news any longer.

"Next fall Dad's going to take me hunting. And next year maybe I can have a gun. A family our size is going to need a lot of meat—rabbit and partridge and deer and moose. Dad doesn't want to have to worry about a family when he goes out to run his trap line."

5 NEIGHBORS

IT was late when Ann and Philip wakened the next morning. Their mother called them to breakfast as though nothing unusual had occurred, but as they sat at the table she stopped often to ruffle Philip's hair or pat Ann's shoulder.

While they were eating, their father came from the cabin. He carried several pieces of freshly hewed wood.

"Made some tools for you," he said.

He gave two to each and Ann examined hers

59

curiously. One was a stick a foot long, flattened at the end like a chisel. The other was a smooth round club.

"What they for?" Philip asked.

"Chinking," his father said. "You stuff a bunch of moss between the logs, hold the wedge against it and pound it in tight with the mallet. Like this."

He demonstrated. "And you'd better get busy or I'll have the cabin built before you finish your job," he said.

"But we haven't any moss," Philip said.

"I saw two sacks of it at the spruce swamp."

Their father went back to work and Ann looked quickly at her mother. Even she didn't seem worried.

"You'll hurry back, won't you?" Mrs. Jackman said. "Your father is anxious to get the cabin chinked."

As soon as they had eaten, Ann and Philip started.

"Do you suppose they aren't going to say anything more about last night?" Philip asked when they were on the ridge.

"Of course not," Ann said. "They're only—"

She didn't know what she intended to say. Being sent right back to the spruce swamp meant something, and yet somehow she felt comfortable about the errand.

"They're just giving us another chance," Philip guessed.

"No," Ann said. "I think—I think they're letting us give ourselves another chance."

The sun was bright. Even the swamp looked pleasant as they peered in. It didn't seem possible they had known darkness and terror in such an inviting place. The sacks were where they'd left them and they filled them with moss until they bulged and carried them to the cabin.

Chinking was fun at first. But pounding moss into long cracks can soon become monotonous. Their father came to inspect their work and pointed out holes and soft places. He pushed several feet of chinking right through into the cabin.

"Maybe you don't care if winds and snow come into your bedroom," he said. "But your mother and I'd like a snug home this winter."

They worked more slowly and their father's eyes shone with pleasure when he saw how well they'd done. "A good job," he pronounced it.

After supper that night Mr. Jackman did not go back to the cabin. He usually worked on until dark.

"I'm wondering," he said, "what's at the east end of this ridge."

Ann and Philip jumped up eagerly and started up the trail. But their father turned from the clearing.

"We know the portage," he said. "Let's see new country."

They pushed through brush and climbed a more open slope beneath jack pines. Philip walked in a stealthy crouch and stopped to peer around each tree.

"He's pretending he's an Indian," Ann said.

"Not a bad game if he played it right," her father said. "That's how I learned to find my way in the bush."

"But Indians don't have to learn," Ann said. "They always know where they're going."

"Ever hear about the Indian who couldn't find his way to camp? When he met a white man he said, 'Me no lost. Wigwam lost.'"

Ann and Philip laughed; but neither concealed his disbelief. They were sure Indians were born with a sense of direction. Their father said an Indian would get lost more quickly in a strange country than a good white woodsman, that he'd never seen an Indian born with a compass in his head.

62

"I'll play Indian with you, Philip," he said. "Now watch where we go."

He led through bush, over windfall, up a slope and around a big rock. Suddenly he stopped.

"Now, Philip, take us back," he said.

Philip started, then stopped helplessly.

"Like to try it, Ann?"

But she was as bewildered as Philip.

"An Indian in strange country would remember rocks and trees and windfalls," Mr. Jackman said. "He'd remember them in order. He carries a picture in his head. We'll try the game again."

They followed him as he twisted and turned through brush, ducked around a clump of birches and ended by encircling a jackpot. It was like a game of hare and hounds. Philip thought he knew the way back, but after a half dozen steps he gave it up. Ann was sure she knew, and didn't do any better.

"I don't know," she confessed.

She'd tried hard to remember and as she stood there chagrined she heard the murmur of water. She'd heard that sound often as she lay in bed.

"I can't back-track, but I can lead you home," she said.

Her father smiled his disbelief. "Try it," he said.

Ann turned toward the sound. It grew louder as they climbed the ridge and she was sure she was right. It was the waterfall. Then she glimpsed the lake through the trees, turned down the slope, and a few minutes later they came out on the shore only a few yards from camp.

"That's using your head, Ann," her father said.

She didn't know how pleased he was until she heard him tell her mother. They described the new game of playing Indian. Mrs. Jackman smiled.

"You won't be satisfied until they grunt instead of saying 'yes,'" she said to her husband.

The next evening Mr. Jackman carried an ax when they left camp. At the back of the clearing he began to blaze a trail, cutting off small slabs of bark on the opposite sides of a tree every few yards.

In less than half a mile they came to the head of a narrow bay from which they could see down Far Lake. Mr. Jackman drew a map in the sand, tracing the shore from their own bay. It showed a long narrow peninsula with the freshly blazed trail across the end.

"That's your country," he said, pointing to the enclosed area. "Roam through it as much as you please. If you get lost, keep walking till you strike the lake or the trail, and then come home."

That became known as "our woods," but Ann

64

and Philip could not spend all their time there. Every morning they gathered moss and chinked the cabin walls, which grew higher every day. Evenings were spent with their father, on errands in the forest, "playing Indian," or sometimes just sitting on a windfall and talking about the wilderness and its ways. Every bird, animal and footprint reminded him of a story.

But in the afternoon they explored their own country, and it was not long before they knew almost every tree and rock, every little swale and slope, every opening and dense thicket. They could go straight home from any place.

Even the animals in "our woods" seemed more theirs than those encountered elsewhere. They knew the runways of snowshoe rabbits which criss-crossed an alder swamp. Philip learned a sharp whistle which would make the big brown hares stop and sit up, their long ears upright while their large black eyes looked about to locate this new danger.

They spent hours in the partridge nursery along the top of the ridge where mother partridges took their broods walking. Sometimes they were lucky or quiet enough to come upon a dozen or more baby partridges scampering around the hen.

The magic disappearance of a brood fascinated

them. At the mother's warning cry, the tiny birds seemed to disappear into thin air. When asked about this mystery their father told the wood's myth.

"Some woodsmen believe each chick seizes the stem of a leaf in his bill and flips over onto his back. He lies under it until the mother calls that everything is safe."

The next time a brood vanished before their eyes, Ann and Philip turned over every nearby leaf, stick and piece of moss. The mother bird, dragging a wing in pretense that it was broken, tried to lead them away. When their careful search didn't reveal a chick, they hid in thick brush. They didn't speak or move or even look out as the mother returned at last, calling to her brood. From her clucking and cries of the baby birds, they knew she had collected her family from the very ground they had searched.

"Maybe we'll never learn to see as well as an Indian," Philip said that night at supper. "I bet an Indian would have found them."

"You both are getting pretty fair," their father said. "Are you as good in the canoe?"

"Better," Ann said. "Now we can put that big Peterborough where we want to."

Ann really liked the water better than the

66

woods, perhaps because she was the captain, and her growing skill promised to keep her in command. Her father said she had a natural instinct for the water, while Philip was too ready to take chances. Instead of liking to paddle for its own sake, as Ann did, Philip thought a canoe was only something to take them places.

"I bet we could paddle across Far Lake," he said one day when they had paddled to the point.

Ann didn't answer. The whole vista of the lake opened before her. Far out was the big island on which their father planned some day to start a fur farm. They would live there in a big cabin of hewed logs as soon as the new railroad came through the wilderness and reached the end of Far Lake. Then they would have a dog team and she could drive to a real store. With the railroad practically at their door, they would have many things they now must go without. Then no longer would everything they ate or used or wore have to be brought in many miles by canoe and carried across portages.

Ann's mind played with a fanciful picture of the future. She'd heard her father and her mother talk for hours of the cabin and the fur farm and the time when the family would be established and secure in the North. Now as the canoe drifted she planned their future home. Her imagination borrowed from every romantic story she had read. She had filled the huge log rooms with massive furniture, gleaming silver, huge bearskin rugs and hunting trophies and she was installing a grand piano when the canoe tipped violently.

"Bear!" Philip hissed.

"Where?" she whispered.

Something dark moved on the point and they hurried toward it. But when they were closer Ann stopped paddling.

"It's only a porky!" she cried.

"Let's go ashore," Philip said. "I want to see his quills."

Twice they'd seen porcupines in trees, but this one was on the ground. As they landed, the porcupine saw them and started for a tree. They ran to head him off. Philip prodded with a pole. Ann waved a branch. The porcupine lifted the long quills on his back until he looked like a great pincushion and he slashed at Philip's stick with his armed tail.

"Look at how mad he's getting!" Philip cried. "We got him now."

But despite their herding, the porcupine outflanked them and reached a tree they had not seen. Philip examined his stick to see if he had captured

68

any quills. Ann looked lakeward and saw the canoe, adrift, and floating from the shore.

"The canoe!" she cried. "You never pulled it up!"

Philip stared in horror at the escaping craft. It was his job as bowman to hold the canoe until Ann got out and then pull it high. He didn't speak, for he knew as well as Ann that excuses couldn't explain this catastrophe. A lost canoe meant all were stranded. They couldn't travel. They couldn't even search for it in the miles and miles of shoreline of the big lake.

They stood too horrified to think, and then the breeze drove the canoe faster. As she saw water widen between shore and craft, Ann came to life. There was not a moment to lose.

She ran to the lake, pulled off shoepacs and breeches and leaped in. The water was colder than in the home bay, but Ann didn't notice. Her only thought was to save the canoe.

Once the craft was almost within arm's reach. She thought she had it, but as she stretched out to grasp it a breeze blew it on. The canoe danced off before her. She spurted, overtook it, finally got a hand on the gunwale.

Ann had expected that catching the runaway would end the danger. She had intended to climb in and paddle back, but when she tried to get aboard she found she couldn't. Each time she lifted herself on the gunwale the canoe threatened to tip over. At last, tired, she merely hung on.

Philip called and his voice sounded a long way off. Ann looked back and saw that the wind had blown her far from shore. Little waves slapped against the canoe and it was traveling fast. She doubted now if she could swim back to shore. She was tired and even hanging on was difficult.

Ann rested and looked ahead. The wind was carrying her past the point across a small bay. She knew she could not swim and drag the canoe against the wind, but there was a chance she could pull the craft across the wind and reach the point. It was her only chance. If she didn't make it she would be carried out into the big traverse of Far Lake. There, when she had become exhausted and could hang on no longer, she would surely drown.

She began the hard struggle. There were moments in which she thought she could never succeed. Then fright brought strength. Swimming with one arm and her legs, she fought to force the canoe nearer the point. At last she was too tired to struggle further. She was sure she would be carried past. Suddenly her feet struck bottom.

She was panting and chilled when she'd pulled

the canoe onto the beach. Across the bay she saw Philip pick up her clothes and start around the shore. She knew it would take some time for him to reach her and she hung her wet shirt to dry and lay down in the warm sun.

She felt better when Philip came. He, too, had had a fright.

"Gosh, Ann!" he exclaimed. "I was scared. It was my fault the canoe got away."

"I shouldn't have hung on until I couldn't swim back," she said. "I didn't think."

"Dad and Mother will be awful scared. I don't suppose they'll let me—"

Ann had thought she was angry with Philip. Now she found she only felt sorry for him.

"No need to tell them," she said. "If I get my shirt dry they'll never know."

Philip sighed in relief. He sat down beside Ann and began throwing pebbles at a tree.

"Look at that tiny house!" he exclaimed. "Looks like someone had made a doll's cabin."

He ran to the brush and Ann followed. They bent over the low structure. Two-foot stakes had been driven into the ground in a circle. One was left out to make a door, and the roof was a thatch of boughs. Even a baby couldn't have crawled through the opening.

Philip was mystified but Ann was not. She and her father had found a similar hutch near their first camp after leaving the railroad, and Mr. Jackman had explained how trappers built them to shelter trap and bait from snow. But Ann looked serious.

"That's a trapping cubby," she said. "And it means someone's here ahead of Dad."

"You mean a trapper? In the bay right next to ours?"

"Yes," Ann said. "Let's see if there are any more."

They didn't find another cubby but down the shore they came to an open space in the brush. The bare poles of a wigwam stood in the center.

Ann and Philip had never seen a wigwam, but they guessed at once what it was. A blackened spot in the center showed where the fire had been. The ground was trampled and in the brush they found quantities of rabbit hair.

"An Indian camp!" Philip cried in excitement. "Wait till Dad finds this out!" Then he stopped and looked at Ann. "How are we going to tell him about the trapper without telling how we got here."

"He's got to know about the trapper," Ann said.

"Sure, but that means we've got to tell about the canoe and everything."

They were sober as they paddled home. Ann didn't feel quite as blameless as she had tried to appear. She knew that when they'd run to head off the porcupine she hadn't even thought of the canoe. She'd been as excited as Philip. To be sure she'd caught the canoe afterwards, but even that swim might be regarded as one of those things into which she was always rushing without stopping to think.

They found their mother cooking supper. She told them to wash quickly and call their father. Absorbed in the final moments of browning a bannock, Mrs. Jackman didn't even glance at Ann's barely dry shirt. She and Philip walked slowly toward the cabin.

"Let's just tell Dad about it first," Ann suggested.

While Mr. Jackman listened to the story of the runaway canoe and the Indian trapper he cleaned his pipe and filled it. That made it harder for them to talk, for they couldn't see his eyes or guess what he might be thinking. At the very least, Ann thought, they wouldn't be allowed to paddle any more.

"There wasn't a trail or snowshoe track around

73

here last February," their father said when they had finished. "That Indian must have come after I looked over the district."

He hadn't commented on the drifted canoe. Ann looked at Philip. It was his turn to talk. So far she had been the spokesman.

"But we knew you'd want to know about the trapper," Philip said in a righteous tone. "Even if we—"

"Sure!" his father interrupted. "Square of you two to tell me."

"And this is your district, isn't it?" Philip said.

His father puffed at an unlighted pipe. He looked disturbed.

"It's just about got to be my district," he said at last. "I was here first, and our cabin is here. I don't want any trouble, but I don't intend to be run out."

Philip would have liked to discuss the Indian trapper, but his father asked about Ann's swim. She told him and then she asked how much they'd have to tell their mother.

"She might be worried. And—and—maybe we won't paddle any more. That way you wouldn't have—"

"Of course, you'll paddle," her father said.

"After that lesson the bush taught you today, you'll never let another canoe go adrift."

Mrs. Jackman called that supper was waiting. Halfway to the tents Mr. Jackman stopped.

"No need to worry your mother about the canoe," he said. "After supper we'll go for a walk and discover the wigwam."

That evening Mr. Jackman looked over the Indian camp. He stood in the camp site for a long time. He was troubled, but he didn't say much except to tell them things they had missed. The Indians had come in late winter. They'd shot a moose and perhaps they'd only camped while they ate it.

"Easier to move to the moose than to carry the moose to camp," he said.

When they reached home he told Mrs. Jackman what they'd found. Instantly she was anxious.

"Now this is nothing to get stirred up about," he said. "It was probably only an Indian traveling through who stopped to do a little trapping. I'll ask Gillepsie about it when we go to the Hudson's Bay post."

6 A STRANGER

A few days later Ann and Philip returned from a paddle to find a pleasant air of excitement in camp. Their father was filling food sacks and their mother was examining a wrinkled dress that had been packed away. Doubtfully she hung it on a line and said she hoped a day's airing would take out the worst of the wrinkles.

"You'd better hang your clothes too, Ann," she said. "We're going to Fort Caribou tomorrow.

Your father wants to hire an Indian to help finish the cabin and freight the winter supplies."

Ann and Philip had looked forward to this journey to the Hudson's Bay post ever since their arrival at Far Lake. Indians, a store, furs and all the strange new sights of a remote trading station of the great company would be thrilling, but Ann hadn't thought of it as a social occasion.

"Do we have to dress up?" she asked.

She hadn't worn a skirt for weeks. Breeches were more comfortable and she thought they made her seem tall and slender.

"Mr. Gillespie may invite us to the dwelling house," her mother said. "You wouldn't want him to think you were a wild Indian."

The camp buzzed with activity. Laundry and packing were under way and a large kettle of mulligan hung over the fire so they wouldn't have to cook while they traveled. Even Philip did not escape the preparation. Mrs. Jackman swathed him in a towel and cut his hair.

"I thought Fort Caribou was only a fur post," he muttered.

"It's also the home of our only white neighbor," his mother answered, as the shears snipped vigorously. "And, fur post or not, remember that the Hudson's Bay Company has been in existence since 1670, more than a hundred years before the Declaration of Independence was signed."

Mr. Jackman added that Fort Caribou had not been built then. The first posts were only on the shores of Hudson Bay.

"But Caribou Lake Indians live much as they lived a hundred years ago," he said. "This post is so far from the railroad its hunters are still rather primitive."

Philip brightened. This promised to fulfill his expectations. Ann had already been infected by the general anticipation. For weeks they had not left their bay, had seen no one except themselves. Now she laundered her favorite blue shirt and a bright handkerchief for her neck and packed a duffle bag for the journey.

The next morning breakfast was eaten early. Sunrise was only a pink flush above the pine-covered ridges. Mr. Jackman stowed a camping outfit in packsacks and stored tools, extra supplies and clothing in Ann and Philip's tent.

"You're not going to leave everything we own in plain sight!" Mrs. Jackman protested.

"It's as safe as if we were here," Mr. Jackman said.

"Doesn't anyone ever steal in the bush?" Philip asked.

78

"Not from a cache," his father said. "Everybody knows that sometime he may have to cache his own things. Indians always store traps and snowshoes through the summer. Even food is often left for a return journey."

He carried a packsack to the lake. Mrs. Jackman started to follow and then ran back to see that the tent flaps was firmly tied.

"I know anyone can undo them," she admitted, "but those knots make me feel better," and she looked back at their unlocked home with some misgiving when the canoe swung past the point and into the open lake.

All paddled, Mrs. Jackman still in the place of honor in the bow, Ann and Philip kneeling amidships. But even with four blades working, a long day lay ahead. On the map Fort Caribou hadn't seemed far, but now Ann could not see the other end of Far Lake, where they would turn into Wolf Jaw River. This in turn led to Lake Caribou, for which the post was named.

In school Ann had learned about the great English company which had been granted a charter by the king to trade for furs in Hudson Bay. "Company of Gentlemen Adventurers" had sounded thrilling. She had repeated the sonorous phrase and liked it, little dreaming as she studied her history lesson in Bradford that she would be starting in a June morning to buy supplies from the "ancient gentlemen."

The sun rose to end the morning chill and the blue lake sparkled as the crest of each wavelet became diamond edged. Their wet blades flashed in the sunlight and the freshness of a new day lifted their spirits. Mr. Jackman began a song of the early voyageurs, one he had often sung in Bradford, but here the words seemed to belong. Paddles dipped in time with the music.

"Isn't this great, Mary?" Mr. Jackman asked. "I told you it was time the Jackman family lived in real country."

They stopped for an early lunch. While the mulligan was being heated, Philip ran up and down to work the stiffness out of his legs. Ann stretched out on the warm sand. She liked the feel of the sun on her body, and the wind in the pines formed singing words.

"Never saw you still so long," her father said. "What's the matter? Knees sore?"

She sat up, intending an indignant denial. Not for worlds would she have admitted her knees ached, for she and Philip had tried to out-kneel each other and be the last to give up and sit on a packsack.

"Our knees will all grow calluses," her mother answered for Ann.

"Once you're used to it, you'll like paddling from your knees," Mr. Jackman said. "And it's a lot safer if you learn to keep your weight low in a canoe. Before the summer's over you'll be squatting like Indians."

"The way you do, Dave," his wife said.

He denied this, but later Ann saw him sitting on his feet while he ate lunch. He grinned and admitted he found the position convenient. Ann tried it and thought it only uncomfortable. Much as she wanted to be like her father, she doubted if she would form that habit.

When the dishes were washed, the packsack was carried to the canoe and the kettle of mulligan stowed in the bow. Generous second helpings hadn't finished the stew and the meal had made the Jackmans reluctant to begin paddling.

Mr. Jackman threw himself down in the shade, leaned against a windfall and lighted his pipe. Ann nestled beside him. She loved these short noon halts when they rested, content and drowsy.

"We haven't had days like this since we paddled up the Brule River," Mrs. Jackman said. "Remember, Dave?"

He nodded. Ann watched his slow smile. When a light shone far back in his eyes, she knew he was especially happy, and since they'd come to Far Lake he seemed always to be so. Even while working on the cabin he laughed and whistled, and the long days never seemed to tire him. Now when Ann would have liked to rest her sore knees a little longer, he jumped to his feet and lifted the canoe into the water.

"Hey, crew!" he called. "Time we were under way."

That afternoon they left the sun-drenched lake and turned into the cool river. The channel twisted through a spruce forest and the banks were shelving rock past which the stream flowed swiftly.

Paddling had become hard work in the lake, but here it was fun again. The canoe leaped forward with the current. Ann forgot she was tired as her mother caught the excitement and set a faster pace for the four flashing blades.

On the journey from the railroad Ann and Philip had liked rivers better than lakes. The banks were close and they'd learned that if they kept quiet they would see forest animals. Now, as they rounded the first bend, Philip pointed at a small dark animal running along the water's edge.

"Mink!" his father whispered.

The mink heard even that slight sound and looked up. Ann had only an impression of two bright eyes and a long snakelike body before she heard a splash and found herself staring at widening circles in the water.

The next stream traveler was in midchannel. An animal swimming across the river appeared to be towing a large cylinder a foot or more behind his head.

"It's a fox," Mr. Jackman said. "His tail's floating high and dry. I never saw one swimming before."

The fox heard them and put on a frantic burst of speed. After he had disappeared ashore, the river was empty and soon its whole character changed. Rocky banks gave way to low land and grass and the trees to open muskeg. The current was sluggish and their paddle strokes lost snap and exhilaration. The sun was hotter here, and there was no wind.

Ann was drowsy and was wondering if it would be all right to take a nap, when her father uttered a warning hiss. All stopped paddling. Ann could feel excitement and peered past Philip and her mother. Then the canoe swung around a bend and

83

she saw a moose standing in the middle of the river.

The moose was facing downstream and did not see them. It was a cow, and as the current carried the canoe Ann realized they would pass very close.

Philip lifted a hand to point, and his hand trembled with excitement. A moose calf stood in shallow water near the bank. With his high shoulders and long knobby legs, he would have been ugly, except that he was so young and innocent.

Suddenly he stood on his hind legs and pawed the water with his forelegs, covering himself with spray. Then he reversed the operation and kicked so hard with his hind legs he splashed the approaching canoe. Mrs. Jackman gasped as water struck her face and the calf heard her. He stopped kicking, took a few steps nearer, amazed, curious and wholly unafraid. He stared like a small boy who had been caught playing in a mud puddle.

They tried not to laugh aloud, but their shoulders shook until the canoe trembled. The calf was only a few feet away and his baby stare was ludicrous.

"How about it, young fellow?" Mr. Jackman said. "Going to let us pass?"

The cow heard his voice and saw them for the first time. Water churned as she plunged for shore.

She didn't even look toward her offspring as she leaped.

"I could have touched her with my paddle!" Mrs. Jackman cried.

No one tried to be silent after that. The small-boy antics of the calf had sent them into gales of laughter which would have warned any animal ahead.

The river left the swamp and again flowed between rocky banks. The current was swifter and waves slapped against the canoe. The stream growled a bit as it danced through a stretch of rapids. Water splashed over the gunwales and the banks raced backwards.

"Only rips," Mr. Jackman said.

They swept through several swift places and at last heard a dull roar around a bend ahead.

"Dave!" Mrs. Jackman cried. "We can't go through that!"

"I should say not," her husband said. "Where's the take-off of the portage?"

"There," Philip said proudly, and pointed to an open space on the bank and a trail leading into the forest.

They turned in, stepped ashore, unloaded the canoe.

"Everyone grab his load," Mr. Jackman said as

85

he swung the canoe up and over and lowered it onto his shoulders.

Mrs. Jackman followed with a small packsack, Ann with another. Philip carried an ax, the paddles and the kettle of mulligan. The portage led across a bend in the river and at the top of a rise Mr. Jackman stopped.

"Here's the trail to the rapids," he said. "Want to take a look?"

Ann and Philip turned aside. They could hear the rapids roar as they walked through the forest but when they emerged on the river bank they saw spray flung high above the rocks.

"No wonder we have to portage," Philip said. "A canoe would be rolled over and—" He broke off to point at a dark object on the shore. "There's a dog!"

Incredible as it seemed, a black dog was sitting on a rock high above the water and staring into the boiling rapids below. Ann and Philip called and went toward him, but as they approached, the dog retreated into the bushes. Philip set the kettle of stew on the ground.

"Let him eat and then maybe we can catch him," he said.

They stepped back and the dog came forward.

86

He sniffed hungrily at the stew and then suddenly his head disappeared in the kettle.

"He knows we're friends," Philip said.

The dog looked up in swift agreement and then gave his entire attention to the food. While he was eating, Ann and Philip went closer and at last stroked his shoulders. He was licking a bare kettle when Mr. and Mrs. Jackman came down the trail.

They listened to a chorus of explanation from what was now a trio. Philip patted the black head. Ann caressed his muzzle and the dog added a wave of his tail.

"I told you we'd get a dog," Philip boasted. "That's why I built the dog house."

"This dog couldn't get in it," his father said.

"I'll build another. A good warm one for winter."

"Stop teasing and tell them they can keep him," Mrs. Jackman said.

"But he must belong to someone!"

"You wouldn't think so if you'd seen how glad he was to see us," Ann insisted.

She knew her statement didn't quite describe the first moments of the encounter, but it was better to say as little as possible about how hard they'd worked to establish the friendship.

87

"Come here, old fellow," Mr. Jackman called.

The dog sat down and thumped his tail. Mr. Jackman repeated the command in a firmer tone, but the dog did not move. Ann and Philip looked serious, for their father liked animals that obeyed. Then Mr. Jackman chuckled. "I'll try Ojibwa."

"*Om-beh*, *om-beh*," he said, and the dog bounded toward him.

Mr. Jackman patted the heavy shoulders. "Put a little meat on your bones and you'd be quite a fellow," he said. "He's got a good broad chest."

Ann and Philip looked relieved. Ann said quickly that they were lucky to find such a good dog. Philip added that anyone who left so fine a dog to starve deserved to lose him.

"We'll take good care of him now," he added, looking at his father.

"Not so fast, son. We're not going to stir up trouble by walking off with an Indian's dog."

"But we can't leave him here to starve!" Mrs. Jackman protested.

In the end it was agreed that the dog could be taken to Fort Caribou, although of even this temporary adoption Mr. Jackman had misgivings. These were increased by the dog's strange behavior when they started down the trail. They called to the dog to follow, but he ran whimpering to the river.

"He's waiting for someone," Mr. Jackman said. "If he doesn't follow, don't coax him."

Ann and Philip walked slowly. The dog watched them. Ann feared he was not going to come on. Then suddenly he left his post and followed. Once started on the portage, he never hesitated. At the end of the trail he waited until the packsacks were in the canoe and everyone was seated. Then without orders he stepped carefully over the gunwale and settled down between Ann and Philip.

They might be warned that the adoption was still in doubt, but he most evidently considered himself a member of the family. He had shown that he knew the proprieties of a portage and now he added exemplary conduct in the canoe. When Philip tried to start a wrestling match, the dog was gravely disapproving.

"He's not over two years old and you're eleven," his father said. "But he knows enough to sit still in a canoe."

Mr. Jackman's tone was thoroughly approving. All found canine qualities to admire and Mrs. Jackman turned often to pat the dog's head. Ann and Philip discussed his future name and decided it should be an Ojibwa word. They'd both wanted a dog, but had never hoped to have one that already knew his woodcraft.

It was late afternoon when they reached Caribou Lake and another hour before the Hudson's Bay post came in sight, a cluster of whitewashed buildings behind which stretched an enormous clearing. A two-story house stood apart in the center of a green lawn enclosed by a white picket fence. A big red flag with "H.B.C." in white letters flew from a tall pole. Off to the right were two other buildings flanked by a row of small cabins.

This was really a village and demanded something better than breeches. Now all Ann could do was rummage in the duffle bag for a comb and a bright handkerchief. Her father laughed.

"And only yesterday Ann was asking if she had to dress up," he said.

"None of us expected a lawn or a flagpole," Mrs. Jackman said. "Ann, while you're rummaging, please get my scarf."

Mr. Jackman was disturbed by the flag. He thought it flew only when important officials visited the post or the manager was away.

"I hope Mr. Gillespie is at home," he said. "I must talk to him about that trapper."

The post was at the head of a crescent-shaped bay. A hundred years of fuel gathering had cleared every tree within a half mile. Ann, accustomed now to vast stretches of unbroken forest, thought the place desolate. Only the two points of the huge crescent were forested.

The nearest of these lay directly ahead. As the Jackmans paddled toward it they were startled to hear the shrill cry of a child and looked up to see a dozen or more wigwams on the nearby shore. Smoke of cooking fires rose lazily.

An Indian boy stood watching. Suddenly he became excited and ran back to the wigwams. Indian women and children gathered around him, and then all ran down to look at the Jackmans. The shore was lined with excited natives who stared and pointed and jabbered.

"They're not used to white strangers," Mr. Jackman said.

"But that isn't it," his wife said. "See how they're pointing. And what's that word they keep repeating?"

"*On-a-mush, on-a-mush,*" drifted across the water.

"What's it mean?" Mrs. Jackman asked.

Mr. Jackman frowned and looked at Ann and Philip.

91

"It's Ojibwa for dog," he said. "They're making such a racket I can't tell what they're saying. But it's the dog that's stirred them up. Sorry, young 'uns. I warned you he probably belonged to someone."

7 FORT CARIBOU

A disconsolate family disembarked before the Hudson's Bay Company post. Philip argued and protested, but Ann was silent as she stood with a hand on the dog's shoulder. The feel of his thick coat strengthened her determination that, no matter how excited the Indians were, the Jackmans were not going to lose him.

"We'll stay here," Mrs. Jackman said, "until your father has talked with Mr. Gillespie."

Mr. Jackman brought disturbing news from the

store. The post manager was absent with the fur brigade and was not expected back for two weeks. Many hunters had gone with him as boatmen and their families were living in the wigwams past the point. Fort Caribou was in charge of a young man who was part white and understood a little English. His name was Michel.

Ann and Philip demanded news of the dog.

"I didn't mention him," their father said. "This other—we'll ask Michel later."

Mr. Gillespie's absence was a blow to Mr. and Mrs. Jackman, but Ann and Philip were much more concerned about the dog. Even being at a fur trading post no longer held their interest and the dog seemed to sense their dejection.

"Maybe we can buy him," Ann said. "I've brought my birthday money."

"His owner might not want to sell," her mother said.

Mr. Jackman carried the packsacks from the shore. Camping at the post meant they would be bothered by thieving Indian dogs and Mrs. Jackman suggested that they pitch the tent inside the picket fence.

"It isn't a lawn, really," she said. "Just wild grass."

Mrs. Jackman lifted a packsack over the fence

and was turning for another when Michel hurried from the store.

"Nobody go there," he said. "That for the trader."

Mr. Jackman removed the offending packsack. It was not a propitious moment to discuss the dog and Ann tried vainly to motion Philip to the background. But as Philip was about to speak, Michel saw the dog.

"How you get him?" he demanded in amazement.

Mr. Jackman told the story. Michel's black eyes glowed and his English became incoherent as he pressed for details. He drew a map on the ground and had Mr. Jackman point to the spot beside the rapids where they had seen the dog.

"Wah!" Michel exclaimed.

Ann's hopes sank. Philip began to argue.

"Easy, son," his father said.

"That dog he belong Mis-tay-os-sin," Michel said.

Ann couldn't stand it any longer.

"Whoever owns him doesn't deserve such a nice dog when he leaves it to starve!" she burst out.

Michel looked at her, his eyes without expression.

"You know *o-ge-ma?*" he asked.

"That means 'chief,'" Mr. Jackman said. "Is Mis-tay-os-sin a chief?"

"This dog's name Ogema," Michel said, "When he's little with brothers and sisters he's the boss."

He seemed to think that of interest and importance and told how Ogema had been the finest dog in the litter, how proud Mis-tay-os-sin had been of the puppy and later of the grown dog.

Ann's heart sank. No amount of money could purchase such an animal. She was sure of this when Michel continued his story, embellishing it with the narrative detail an Indian loves. He told of smart things Ogema had done. Most Indians, he said, let their dogs run wild in summer and did not feed them much, but Mis-tay-os-sin always kept Ogema with him. Michel had never known an Indian to care so much for a dog, though it may have been because Mis-tay-os-sin had no family.

Philip couldn't stand any more. His face twisted as he tried to choke back the sobs. Ann felt tears in her eyes.

"I don't care!" she cried angrily. "Mis-tay-os-sin lost any right to the dog, treating him so."

"Mis-tay-os-sin," Michel said, "he dead."

Ann gasped. Suddenly she felt ashamed.

"In the rapids," Michel said. "He think he boss and Wolf Jaw rapids no like that. Indians find canoe but no Mis-tay-os-sin. They find dog, but the dog no go away. Everybody try, but Ogema stay where he see Mis-tay-os-sin last time."

The Jackmans were silent. Ann wondered how long Ogema had been sitting beside the rapids. It must have been many days, he was so thin and hungry.

"When Indian feel bad," Michel said, "maybe he die from sad thinking. Guess maybe Indian dog same as Indian."

"He'd have died if we hadn't found him," Philip said.

"Poor fellow," Mrs. Jackman said, and patted Ogema.

"But if Mis-tay-os-sin is dead!" Ann cried. "And if we found Ogema!"

Michel shrugged, but his eyes were kindly.

"Ogema no want new Indian boss," he said. "He think you good boss. So you get fine dog."

Ann could scarcely believe it. She had lost all hope of having Ogema in the family, but Michel accepted the dog's decision as final. She dropped to her knees and threw her arms around Ogema's neck, and she let the tears flow now.

Ogema seemed to understand. He dabbed at her cheeks with his tongue and then turned quickly when he heard Philip's choked voice say, "Ogema!"

Ann thought supper that evening was the happiest meal the Jackmans had ever eaten, even if they had been forced to make camp on the lake shore outside the picket fence. Her father and mother were as pleased as their children and, after the dishes were washed, all five went for a walk around the post buildings.

The store was closed, but in front stood the tall press with which bales of fur were squeezed into compact bundles. The Jackmans were examining the heavy timbers when several Indian women came around the corner.

"Good evening," Mrs. Jackman said.

"*B'jou'*," her husband interpreted, but the women did not reply.

They stared incredulously at Ann, and soon a suppressed murmur broke forth and grew to excited comment. Ann looked down at her shirt and breeches to see what was awry.

One of the women came forward. She spoke in a low tone that was soothing and musical and her eyes were soft and kindly. Ann had no fear as the woman came nearer, the first Indian who had ever talked to her.

The woman stopped, but the soft liquid words

98

continued. Slowly she lifted a hand and touched a lock of Ann's blond hair. She tugged it, just a little, as if making sure it were really growing from Ann's scalp, and then called to the others.

At once Ann was surrounded by the women. All touched her hair and made little sounds of wonder.

"They've never seen anything but black hair," Mrs. Jackman said.

Ann liked being the center of interest and the women were still exclaiming when Michel appeared.

"Wah-bo-sence! Wah-bo-sence!" they called to him.

"They give you a name," Michel said to Ann. "Indians always do that first time they see somebody."

"A name!" Ann exclaimed delightedly. "What does it mean?"

" 'Little rabbit.' "

Michel evidently considered that a great compliment to her blond hair, but Ann wasn't sure she liked being a rabbit's namesake. A rabbit was such a timid creature.

"Rather be called a weasel?" her father asked. "He's white in winter too, but he's a bloodthirsty little beast."

99

"Wah-bo-sence," the Indian woman murmured, and as she patted the blond head and then turned to lead her companions away, Ann thought the name had sounded like a song. And she was the only one in her family who had been honored.

That evening, when he returned to camp after a talk with Michel, Mr. Jackman was more cheerful about Mr. Gillespie's absence. He'd have to return to the post later, but meanwhile Michel had sent a messenger for an Indian to help freight winter supplies and household goods from the railroad to Far Lake.

The man was John Ottertail, who had worked in a large post on James Bay and was the only Indian at Fort Caribou who could speak a little English.

"He's coming tomorrow," Mr. Jackman said, "but he may not take the job. Michel says his wife might have other ideas."

"We'll tell her what a nice place Far Lake is," Ann said.

"Try it," her father said. "She can't speak a word of English."

That night Ogema proved he understood campfires as well as portages and canoe travel. As soon as the blaze began to die he lay close to it, just near enough to get the heat without singeing his hair.

In the morning he arose, shook off the ashes and was ready for the new day.

Ann and Philip took him for an early walk. More than anything else, Ann wanted to visit the dwelling house. Being a guest of the great company seemed infinitely more desirable now that it was impossible. All through breakfast she watched the house for signs of life, but it remained aloof and silent. Its doors were closed, its shades down.

Later an Indian woman came along the shore with a heavy load of wood. Although there were gates on the two sides of the enclosure, she walked around to reach the servants' cabins.

"Why doesn't she cut through?" Ann said indignantly. "Who wants to go inside that old picket fence anyhow?"

"Most evidently you do," her mother said.

The Jackmans, too, walked around on their way to the store, though Philip dared drag a stick along the pickets.

"Michel will lock you in the Indian house," his father said.

But Michel was too busy. A hunter had arrived from the farthest corner of the Fort Caribou district, bringing his family and late winter fur and when the Jackmans entered the store Michel was grading the pelts, putting them in piles according to animal and quality.

Even the hunter lost interest in the grading when the four white people entered. He and his family stared in wonder. The wife and three children sat on the floor and as soon as a little girl saw Ann's hair she hid under her mother's shawl.

"They think you're not real, Ann," Mrs. Jackman said.

Michel, after much painful figuring, looked up from a paper on which he had been writing and adding. The hunter was all attention now.

"*Ah-nim-i-nick ah-mik?*" he asked.

"He's asking, 'How many beavers?' " Mr. Jackman said. "He means 'dollars,' because once they used beaver skins for money."

Michel gave the total, and from that he subtracted the Indian's "debt," or value of goods advanced the previous fall and winter. It was a difficult task for Michel and he twisted his face and stuck his tongue out of a corner of his mouth. Philip giggled.

"I've seen a Jackman boy who looked like that in school," his mother said.

At last Michel told the Indian all "debt" was settled and he still had more than a hundred dollars. At once the hunter began to run up and down beside the counter, searching the shelves. His wife and family joined him and all talked at once and pointed and grew more and more excited.

Other Indians came into the store and became as excited as the hunter. They pointed, too, making suggestions. Evidently the hunter was anxious to spend his money all at once, and the others were as anxious to advise him. Michel set out bolts of dark-colored plaid woolen cloth, beads, thread, needles. He measured off yards of duffle, a thick white woolen cloth which, he told the Jackmans, the Indians used for socks.

The hunter bought big balls of gilling twine to make a fish net. He bought tobacco, shirts for the two boys, trousers for himself, some powder and lead, tea, finally a hat which he pulled on over his stiff black hair.

The woman who had named Ann "Wah-bo-sence" came into the store. She came close to Ann, called the new name softly and stroked the blond hair. Ann smiled at her and wished she could say even a few Ojibwa words. She was sure those soft sounds meant something nice.

The woman went to the end of the counter and called to Michel. He set out a box of beads, the sort Ann had called "wampum" in school. After much study, the woman selected a bunch, but

Michel shook his head. With all the din of purchasing and advising going on around them, the two argued. At last the woman laid down the beads and went out.

Michel returned to his first customers and began to list the purchases. The excitement died suddenly when he announced that more had been selected than the hundred dollars would cover.

Everyone started to advise again while the hunter and his wife tried to decide what they should return. The account was settled at last and quiet came. The hunter turned to see his youngest child, clad in a coat made of rabbit skin, sitting in a corner. Tears ran down the little brown cheeks.

The father took off the hat and threw it on the counter. He argued, and Michel shook his head, until every Indian in the store gathered behind the hunter. At last Michel went to a back room, returned after a few minutes with a paper bag half full. All the purchases were gathered and the jabbering crowd filed out. The last to go was the beaming, hatless father leading a white-coated little girl clutching a precious bag. Her cheeks were stuffed with candy.

"I never saw anything so sweet!" Mrs. Jackman exclaimed. "And he did want a hat."

"Every year just same," Michel said. "He never have a hat, that hunter. Some day maybe."

"We'd better start running up and down and yelling," Mr. Jackman said. "Got your list, Mary?"

She had, and she read it: sugar, coffee, dried fruits, bacon, baking powder, rice, canned milk, silk thread, all the common things Ann and Philip had been sent to buy in Bradford. Ann thought she couldn't get excited about them and that her mother didn't need advice.

But with each item Michel shook his head.

"No got," he said. "Indian no buy um."

Ann looked around, startled, not comprehending. She had been so fascinated by the excitement of the Indian family's shopping she had not noticed the shelves were almost empty. The store had no store cases, no candies, not even boxes of cookies or bottles of catsup and pickles, none of the familiar canned goods or hams and slabs of bacon.

Kettles of many sizes hung from beams. She saw axes and old fashioned muzzle-loading guns, powder horns, steel traps, a few imitation astrakhan caps. No bright cotton goods relieved the somber colors of plaid woolen cloth, but on a high shelf were many thick blankets, some white, others brilliant green or red. Below were big bolts of duffle and white and blue strouds, a tough woolen cloth. Ann shivered. Everything seemed designed to keep the wearer warm.

She was drawn by one spot of color and when she spoke to Michel he handed her a band of wool woven with white, red and green strands. It was six inches wide and, with the tassels at each end, six feet long.

"L'Assomption belt," he said. "Indians wear um. Like this."

He drew down a coat of white wool and held it for Ann. The skirts were long, reaching her knees, and an attached hood pulled over her head. It had no buttons or buttonholes but Michel found a smaller l'Assomption belt, wrapped it around her waist twice, tucked in the tasseled ends, and the coat was held snugly around her.

"Capote," Michel said. "For winter. Every Indian have um. Babies too," and he held up a tiny coat for a child of three and a tiny belt to go with it.

Ann was entranced and turned instinctively to see herself in a mirror. But of course there was none in that store. She was sure, however, she looked most attractive in the costume. Her mother's eyes told that.

"Ann would swelter in it for the effect," her father said. "Can you wait until winter?"

"Yes," Ann said, "only—"

She took off the coat and refastened the belt about her waist, the long tassels hanging at either side. Her father looked at her admiringly.

"No Indian dad is getting ahead of me," he said. "She'll keep it, Michel."

Michel gathered the pelts he had purchased to take them up the stairs, and he agreed readily when Mr. Jackman asked if his family could climb to the fur loft. Michel was proud of his position as head of the great company's post in the absence of the manager and was becoming more friendly.

He delighted now in displaying the great quantity of pelts hanging from rafters and piled on the floor. The first brigade had taken a hundred bales, he said, but all this remained for the second.

Many were "cased" with the fur inside and all Ann could see were the white and stained skins, stiff as shingles. But fox, lynx and fisher pelts had been stretched with the fur outside and Ann and her mother exclaimed over the great quantity of loveliness. Ann thought the cross fox skins with their dark shoulder markings the best and Michel draped half a dozen around her neck.

"I never imaged anything so gorgeous!" Mrs. Jackman exclaimed.

"If it weren't for you women, there'd be no trapping," her husband chuckled.

He picked up a bundle of mink skins and looked at the black fur inside.

"Finest mink in the world in this district," he said. "And I'm going to get my share this winter."

Michel turned swiftly. He was no longer smiling.

"You hunt here?" he demanded.

"Sure," Mr. Jackman said.

Ann was proud of the way her father said it. He would trap as much fur as an Indian, she was sure, and she expected Michel to be impressed.

But all the friendliness had gone from Michel's face. He led the way from the fur loft.

"I lock store now," he said curtly, and when they were outside he hurried away without a word.

"What happened to make him act like that?" Mrs. Jackman asked. "As soon as you mentioned trapping."

"He's afraid Dad will get all the fur," Philip said, "and there won't be any left for the Indians."

Ann laughed, until she saw her father's face.

She had never seen him so disturbed since they came to Canada.

"You can ask Michel," Mrs. Jackman said.

"And never get a word out of him," her husband said. "When an Indian shuts up like that, you can't learn why. But you can be sure he doesn't want you around. I wish Gillespie were here. Something's wrong, and I've got to know what."

8 ANN'S LOBSTICK

Ann and Philip went back to camp with their parents. No one spoke. Ann didn't know what the change in Michel meant, but her father's silence and troubled face told that it was serious.

Philip shed any sense of depression most suddenly and completely when two Indian boys came along the shore. They carried bows and blunt-headed arrows and a black bird attested to their skill. As naturally as a creek flows into a river, Philip and Ogema joined them. The Jackmans did not see the pair again until Philip rushed back at lunchtime.

"They're lending me a bow and arrows," he said between hasty bites. "And we've got a birch bark canoe and put boughs in the front end to hide behind and we're going hunting in the marsh down the shore and kill a lot of birds."

"But, Dave!" Mrs. Jackman exclaimed. "They can't even talk to each other."

"Boys don't need a language to go hunting," her husband said.

"We make signs," Philip said. "And they're teaching me Ojibwa and they think Ogema's the finest dog they ever saw and they don't have sisters along. Hunting is a man's job," he added loftily.

Ann resented this male superiority the more because she was a better canoeman than her brother.

"All right for you, Philip Jackman," she retorted. "But you'll wish you were with me this afternoon."

Later she wasn't sure she could make the boast good as she listened to her father urging John Ottertail and his wife, Es-quay-gee-she-gok, to come to Far Lake. John was as thin and serious as his wife was fat and merry. Despite her lack of English she had no trouble making friends with the Jackmans.

But she had to be convinced of the desirability of going to Far Lake. Mr. Jackman spoke slowly, repeating words to make sure John understood, and then the thought had to be conveyed to Esquay-gee-she-gok. Ojibwa volleyed back and forth in family conference, after which her objections had to be haltingly translated for the Jackmans.

"Doesn't she want to come?" Mrs. Jackman asked when this had gone on for some time.

"At least she hasn't said 'No' yet," Mr. Jackman said. "These things can't be hurried."

The discussion threatened to go on for hours. Ann tired of it and when she saw Michel leave his cabin she went to the "trade shop," as Michel called the store. She hoped another Indian family had come to trade, but Michel was alone, laboriously adding figures in an account book.

Ann stood in the door and stared at the lake. Past the timbered point, she could see smoke from the fires of the Indian village.

"Does that nice woman who called me 'Little Rabbit' live down there?" she asked.

"Yes," Michel said. "Her man Pe-tah-bo, he with fur brigade."

"What is her name?"

"Wah-be-goon."

Ann repeated the word several times to make

sure she could remember it, for suddenly she had decided to pay a call. She considered asking parental permission, but concluded this might be unwise. A visit to the wigwams had never been expressly forbidden and she reasoned that her parents were far too occupied with the Ottertails to be bothered with unimportant matters. If Philip could go hunting in a canoe, she certainly could be trusted to take a walk ashore.

Ann foresaw awkward formalities in a call on a wigwam. They might be evaded if she arrived bearing a gift and she remembered the beads Wah-be-goon had selected that morning and asked Michel for the box. After finding two bunches of the correct colors, she asked, "How much?"

"*Ap-tah wah-bik*," Michel said.

Uncertainly she laid her birthday dollar on the counter, hoping it would be enough. She was relieved to get fifty cents in change.

The beads put an entirely new light on the visit. Ann was now bound on an errand and she hurried from the store and past the servants' cabins, where an old man sat in the sun smoking.

"*B'jou*'," Ann said.

His smile and own quick "*B'jou*'" were encouraging. Not only had she successfully used the

Ojibwa greeting but the old man had seemed friendly.

As Ann followed a well-worn trail along the shore she practiced the few words she had learned. They might not be sufficient for a whole afternoon's visit, but at least she could say "thank you," and she knew "come," "go," "good," "boy" and "sister." These, and the beads, would have to serve, and perhaps they would, she decided comfortably. Ann didn't believe in anticipating trouble, for difficulties in which she found herself were never like anything she could have imagined. And her solutions, she had discovered, were always better if inspired on the spot.

The clearing was sunny and hot and she was glad when the trail entered the cool forest. Here she could no longer see the smoke of cooking fires, but she caught glimpses of the lake through the trees. The cries of children told her she was nearing the encampment and she began to look eagerly ahead for the wigwams.

Then a dog barked. Shrill yelps echoed in the forest and Ann stopped. She had not thought of the pack of Indian dogs, except as a menace to Ogema, and now she wondered about their number and ferocity. She hoped she wouldn't encounter them when there was no one to protect her and she decided to approach the village noiselessly.

Despite her care, a stick snapped under a foot. At once a dog growled and Ann saw him in an opening beside the trail, his lips drawn back in a snarl. He was a dirty white and ill-conditioned. Ann had never seen a less prepossessing dog, but she managed an uncertain "Hello, boy," and stood her ground.

Most dogs, she had felt sure, would respond to friendliness, but all thought of peaceable overtures vanished now. The muscles of the animal's throat quivered from a deep-throated growl and he started toward her. Ann turned and ran.

With her first step she recognized her mistake. She couldn't run faster than a dog and looked wildly around for a tree she could climb. The next moment she was scrambling up a spruce.

Its low branches were like a ladder, though they tore her face and hands, but Ann cared nothing for scratches as the dog's jaws snapped close to her heels.

She reached safety and looked down into the beast's eyes. They were incandescent with hatred as he leaped up the trunk and tried to reach her.

Then, to Ann's horror, more dogs came rushing down the trail. Brown dogs, black dogs, yellow dogs and all mixtures gathered around the tree.

They leaped and plunged, barked and snapped even at each other. She heard the sharp click of fangs and clung to the branches in terror lest she fall into the shrieking pack below.

Pandemonium reigned in the forest. Ann screamed but her voice was drowned. All she could do was cling there, trembling. She was too frightened even to think of rescue when she heard a shout. Through the branches, she saw a boy running down the trail.

He stopped and looked at the spruce around which the dogs leaped, then came closer to learn what they had treed.

He stood staring up at Ann in astonishment. The sight of a white girl clinging high up in a spruce seemed to have paralyzed him, but only for a moment. He charged into the pack, swinging right and left with the handle of an ax.

At first the dogs did not heed his blows. Some even snapped at him and Ann wondered if he would be torn to pieces.

But the boy shouted and redoubled his efforts. He was not in the least afraid and the ax handle rattled on ribs and thudded on skulls. The smaller and weaker dogs began to slink away and at last the larger animals retreated. The big white dog was the last to go.

When the boy stood alone he beckoned Ann to climb down. As she reached the ground, he smiled. Ann smiled too, and then to her dismay she could not remember one of her Ojibwa words. She could not even thank him.

The boy, she decided, was about her age, although it was hard to tell. He wore a torn shirt and the shortened remnants of a man's trousers. But she liked his eyes.

He watched her pick pine needles from her hair.

"Wah-bo-sence," he said.

Her Ojibwa name helped to recall the word for thank you.

"*Me-gwetch*," she said.

He smiled to show he understood and then they looked helplessly at each other. Ann wished she knew a sign language so she could tell him how brave he had been to drive away the dogs. A rescued maiden should not walk away without a word. Now she didn't even know his name.

She pointed at herself and said, "Wah-bo-sence," then pointed at him.

He shook his head, but when she repeated word and gesture his face brightened.

"Wen-dah-ban," he said, and she liked the way his name sang.

"Wen-dah-ban, Wen-dah-ban," she repeated,

trying to draw out the second syllable softly as he did.

Ann was wondering what more she could say when several Indian women hurried down the trail to see what all the noise was about. Wen-dah-ban told what had happened and there was much clucking and excited chatter. Wah-be-goon was one of the last to arrive and she had to be told all over again. She stood near Ann, but her glance rested on Wen-dah-ban.

Before he had finished his story Mr. Jackman and Michel came running from the post. Both were gasping from the run, but Ann's father had enough breath to scold her.

"What a crazy thing to do!" he exclaimed. "You might have been torn to pieces."

"But I was up a tree," Ann said.

"And what if you hadn't been able to climb a tree? We heard the rumpus, but never imagined you were in danger until an old man came to tell us he had seen you going to the wigwams."

"And anyhow," Ann said, "Wen-dah-ban drove the dogs away."

Mr. Jackman sat down to recover his breath and Ann told how she had been rescued from the yelping pack. The story lost none of its drama in her telling, and when she had finished, Michel added to the general hubbub by interpreting to the women all that Ann had said about Wen-dah-ban.

Mr. Jackman stood up, and now that Ann was safe he was more angry than relieved.

"Why did you come without asking us?" he demanded.

"I was going to visit Wah-be-goon," Ann said, and she added righteously, "I was bringing her a present."

She drew the beads from a pocket, thankful that she had something to produce, and handed them to Wah-be-goon. The Indian woman's face broke into smiles.

"*Me-gwetch, me-gwetch, me-gwetch*," she said, and when she saw the colors many "*nish-i-shins*" flowed from her lips.

"She say, 'Good, good, very good,' " Michel interpreted. "And Wen-dah-ban glad you give um to his mother."

"His mother!" Ann exclaimed.

The excitement of this discovery spurred her memory and she recalled the word for "you" or "yours." Michel had used it in the store that morning.

"*Keen?*" she asked, delighted that at last she had found something she could say. "*Keen?*" she repeated to Wah-be-goon, and pointed at Wen-dah-ban. "*Keen?*"

"*Neen, neen!*" Wah-be-goon answered, meaning "mine," and then the "*keens*" and the "*neens*" flew back and forth and everyone laughed and seemed suddenly to be great friends. Even Ann's father looked at her approvingly.

The Indian women admired the beads and appeared to think Wen-dah-ban's heroism had won his mother a present. But Ann wanted Wah-be-goon to know she had been bringing the gift when she met the dogs. She tried to say so with signs and then appealed to Michel to say it for her. When he finally understood he spoke for a long time and his audience seemed impressed.

"I think, Ann," her father said, "that it's our turn to say a few '*me-gwetches*' and '*nish-i-shins*.' Where's the young hero?"

They looked around for Wen-dah-ban, but he was nowhere in sight. They heard sounds of an ax and Michel hurried toward the lake shore. He called the others. Wen-dah-ban was in a tree that stood alone on a little point. He had climbed almost to the top and was cutting off the branches. He pointed to the untouched tuft above him and called something to the group below.

ANN'S LOBSTICK

A wave of laughter broke from the women. Michel chuckled.

"Now he cuts lobstick," he said. "You know it?"

"You mean the tree to mark a great event?" Mr. Jackman asked.

Michel nodded. "You see tree like that long way off. You know man cut um. Maybe man kill a bear, he cut a lobstick. Maybe he meet friend on river. Maybe fur brigades join together. Maybe big boss of the company come along. Maybe just because man is happy. Always he cut a lobstick. Then every time people go by they say, 'That lobstick cut when such thing happen.' Now Wen-dah-ban cut lobstick."

Wen-dah-ban, hacking branches from the trunk, worked swiftly down the tree. At last he reached the ground and stood there. He pointed upward at the conical crown and made what sounded like a speech. The women shrieked with delight, but Wah-be-goon's eyes were proud. Ann didn't know what all the laughter was about for Wen-dah-ban's face was serious. She clapped her hands and said, "*Me-gwetch.*" Michel shouted with approval.

"He say he cut lobstick for day that Wen-dah-

ban drive dogs away for Wah-bo-sence," Michel
interpreted.

Mr. Jackman looked at the lobstick, and a smile
lurked at the corner of his mouth.

"Think you can find some more candy in the
store, Michel?" he asked.

Michel shook his head and explained they never
had but a little and Mr. Gillespie had told him to
keep it for special occasions.

"This is one," Ann's father said. "Tell Wen-
dah-ban the father of Wah-bo-sence gives him
regale. Come on!"

Wen-dah-ban looked up alertly at the white
man's word for a special feast, reward for service.
He needed no further urging to return to the post
with the Jackmans. In the store Michel disappeared
in the back room, to return with a bag of highly
colored and very hard candy. As he handed it to
Mr. Jackman he said it was right that all share in
the regale, and Michel began at once to eat with
Wen-dah-ban and Ann. He and the Indian boy
were still munching when Mr. Jackman took Ann
to camp for supper.

Ann knew she still faced an explanation when
her mother learned she had gone alone to the Indian village, but she felt that any possible unpleas-
antness had compensations. No girl Ann had ever

known had been saved from great danger by a brave young Indian and had had a lobstick cut in her honor.

And she was sure her mother must understand what an important occasion the day had been.

9 ES-QUAY-GEE-SHE-GOK

John Ottertail had promised to leave with the Jackmans at sun-up the next morning. Breakfast was eaten, tent down and canoe stowed when the first shafts of sunlight gilded the lake. But John was not in sight. Mr. Jackman said they couldn't reach home that evening if they didn't start at once and he threatened to leave without John, trusting he would follow. Mrs. Jackman reminded him of the afternoon spent in helping Es-quay-gee-she-gok make up her mind.

124

"You must have a man," she said, "to help finish the cabin and do the freighting if you cut trapping trails by fall."

Mr. Jackman agreed and they sat down. An hour went by. Mr. Jackman was becoming explosive in his impatience.

"If there was another Indian who could talk English, I'd hire him," he said.

"And spend another day convincing his wife," Mrs. Jackman added.

Mr. Jackman grinned and admitted that she might be right. There was nothing to do but wait. The servants' cabins came to life. Smoke rose from chimneys and the sound of chopping was heard. Ann suggested a walk, but their father frowned and said he wanted them within sight and ready to depart the moment the Ottertails arrived.

At last John's canoe appeared around the point. The birchbark was golden in the sunlight and the early morning refraction seemed to make it float above the water. John paddled in the bow and Es-quay-gee-she-gok, her broad face wreathed in smiles, was in the stern. In front of her enormous figure were bags, bundles, pails, rolls of birchbark and kettles. Ann wondered how they'd ever carry all those things across the portage.

Mr. Jackman was hurrying his family into their canoe when John came ashore.

"I get something," he said.

He disappeared among the servants' cabins. The Jackmans waited. John returned bearing another bundle. He and his wife discussed this volubly and then she scrambled out.

"Here!" Mr. Jackman called. "You can't go away now."

Only John understood her answer.

"She get something," he said softly.

"Remember, Dave," Mrs. Jackman said, "you explained that these things can't be hurried."

Es-quay-gee-she-gok reappeared with several women and there was much talk and restowing of the canoe. When everything was arranged to Es-quay-gee-she-gok's satisfaction and she was settling herself among her belongings, John thought of an errand and disappeared.

So it went for another hour. The Jackmans waited while one or the other, or both, went to "get something." They waited through long conversations.

Always Indians were arriving, women and children and a few men, and it seemed that every one had some advice to give John and his wife. The

Jackmans went ashore to wait more comfortably.

"Mother," Ann whispered as she watched the crowd, "there's Wah-be-goon and Wen-dah-ban."

Mrs. Jackman looked at the Indian woman and her son.

"Ann," she said, "how do I say 'thank you'?"

Ann spoke the word and her mother repeated it several times. "Come with me," she said.

They went back among the Indians until they reached Wen-dah-ban and Wah-be-goon. Ann was proud of how her mother did it, calmly and with the same poise she had presided over a classroom of children. She stopped before Wah-be-goon and held out her hand.

"*Me-gwetch*," she said, and there was something gracious and fine in her manner.

It brought a light to Wah-be-goon's eyes and even Wen-dah-ban felt it and seemed proud to have the white woman thank him.

"I wish I could say more," Mrs. Jackman said. "Maybe someday I will. And here are the Otter-tails at last."

John and his wife were getting into their canoe, and this time they seemed to mean it. The Jackmans hurried to their craft. The sun was high and the morning half gone.

"Have to travel fast now," Mr. Jackman said.

John pointed at the Jackmans' four paddles and at their own two.

"Four go too fast," he said.

Es-quay-gee-she-gok caught his meaning and shook with laughter.

"Let me paddle with them," Ann said. "I'd love to."

"But, Dave—" Mrs. Jackman began uncertainly.

"Why not?" Mr. Jackman said. "Ann might help keep their canoe in sight."

Ann's change to the birchbark necessitated more restowing and considerable advice from onlookers, but at last the two canoes started amid much waving and shouts and laughter from the shore. It was all very jolly, and secretly Ann was delighted that they had not gotten off at sunrise. This was much more fun.

Six paddles dipped. At last the crowd ashore and the white buildings of the post were shut from view. The Ottertails, now that they were started, were as happy as children going to a picnic.

A loon floated motionless on the glassy water. It gave its piercing call and John imitated the mad laughter of the cry. He told Ann the bird's Ojibwa name and she asked the words for other birds and animals, for trees, the lake and river. Some were too long to remember and she resolved to write them. When she asked John if he would help make a list, he wasn't at all astonished. He said white men often did this when they came among the Indians. Until then it had never occurred to Ann that dictionaries could be homemade.

Try as she might, Ann could not say Es-quay-gee-she-gok. John repeated the name slowly and explained that it meant "round-cloud-in-the-north," but that didn't help.

"It's no use," Ann said at last. "Would she mind if I called her Es-quay?"

The Ottertails laughed so heartily Ann knew she'd made a joke. Es-quay was round and almost as large as a cloud. But why the north? Finally Ann dared ask the reason.

John explained Ojibwa christening. A child was named for the thing which the father first saw as he stepped outside the wigwam after the baby was born. John appeared to think it all very natural, but Ann thought the custom might not always work out well. She asked the meaning of Wah-be-goon.

" 'Flower,' " John said. "Her man name Pe-tah-bo. His father see tea water first."

Ann felt a father should be careful about what he saw and she hoped Wen-dah-ban meant something pleasant.

"It mean 'coming dawn,'" John said. "Baby born early."

"Coming dawn" had a brave sound. No wonder he had dared attack the dogs. Es-quay, who had demanded that everything be interpreted, now asked a question.

"She say what your name mean?" John said.

It had never occurred to Ann that English names might have a meaning, nor had she wondered how they were evolved. Es-quay was astonished when Ann admitted she didn't know, and Ann determined to learn more about the white man's culture so she too could answer questions.

John and Es-quay paddled with a quick short thrust much faster than the stroke to which Ann was accustomed, but the Ottertails stopped often to laugh or talk. Often they skirted the shore, not because they were timid, as Ann first thought, but to watch for game. Ann saw nothing the first few times the Ottertails grew tense and watchful, but later her eyes became accustomed to the dark forenoon shadows that lurked beneath the spruces. Once Es-quay hissed softly and John picked up his rifle. A deer stood in the forest, his head up-lifted, his tawny body splashed by sunlight. He was so lovely Ann cried out. The next moment the deer had vanished.

Es-quay made a quick sound of disappointment, but John was cheerful.

"Next time I shoot quick," he said.

Ann was afraid he might suspect she had cried out to keep the deer from being shot, but evidently such a thought never occurred to him.

Time passed so quickly Ann was astonished when they reached the portage at the rapids. The Jackmans were waiting. Ann had expected to help the Ottertails make several trips across, but Es-quay collected her household possessions in a huge blanket pack, adjusted the headstrap, piled rolls of birchbark on top, gathered two handsful of kettles, ax and baskets, and trudged off up the trail.

Philip and Ogema were not in sight. Mrs. Jackman said they had gone to look at the rapids.

"But Philip shouldn't have taken Ogema there!" Ann cried.

She sped up the trail to overtake them. It was much too soon to let Ogema revisit a spot that held such poignant memories. What if he decided to resume his vigil? But to Ann's great relief she met the pair returning. Philip defended his action.

131

"I knew Ogema'd want to see the rapids," he said. "And you ought to have heard him whimper. But he turned right around and came away again."

Philip stopped to pat the black head.

"I don't think he feels so bad about Mis-tay-o-sin now," he added. "It sort of helped him to know he belongs to us."

Philip's faith in Ogema's devotion had been unshaken, and now Ann realized her own was strengthened.

"I'm so glad you took him!" she cried. "We needn't ever be afraid he wants to leave us."

When they reached the end of the portage Esquay already had a fire started. A kettle of tea hung from a blackened tea stick thrust obliquely into the ground.

Ann had thought her father's camping methods simple, but that evening she learned how much more simple overnight camps and meals could be. The Jackmans were still eating supper when the Ottertails, fed and rested, crawled under a shelter of sheets of birchbark spread over slanting holes.

"No wonder they don't care when they start or where they stop," Mrs. Jackman said. "They're no more trouble to themselves than a pair of birds."

Indian housekeeping was not quite so simple as

that, Ann discovered, when they arrived at Far Lake the next day and she and Philip watched Es-quay build a wigwam. To their delight, she chose to camp down the shore in their own woods, but they did not realize how deep a trail they would wear to it.

Es-quay, and now even Mr. and Mrs. Jackman called her that, arranged her kitchen in a few minutes. She cut two dry poplar logs, laid them an inch apart on the ground, started a tiny fire between them and set a kettle of meat on the smoldering timbers.

Dinner started, she tied the tops of three poles together and stood them up as a tripod. More poles were leaned in the crotch so that their butts formed a circle on the ground. Wide sheets of birchbark, long mellowed by weather and bent to the cone-shaped frame, were unrolled and laid over the poles until they were entirely covered except for the tip, where a smoke hole was left, and a space for a low door. Es-quay hung a piece of old blanket over this and her nomadic home was complete.

"You can't knock on that door," Philip said.

Es-quay didn't understand what they meant until Ann acted out a visit, coming from her own camp. Then Es-quay pretended to be the visitor. Her moccasins made no noise as she approached the wigwam and she indicated that anyone inside would not hear her. Then she stopped at the door and scratched the birchbark with a fingernail.

Ann saw where many fingernails had scratched the bark at Es-quay's door. "People must like to visit her," she said.

When the wigwam was completed, Es-quay cut flat cedar boughs and spread them on the ground inside, placed blanket rolls and other possessions around the walls, and the Ottertails had a home, complete with carpet and bed. Even a meal was ready, for she had stopped occasionally to push the smoldering logs together beneath the kettle.

"And did that moose meat smell good!" Philip reported in his own camp.

Philip's growing appetite had aroused the wonder of his family, but Mr. Jackman said even Philip wouldn't care to eat Es-quay's food when he found a bunch of moose hair in the stew.

As Ann and Philip became daily callers at the wigwam, they discovered their father was right. Moose meat and whitefish went into the kettle without being well cleaned. There were no dishes and even the kettle from which the Ottertails ate was seldom washed. It was usually on the fire with a meal simmering.

"But there's always hot grub ready when they're hungry," Philip said a bit enviously.

"And no cookies, cake or brown sugar on bread between meals," his mother added. "But how in the world can you and Ann carry on a conversation with Es-quay?"

Talk among the three was limited. Es-quay steadfastly refused to speak a word of English and Ann's and Philip's Ojibwa, although increasing daily, did not cover a wide range. They used words they knew and acted out the rest, and were amazed at how much they could convey. It was like a game of charades, and they knew the other side had guessed the word when Es-quay's fat face broke into smiles. But when it was her turn to act the answer she showed her powers of mimicry. One waving motion of her hand was unmistakably a fish, another was surely a bird. Pain, astonishment, despair and joy were all acted out in pantomime. They knew just how she felt when she found a sprung and empty rabbit snare, or when the fish net held nothing.

Everything Es-quay did was new and exciting, and she was always busy. Each morning the blankets were rolled to the wall. She swept by the simple process of pushing the rug into the fire, which always burned in the center of the wigwam on rainy days, and laying a new rug of fresh cedar boughs.

Each day she lifted her fish net and gathered wood. She dug spruce roots. When washed, peeled and split, these became the threads with which she sewed slats to new wide sheets of birchbark to replace old ones. A new roof was as simple as that.

In the afternoons Es-quay sewed, either on moccasins or making a buckskin bag to hold some trifle. She made a new fish net of gilling twine. And always she was ready to stop for laughter or questions, to show how she sewed buckskin with a three-sided needle and puckered the leather above the toes when she made moccasins.

Like all Ojibwa women, she loved children and her disappointment over having none of her own made her a more eager and responsive companion. A very real affection developed between the three, and Ann and Philip loved the hours they spent in the wigwam.

The afternoons when Es-quay brought out her bead work were never as merry. Then she was intent and serious, and if Ann and Philip stayed they must sit quietly and watch as she sewed colored beads into a flower pattern, hour after hour. When she sewed on beads she wore a pair of steel spectacle frames without lenses. When they saw Es-quay wearing her spectacles they never loitered, for they knew serious matters absorbed her. The mystery of the glassless spectacles fascinated Ann and Philip. They asked John one day why she wore them.

"She see good that way," he explained. "White people wear glass. So she do."

John killed a deer and Es-quay tanned the skin. Ann thought tanning very messy, but Philip helped to scrape the hide of hair, and then to rub in a mixture of deer's brains and soap. A few days later he and Es-quay washed the hide in the lake and then they sat on the ground and pulled the skin between them to make it dry and soft. Compared to Es-quay, Philip was very light and it took all of his strength to pull against her. Once suddenly she let go and Philip went backwards, heels over head down the hill. Es-quay's enormous body shook with laughter.

Philip laughed, too, when he had recovered from his astonishment. The practical joke was on him, but Es-quay had been just as quick to laugh when the joke was on her. She was never cross and thought it funny when they hid her paddles or fastened stones in her fish net. Ann, who had always believed Indians were taciturn and sullen, was amazed to discover their love of gaiety and laughter.

But Ann and Philip could not spend all their time with Es-quay. Mr. Jackman had finished the log work on the cabin before going to Fort Caribou and now, while he hewed planks for doors and logs for the floor, John Ottertail cut spruce saplings and limbed and peeled them for roof poles. Ann and Philip dragged these to the cabin, and they thought their father would never be satisfied with their rate of progress.

John rigged a harness for Ogema so he could drag four poles on each trip. Ann and Philip didn't bring poles any faster that way, but getting them became fun and Ogema was much happier when he worked.

They built a house for him. John thought this was funny and said an Indian dog liked to sleep in a nice warm snowdrift, but Philip insisted Ogema was now a white man's dog and would follow white ways. Ogema said nothing, but achieved a nice compromise by sleeping on the roof of his house in daytime and beside the campfire at night.

As soon as the roof poles were in place, Mr.

Jackman set Ann and Philip to gathering moss once more.

"I want a thick layer between poles and tar paper," he said, "so don't stop with a dozen sacks. And have it ready when I get back from the railroad."

He and John were gone six days. It was the first of several trips that would have to be made before all the household goods and winter supplies would be brought to Far Lake. Mr. Jackman was tired as they unloaded the canoe.

"Ten portages," he said. "The longest nearly a mile. And we brought eleven hundred pounds."

Several rolls of roofing paper were in the canoe. Ann and Philip had a great mound of moss ready and the next morning this was spread thickly over the poles and then the paper was placed on top and fastened with strips of cedar.

The cabin seemed more like a house now, with a roof that would shed rain, but it was still bare and empty inside. Ann tried to think how it would look when they moved in. It didn't seem promising.

"Now we've got a place to store supplies, John and I will rush this stuff in," Mr. Jackman said as the two men again departed southward.

They returned a week later. The canoe was

loaded to the gunwales and Mr. Jackman looked thin and worn.

"Take a rest before the next trip," Mrs. Jackman said.

"Work for the big company, always rest Sunday," John said, and he drew a small notched stick from a pocket.

He was counting the notches when Mrs. Jackman brought a calendar from the tent.

"We haven't looked at this since we came," she said. "And if—here's the day we left Fort Caribou —why, tomorrow is Sunday."

"All right," her husband said. "I'm willing to lay up. And John needs a rest. What that man can carry on a portage!"

But John didn't rest the next morning.

"Kill moose," he said as he set his canoe in the water.

"Take us!" Ann and Philip cried together.

"Talk too much," John said. "You tell moose we come."

"But we won't," Ann said.

John shook his head but Es-quay laughed and motioned the children into the canoe. John grinned.

"I scare um," he said.

140

"*Kah-win!*" Es-quay shrieked as Ann got into the bow, and Ojibwa sputtered and bubbled from her lips.

Ann knew "*kah-win*" meant "no," and she'd often thought the Indians used it more than any other word. Now she feared Es-quay had changed her mind. But again John grinned.

"She say you paddle here," he said to Ann, and indicated the stern. "Man paddle in front so he can shoot."

Thus they went off, Ann in the stern, Philip in the center, John with his rifle in the bow.

"*Tib-ish-ko nish-ee-nah-bee,*" Es-quay chanted from shore.

"Same as an Indian," Ann interpreted, "but she meant me, Philip."

"You can't shoot a bow and arrow," Philip said.

"Too much talk," John said.

They paddled far down the lake, into bays and around points, watching always, and without seeing a moose. Philip fidgeted and squirmed and Ann thought she'd never been silent so long in her life. She was wondering if she could stand it any longer when John laid down his paddle and lifted the rifle.

"*Muk-wah,*" he whispered.

That meant "bear" and Ann saw something small and dark at the edge of the brush on a point.

"*Muk-wonce*," John said, which meant "little bear," and he began paddling again.

The little bear lay on the moss as they approached but he didn't run away. He didn't even lift his head. They landed and walked closer.

"Sick," John said, and he looked at the ground and walked into the brush.

"Hungry," he said when he returned. "Indian come by. Kill mother. Skin um back there. No see *muk-wonce*. Now he big hungry."

The cub was very thin and his hair was dull and tangled. His head was much too big for his thin little body and his black eyes were dull.

"The poor little thing!" Ann cried.

She dropped to her knees beside the cub. He drew back his lips and let out a tiny growl when she reached for him, but with the first touch of her hand he whimpered. The next moment he was cuddled in her arms.

"We'll take him home," she said.

"*Kah-win*," John said. "Moose smell um. No get moose."

"I don't care! It's wicked leaving him here to starve. I will take him home."

"He make trouble," John said. "All time run

around. Eat out of kettle. Tear up clothes. Eat pork, sugar, flour. Me kill him now."

"No!" Ann cried. "He's mine," and she ran to the canoe with the bear in her arms.

10 "MUK-WAH" MEANS
MISCHIEF

When Mr. Jackman and John Ottertail departed for the railroad the next morning, no one questioned but that Ann might try to nurse the cub back to health. Her father and mother gave no heed to John's lengthy predictions that they would only have trouble if they kept the little bear for a pet. They didn't believe he had a chance to live.

Ann had doubts that first day. Despite warnings,

she fed him too much warm milk and thin broth. But the second morning he lifted himself on wobbly legs.

"He couldn't cause trouble," Ann said. "He knows he's adopted and he'll learn to mind."

"He snuggles up to you like a baby," Mrs. Jackman said.

"He's as cunning as a baby, Mother. And isn't his nose black?"

"He is cute. I'll make more broth for him."

The cub was cute, more so every day as he grew stronger. Mrs. Jackman cuddled him too, and helped Ann prepare his meals. Es-quay held long conversations with him and rubbed his nose and laughed. The cub looked at Ann with affection, but he listened to Es-quay with strict attention.

"I'd almost swear he understands Ojibwa," Mrs. Jackman said.

Everyone admired the little bear but his care was Ann's sole occupation. She devoted herself to him and when he saw her coming his bright little eyes lighted up.

"I've named him," Ann said when he first scampered at her heels. "He's too little to be Muk-wah so I'll call him Muckie."

Mrs. Jackman nuzzled the small black ball.

"Mickie would be better," she said. "There's

145

laughter and mischief in his eyes. But he's the cutest baby thing I ever saw."

The mischief did not remain in Muckie's eyes. It oozed out of every pore. It flowed from every hair tip as he grew stronger and ran around camp. Nothing was safe from him. He had no difficulty in climbing onto the table, and when he tried to climb to the hanging cupboard even Ann admitted he would be able to reach it in a few days.

He investigated the tent, tore beds apart, rummaged in packsacks and Ann's bureau, scattered her clothes. He attempted the same liberties in Es-quay's wigwam but she stood no nonsense from him, now that he was round and fat and well. Let Muckie so much as look into her wigwam and her stern "*Kah-win*" sent him into swift retreat. She had a way of saying the Ojibwa "no" that even small bears understood. Yet Ann suspected that Muckie liked Es-quay best of all. He learned the trail to her camp and would scamper down it even without Ann and Philip.

By the time the men had made two more trips to the railroad Muckie had fulfilled John's direst prophecies. He was a nuisance, but he had also proved Ann's contention that he would be an engaging pet. Usually she was his only champion. When she saw him running toward her, a look of fright puckering his baby face, she knew he was in trouble even before she learned what he had done. And a moment later an indignant owner of a pilfered or ruined possession would be at his heels.

Muckie was responsible for the disappearance of the pie baked to celebrate Mr. Jackman's first dinner at home in a week.

"I turn my back for a moment and it is gone," Mrs. Jackman cried. "Nothing is safe from him."

"But Muckie doesn't know he shouldn't steal!" Ann protested.

"He knows more than we give him credit for. See how he's hiding behind you. He knows you're defending him."

Mr. Jackman laughed when Ann stood staunchly between her mother and the frightened culprit.

"It isn't funny any more," his wife said. "Something's got to be done."

"How about moving the kitchen into the cabin?" Mr. Jackman said. "A couple of days' work and we can cook and eat inside. And then if that young man steals my pie, I'll paddle him with an ax handle."

John was pleased when he heard they would not

do any freighting while Mr. Jackman built furniture.

"Me kill moose," he said. "This time no little bear."

John liked the cub despite his predictions and taught him to box. Muckie loved the game and he knew it won attention and admiration. He learned that if he stood upright and invited a match he often won forgiveness or softened anger.

John said Muckie could be taught to ride in a canoe and made a small open crate of peeled saplings.

"The cub doesn't mind on land," Mr. Jackman said. "What makes you think he'll behave on water?"

Es-quay went along when Muckie received his first day's training as a sailor. Before the afternoon was over he hopped in and out of his crate at command and sat motionless while they paddled. Like all animals, he loved the idea of traveling with no effort on his part. His greatest fear was that the canoe would depart without him aboard.

Later, when Ann and Philip wished to paddle without Muckie, they had first to chain him to the small doghouse which had become his official home. Even that measure was not always successful for Muckie was adept at slipping his collar.

Many times he was at the water's edge as soon as they were, and pleading so pitifully that they usually took him along.

The quartet, Ann and Philip, Muckie and Ogema, could always stir up some excitement when they went roaming in the woods or paddling on the bay.

"And it's a lot more fun with them along," Philip said one night at supper. "They hear and smell things we'd have missed."

"And in the meantime neither of you are any help around the cabin any more," their father said. "I'm building furniture, your mother's working every minute and you two haven't managed to cut enough hay to fill the mattresses."

"You mean we four," Ann giggled. "But honest! We'll cut heaps of hay tomorrow."

"Believe that, Mary?" Mr. Jackman asked.

"Not quite," his wife said. "Their intentions will be good, but they'll find something to watch at Es-quay's camp, or Ogema will smell game or Muckie will climb a tree. This is their vacation, though. The Ottertails will be gone soon, we'll be settled in the cabin, lessons will begin and they won't have time to run wild."

Life was threatening to become everydayish. The kitchen corner of the big room was completed. Pots and pans now sat on a stove instead of hanging from a crane over a campfire. Ann missed the birchbark table in the open. Wiping dishes was only housework now, not camping. Mrs. Jackman was proud of the easy chairs her husband was making for the living-room corner but Ann thought it was more fun when all four sat on the ground. And schoolbooks, already on shelves, were unpleasant reminders of days of regularity and set tasks ahead.

Ann was glad the bedrooms were not finished. She'd miss the bough bed on the ground. She and Philip talked about it one night before they went to sleep. Moonlight was etching shadows of pine branches on their tent. They could hear small scurryings in the forest about them. The lake was silvered. Ann said that even a log-cabin bedroom couldn't be half as nice.

"If we can't stand living in a house," Philip said, "we'll build ourselves a wigwam. Let's build one anyhow."

"Let's," Ann said. "We're so used to being in Es-quay's."

She thought how Es-quay had fitted into their daily life and how much they would miss her. She spoke of it next morning at breakfast.

"I'm sure I'll miss Es-quay, too," Mrs. Jackman

said. "We can't talk to each other. She might not understand me if a crisis arose. And yet I feel I have a fine neighbor."

"She's been company for Ann and Philip," Mr. Jackman said.

"And for me. I feel safe, too, with Es-quay here. I wish you'd stop worrying about our being alone. And don't rush across portages with heavy loads just to get here a day sooner."

"Loads will be heavy this trip," Mr. Jackman said, "because it'll be the last. But we'll have a winter's supplies under our own roof and I'll have nothing to do but trap."

"And I'm going to help," Philip said.

"I'll bet you haven't even cut hay for mattresses," his father said.

"But we have!" Philip cried.

"And every day we turn it over in the sun," Ann said. "It'll be dry before you make the beds or mother sews the ticks."

"Fine!" her father said. "When it's thoroughly dry, pile it in a bedroom and I'll make the beds when I get back. John and I start tomorrow noon."

All were busy the next morning with baking for the men, food bags to be filled, last-minute jobs around the cabin to be finished. Muckie was underfoot until sternly sent outside.

And there even Ogema refused to play with him. Often Ogema's dignity broke down before Muckie's playful overtures and he joined in a rough and tumble. Usually he took care not to hurt the cub and although he'd hold him under a big paw and pretend to bite him, he never really closed his jaws. Ogema really enjoyed these romps as much as Muckie, if he thought no one was watching. But if he heard laughter he'd stalk off in great dignity.

But this morning Ogema wished to lie in the sun and think dogs' thoughts, and he growled warningly when Muckie approached. The cub could not believe Ogema meant this and tried a bit of humor. He'd slipped up and nipped Ogema's haunches and then scooted for a tree. But Ogema was having a stern moment and he caught the fleeing Muckie.

The small cub's cries were pitiful. Ann flew to stop the punishment, but John held her back.

"Ogema show who boss," he said. "Ogema boss same as Es-quay."

John seldom made a joke and the Jackmans laughed so much he repeated it to Es-quay when she came to see them off. It wasn't such a funny joke, but everyone's delight that this was to be the last hard freighting trip made laughter come easily.

All went down to the lake to see the canoe depart. That is, everyone except Muckie. He still sulked in his house because of Ogema's chastisement.

"It's the last week we'll be left alone," Mrs. Jackman said as they walked back to camp. "Let's surprise your father."

They plunged into an orgy of activity. Curtains were hung at windows, goods unpacked, mattresses filled and shelves arranged. It wasn't the palatial wilderness home Ann had visioned in the future, but she was surprised at how much she enjoyed seeing familiar things from Bradford.

"Dad will be surprised when he sees how nice the cabin looks," she said.

Her mother proudly surveyed the ruffle around her dressing table and agreed they had accomplished wonders. And they had three days left before the men's return, time to gather fruit for preserves.

"If we take our lunch and stay all day we can get enough raspberries to fill our jars with jam," Mrs. Jackman said. "We'll have a picnic and invite Es-quay."

Ann and Philip delivered the invitation. Es-quay understood they would gather many berries and eat lunch but she was puzzled by the charade by which they tried to express "winter jam." At last she concluded it was only another of the mysteries of a strange people, for she dismissed it with "*Shag-e-nash, shag-e-nash.*" This Ojibwa word for "white men" always meant further explanation was useless.

Es-quay was ready the next morning. She had dressed for a party by wearing a very full and very long apron over her equally full and equally long and only dress. Mrs. Jackman, in breeches, looked at Es-quay's volumious skirts and asked Ann if she'd not explained they were to pick berries.

But Es-quay had no doubts about her costume. Evidently she'd never understood why Ann, a girl, wore breeches, and she laughed and chattered and directed the stowing of dog, bear, kettles, pails, lunch and people in her birchbark. The big raspberry patch was within easy walking distance, but now even the Jackmans used a canoe to carry burdens.

Mrs. Jackman had brought small kettles for each to pick in and two large water pails to be filled. Ann wondered how four people could ever gather so many berries, and then was amazed at how fast the big pails were filled as each poured in the contents of his kettle. Es-quay made as many trips as the others. She had no notion why these strange people wished so many berries, but she was willing to assist.

Ogema ranged off on investigations of enticing scents but Muckie never lost sight of the packsack which contained the lunch. His nose told him it held chocolate cake. Es-quay spoke a stern *"Kah-win,"* but Philip refused to trust lunch even to Es-quay's discipline. He hung the packsack on a pole between two trees, where it dangled tantalizingly, and Muckie spent the morning vainly devising ways to reach it. A very disgruntled little bear watched them eat the cake at noon.

Es-quay liked white man's food. Sandwiches and cake melted under her onslaught as she bowed and beamed approvingly at Mrs. Jackman and murmured many *"Nish-i-shins."* When the last crumb had disappeared they stretched out in the warm sunshine and said what a fine picnic it had been. Philip pantomimed that he couldn't hold another mouthful and Mrs. Jackman acted out how good it was to eat together.

"We should invite Es-quay often," she said to Ann. "When the men come home we'll have a party."

Ann had worried because her mother and Es-quay could not talk, but now she realized it wasn't necessary. Thoughts didn't always have to be spoken. When the two women smiled at each other or laughed together over Philip's antics, they were saying they were good friends.

Ann thought a swim would make the picnic perfect but her mother protested that it was much too soon after eating.

"And there's room for more berries in the pails," she added as she picked up a kettle and started toward the laden bushes.

Ann took her kettle and called Muckie. "One kettleful and my dinner will be jogged down," she warned her mother. "Then I'll beat Philip swimming to the point."

Mrs. Jackman and Es-quay picked berries sociably side by side. Ann and Muckie went on to a huge clump of bushes. They were higher than her head and each branch was heavy with red berries. While Ann picked, Muckie stood on his haunches and ate. He loved fruit and was completely occupied and very happy as he held branches with his paws and stripped them with his teeth.

When Muckie was good he was so very good he was captivating. Ann dropped a kiss on his funny little black face and he whimpered joyfully. She moved around the clump, hurrying to fill her kettle, and believed Muckie was berrying near her, when she heard Philip's horrified shout.

"Ann! Look what your bear's done now!"

Muckie was always her bear when he was in trouble, but nevertheless Ann ran to Philip. An overturned water pail of berries lay in a mass of trampled fruit. Philip stood threateningly over Muckie, from whose jaws berries dripped. The cub saw Ann and, relieved that his protector had arrived, waddled toward her.

"Philip!" Ann cried. "You ought to know better than leave a pail of berries on the ground."

"Gosh! I only turned my back. I can't watch that bear every minute. I thought he was with you."

Es-quay and Mrs. Jackman ran up to learn what the excitement was about. Es-quay looked at Muckie and the ruined fruit and burst into a torrent of invective which sent the cub cringing behind Ann's legs. Mrs. Jackman was as angry but not so violent.

"Half a morning's work spoiled!" she said. "Something's got to be done about this bear."

When Mrs. Jackman used that tone her family knew she was serious. It was one thing for Ann and Philip to be cross with Muckie but quite another when the cub had exhausted the patience of their mother.

"I'll tie him up for the rest of the day," Ann

said as she brought his collar from a pocket.

"That's not going to give us winter jam," her mother said.

"Philip and I'll pick another pail," Ann added quickly. "I won't go swimming and you and Es-quay can rest in the shade."

Mrs. Jackman sat on a windfall. She said owners of a mischievous bear cub should make good any damage, and she looked as though she meant it. At least Philip and Ann believed so as they trudged off to the berry bushes. The sixteen-quart pail had seemed large that morning. Now it appeared tremendous. Philip complained that Muckie got worse every day. Ann said nothing, but she looked longingly at the sun-lit lake and thought how cool and pleasant the water would be.

Ann and Philip expected to spend hours picking berries, but when they hurried to the big pail with their first filled kettles they found Es-quay and Mrs. Jackman gathering fruit. Their mother smiled.

"I suppose berries are berries to a hungry little bear," she said, "whether in a pail or on bushes."

It was late afternoon when they started home. Every kettle and pail was filled with raspberries. Ogema was tired. He had run until his long tongue was hanging, but his eyes said he'd had adventures.

Even Muckie had been forgiven. Mrs. Jackman said it had been a *"nish-i-shin* picnic" and smiled at Es-quay, and Es-quay nodded and repeated the speech.

"That's the first word of English Es-quay ever said!" Ann cried. "She must like you very much."

"She knows we like each other," her mother said. "We've both known that for—" She broke off to stare at the Ottertail's camp. "Whose canoe is that?" she demanded.

A birchbark was drawn up on the shore before Es-quay's wigwam. Es-quay looked as astonished as were the Jackmans.

As their own canoe touched the beach an Indian came out of the brush. There was dignity in his bearing, but no friendliness.

Es-quay stared. Most evidently the man was a stranger, but when they had exchanged a few words she looked serious and glanced quickly toward the Jackmans.

Mrs. Jackman gathered pails, kettles and berries. "We must go home," she said. "Es-quay has a guest."

They had turned to the trail when the voices of Es-quay and the visitor rose in excitement. The man was angry and Es-quay was disturbed. Mrs. Jackman stopped.

"We shouldn't leave her," she said. "Can you tell what they're saying?"

As she spoke the Indian turned toward the Jackmans. He began to speak with passion and the word "*shag-e-nash*" was repeated. His rising anger was directed at them as they stood there, too terrified to move. Ogema took a step forward and the hair on his back bristled.

Mrs. Jackman stiffened. When she spoke her voice was quiet.

"Ask Es-quay what he thinks we've done. Have her tell him we are friends."

"But I can't say all that in Ojibwa," Ann said.

The man stopped talking and started toward his canoe. Mrs. Jackman's calmness left her.

"Ann! Don't let him go off thinking whatever he must be thinking. You know some Ojibwa. I don't care what you say. But say something!"

"*B'jou'*," Ann began falteringly.

At least a courteous greeting would give her time to construct some statement of friendship, but the man didn't even glance in her direction as he lifted his canoe into the water.

"Es-quay, what is the trouble?" Mrs. Jackman demanded.

The Indian woman only stared at the lake while

the man got into his canoe, dipped his blade and paddled away. Not once did he glance back.

When Es-quay at last looked up her eyes were troubled. Ann thought Es-quay felt sorry for them as she sadly shook her head.

"*Kah-win nish-i-shin*," she said several times. ("It is not good. It is not good.")

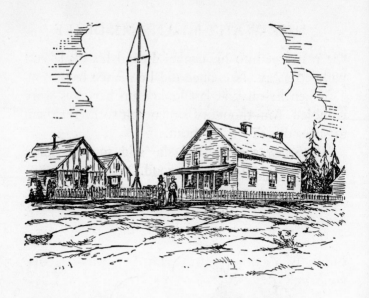

11 A SERVANT OF THE HBC

Mrs. Jackman returned to Es-quay's wigwam with Ann and Philip that evening and several times the next day, but the Indian woman would not or could not explain the reason for the stranger's visit or his angry outburst. She would only shake her head and repeat, *"Kah-win nish-i-shin."*

"It's something she doesn't want to tell us," Ann said.

Mrs. Jackman stirred a kettle of bubbling jam and did not comment. Ann had never seen her mother so troubled and wished her father was home. Apparently Mrs. Jackman wished so, too.

"Why don't you two run to the point and see if he's coming?" she said. "He might get home a day early."

Ann and Philip did better than that. They borrowed Es-quay's birchbark canoe and paddled out of the bay. But the lake was empty.

"Never mind," Philip said when they returned. "Ogema and I'll stand guard all night."

"Heavens, no!" his mother exclaimed. "If that Indian had intended any harm, he wouldn't have gone away."

"But why does Es-quay keep saying, '*Kah-win nish-i-shin*'?" Ann asked for the twentieth time.

"I can't imagine," her mother said, "unless it's for the same reason Michel acted so queerly when he learned your father is going to trap here."

"I bet that trapper's camp we found has got something to do with it," Philip said. "But Dad won't let anybody drive him out. He said he wouldn't."

"It mustn't come to that!" his mother exclaimed. "And I'm sure it won't. But after your father has planned so long and worked so hard, bringing in supplies and building a cabin, after we're all settled, I can't bear to think of his having trouble."

163

"But we won't have to leave, will we?" Philip asked.

"Of course we won't!" Ann cried.

Even she was surprised by her fervor. She hadn't realized how much she loved the wilderness. Suddenly she saw life without forest trails, without the canoe, Ogema, Muckie, the family at home sharing life together, without each morning promising new adventures. She whirled on Philip.

"To hear you talk," she cried, "anybody'd think people had to leave a country just because one man got mad at them."

"We're all talking foolishly," her mother said. "We can't even guess what this means until John gets back to tell us what Es-quay knows."

Mrs. Jackman became briskly cheerful. She laughed at Philip's suggestion that they keep the campfire burning all night.

"And scare your father to death if he did come," she said. "Tomorrow we'll learn it's just a tempest in a teapot."

Ann and Philip pretended to be convinced. There was no use asking questions when their mother had resolved not to discuss a subject. But Ann couldn't forget the angry Indian or stories she'd heard of the red man's revenge. And evidently Philip could not forget.

"Mother's worried," he said when they went to the lake for water. "What you suppose was eating that Indian?"

"Wish I knew," Ann said. "But we can't find out until John comes and talks with Es-quay."

"Just the same, I'm going to keep a watch all night," Philip said.

But Philip was asleep before Ann, and when they wakened late next morning Ann knew her mother had not slept much. None of them spoke of the angry Indian. Daily jobs were attended to, but never was the bay unwatched. Always one or all were looking for the big green Peterborough canoe.

It came around the point at noon. Ann, Philip, their mother, Ogema and Muckie all rushed to the shore. The men looked tired, but they were beaming. Mr. Jackman splashed through shallow water, leading the heavily loaded craft.

"Here's the last of the stuff," he said. "A real homecoming with all five down to meet us." Then he saw their faces. "What's the matter?" he demanded.

When they had told their story, John started toward his camp.

"I see Es-quay," he said.

"I'm coming," Mr. Jackman said.

The others hurried with him. Es-quay, sitting in the door of the wigwam, evidently expected the visit. Everyone waited while John and Es-quay talked.

"What's she saying?" Mr. Jackman demanded.

John only glanced up and Es-quay went on talking. When Ann thought she could bear the suspense no longer, John began the story.

"Pe-tah-bo come," he said.

"He's Wen-dah-ban's father!" Ann cried.

"You know him?"

"Ann!" her father said sharply. "Let John talk."

"Pe-tah-bo much mad," John said. "He say this place where he hunt."

"He's crazy!" Mr. Jackman exclaimed. "I'm here first."

"Pe-tah-bo here all his life. His father here. His grandfather. His grandfather's father. Always same place."

"Indians have no right to do that."

"Fort Caribou Indians always do it," John said. "Place to hunt stay by one family. Pe-tah-bo's father and uncles die. Now he got much bush. Enough for two hunters. Some day Pe-tah-bo die. Then Wen-dah-ban have it."

John stated the facts as if they were divine law. Even Mr. Jackman was impressed.

"Have you known this all the time?" he demanded.

"Me think you know it," John said. "Me think you get place to hunt. Me not know much about Fort Caribou people. Me just come from The Bay."

"You know Pe-tah-bo?"

"Two-three time I see him. Es-quay no see him. Then he come here. Es-quay say Pe-tah-bo much mad. Pe-tah-bo say you must go."

Mr. Jackman sat on a windfall. His face was hard.

"Let's get this straight," he said. "Pe-tah-bo claims the bush around this end of Far Lake is his. He's wrong. The Government owns the land."

John shrugged. "Maybe. But the big company know this is Pe-tah-bo's place."

"But Pe-tah-bo didn't hunt here last winter. I came to look. No camp. No traps. No snowshoe tracks. Nobody here."

John consulted Es-quay.

"Pe-tah-bo bush so big he hunt only half. This winter he hunt this part. That way he get much fur. Last spring he come stay little while. Take few mink. His camp next bay."

Mr. Jackman stood up. His shoulders were back and his face was harder than before. Suddenly

Ann wasn't afraid any more. She knew she wouldn't have to return to Bradford. Her father was the gentlest, kindliest man in the world until he got mad or determined to do something.

"Pe-tah-bo is out of luck," he said now, and he seemed to kick the words out between clenched teeth. "I've built a house and brought in supplies. I stay."

Even Es-quay understood what he meant and she spoke in quick protest to John.

"Pe-tah-bo tell her," John said, "that big company not let you stay."

"Dave!" Mrs. Jackman cried. "This is the reason Michel acted so queerly. Perhaps—"

"We'll find out about it," her husband interrupted. "I'm going to Fort Caribou and see Gillespie. When can you start?"

"In an hour."

"Early tomorrow morning will be time enough. John, I go see big company."

John shrugged as if to say it was no use. For him the ownership of the district was apparently settled, but if the white man wished to go to all that trouble, that was his affair.

"And, John," Mr. Jackman said, "while I'm away you build me a good birchbark canoe. We'll need two from now on."

"You no need another canoe," John said.

"I'm coming back and I'll trap here. You make good canoe while I go talk to the trader."

All this was repeated to Es-quay, who then had a great deal to say to John.

"She say she take care of little bear," John interpreted.

"Thank you, Es-quay!" Ann cried. "*Me-gwetch, me-gwetch.*"

Es-quay patted Ann's shoulders and gravely shook hands with Mrs. Jackman, and they knew she was trying to say she was sorry. No one spoke as the Jackmans walked back to camp. Mr. Jackman looked at the cabin.

"Thought it would be safer with John here," he said. "That's why I set him to work on a canoe."

"But John doesn't believe you can stay to use it!" his wife cried. "Is it possible Pe-tah-bo can force us out?"

Ann and Philip waited breathlessly for the answer. Their mother's question had cut close to their own fears.

"We've got to stay," their father said. "Summer's work and winter's grub here. Fall coming on. I'm not letting any Indian or white man run us out."

169

They were away at dawn next morning, but now there was no eagerness for the journey, no excitement in watching forest creatures. None of the four paddlers thought of anything but the end of the day. All looked anxiously when the post buildings came in view, and sighed in relief when they saw the flagpole was bare and knew the manager was at home.

When they landed, Mr. Jackman left them on the shore. Ann and her mother and Philip were prepared for a long wait but in a few minutes Mr. Jackman returned with Mr. Gillespie.

The manager shook hands, patted Ogema and said how glad he was to meet the white neighbors of whom he had heard. The grizzled Scotsman had a brusque heartiness that Ann liked, but there was also a quiet air of authority in his voice when he called to a young Indian employee to carry the Jackmans' packsacks to the dwelling house.

They went through the gate in the picket fence and a moment later a neatly dressed Indian woman, whom Mr. Gillespie introduced as Louise, his housekeeper, was leading them to their rooms upstairs. She said Mr. Gillespie always had afternoon tea in the living room and it would soon be ready.

Ann and her mother changed to dresses. Philip, impressed by the three bedrooms, combed his hair without being urged, and when his mother laid out a tie he made no protest.

"Rather different from our last visit," Mr. Jackman said. "Isn't Gillespie a fine chap?"

"What did he say about Pe-tah-bo?" Mrs. Jackman asked.

"I didn't mention that in the trade shop with Michel there. Don't want to discuss it with Indian servants about."

Mrs. Jackman gave a little gasp of pleasure when they entered the living room and found a tea tray on a low table. Mr. Gillespie seated her before it.

"It's good to see a woman pour tea again," he said.

Louise brought in a plate heaped with English tea biscuits and the manager nodded towards Ann and Philip.

"Tuck into it," he said. "When I was your age I thought I couldn't survive until teatime."

Ann looked around the room. Easy chairs, a bookcase filled with books, even a piano, assured her that her dream picture of their own future home hadn't been too fantastic. She was glad when her mother asked how they had brought in a piano.

"Indians did it somehow," he said. "Across fifteen portages. A former manager was a good musician and that piano probably helped him through some lonely evenings. Many a time I've wished I could hammer out a little music."

"Would you like me to play something?" Mrs. Jackman asked.

"Would you?" he said eagerly. "It's probably out of tune."

It was badly out of tune and some of the yellowed keys were silent. But Mrs. Jackman played "Silver Threads Among the Gold." When she followed with "Loch Lomond," Mr. Gillespie frankly wiped his eyes.

"Thank you," he said when she had finished. "Now I must lock the trade shop and give Michel some orders. See you all at supper."

During the evening meal talk turned to fur. Mr. Gillespie was interested in Mr. Jackman's theory that the white man could trap as well, if not better than, the Indian.

"Maybe," he admitted. "But I'll back our Indians. They've been hunting for generations."

"The new railroad will bring in white men," Mr. Jackman said.

"And you decided to come in ahead of the rush," the manager guessed. "It's a lonely and hard life you've chosen."

"Not any harder than making a living anywhere," Mr. Jackman said. "Price of fur is going

172

up. Once you bought a prime mink for a couple of dollars and I wouldn't be surprised to see it bring five times that."

The manager nodded. He looked at Mrs. Jackman and Ann and Philip when he added that life in the bush meant isolation and often hardship for a family.

"But Dave won't be a trapper always," Mrs. Jackman said.

"I was coming to that, Mary," her husband said. "A couple of years' good trapping and I'll be fixed to start a fur farm. With prices going up, it will pay to raise furs."

"Not so fast!" Mr. Gillespie laughed. "You're talking to an old Hudson's Bay man. The forest will raise all the fur we'll ever need. Our job is to keep our hunters fed, clothed and happy so they'll bring in pelts. Conditions haven't changed much in a hundred years."

"But they will," Mr. Jackman insisted. "Even the bush is changing. A railroad will reach Far Lake next year. Who knows what's ahead? Perhaps some day Ann and Philip will travel to Far Lake in an airplane. That's the answer to your talk of isolation."

"Man! Man! You're refreshing," Mr. Gillespie laughed. "With such a husband, Mrs. Jackman, you'll never have a dull minute. Now he's talking of you flying outside for a bit of shopping. No paddling. No carrying on portages. You won't even bother with trains. You'll go through the air in one of these silly flying machines. Man, where'd the things find a place to light in the bush?"

"Plenty of lakes here, and already they're building airplanes to land on water."

Ann loved it when her father came alive and talked about the future. His eyes glowed and his voice rang. He made her believe anything was possible. She believed him even as Mr. Gillespie laughed when they left the table and settled themselves in the living room.

Louise cleared the dishes and soon the kitchen was quiet. Now, Ann knew, they would talk about Pe-tah-bo, and when her mother suggested bed, she and Philip begged to stay.

"One late night won't hurt them," Mr. Jackman said. "And they've got a share in this."

Mr. Gillespie listened to the story of the cabin and Pe-tah-bo and as he listened he was no longer the genial host. Ann thought of a phrase from a school history which spoke of old company factors as rulers over vast districts. As she watched his stern face she knew he had wielded power, and that he still did. When her father stopped speaking, the manager silently puffed at his pipe for some moments.

"My dear fellow," he said at last, "I'm sorry you didn't come to me before you built this place or brought in your family. I could have saved you disappointment."

"You don't mean that Indian can keep me out?" Mr. Jackman demanded.

"I am afraid he can."

"But I'm on government land. There's no law—"

"There's a law of tribal custom and company policy," Mr. Gillespie interrupted, "and both still rule in the north. Among Ojibwas in some districts, rights to hunting territory are passed down from father to son or inherited by next of kin. It is the custom in my district and is what Pe-tah-bo means when he says this land belongs to him. He has inherited it from his father and from his father's brothers. It will pass on to Wen-dah-ban, whom I hear you know."

He stopped to smile at Ann. "Wen-dah-ban is a fine lad," he continued. "He will be a fine hunter, like his father. Pe-tah-bo is one of my most intelligent and influential men. I use him as a chief in my dealings with the other hunters."

"But I'm there and I've got to stay!" Mr. Jackman exclaimed.

The Hudson's Bay manager stiffened.

"We want to be fair," Mrs. Jackman said quickly. "But you can see what this means to us."

"I understand that perfectly," Mr. Gillespie said. "I understand even better what it means to Pe-tah-bo. Mr. Jackman spoke of a fur farm. My Indians have been operating fur farms for a century. A hunter knows exactly how much hunting his territory will stand and takes only the natural increase. He knows exactly how many beaver he has, young and old. He operates in perfect confidence that no one will ever set a trap in his strip of bush. And the Hudson's Bay Company will see that he is protected."

Ann's hopes had been sinking lower and lower, and now they vanished utterly. But her father got to his feet and when she saw his shoulder's back and his head high, she found fresh courage.

"Can't you see my side of this?" Mr. Jackman urged. "I settled on government land. I visited Far Lake last winter and made sure no one was trapping there. Now I've sunk practically all my savings in a cabin and supplies. It's too late to move. Pe-tah-bo has a larger district than he needs. Some arrangement can be made with him." He stopped

176

a moment, then added: "I am asking you to help make him see reason."

"You are asking me to advise him to give up his inherited rights," Mr. Gillespie said sternly, "after I have spent my life winning the confidence of the natives. After Pe-tah-bo has acquired implicit faith that the company will protect him."

"Then you're not interested in my rights?"

Mr. Gillespie's face became very grim.

"You have no rights," he said. "You say white trappers are coming in, and you are, or wish to be, one of the first. But Indian hunters have served this company for generations. I would be a poor servant of the Hudson's Bay if I allowed myself to forget that fact."

12 AN EVIL SPIRIT

TO THE RESCUE

When Ann and Philip had said good night and gone upstairs to bed, she had intended to lie awake and devise some means of winning a concession from Pe-tah-bo. She and Wah-be-goon were friends and Wen-dah-ban had cut a lobstick in her honor. Surely she could think of something which would save her family.

But Ann had not realized the soporific effects of

a long day's paddle and the excitement of a visit to the post. She put out the lamp and settled herself to think, and then it was broad daylight and her mother was standing beside the bed.

"You'll have to hurry to be ready for breakfast," Mrs. Jackman said.

Ann and Philip reached the dining room as Louise set large bowls of porridge on the table. Mr. Gillespie and their father and mother were already in their places. The post manager was again the genial host and seemed to want to make amends for his sternness the previous evening.

Mr. Jackman opened the question of the hunting territory when he asked if Mr. Gillespie had any objection to his talking to Pe-tah-bo.

"None whatever," the manager said. "But I know it's useless."

"I can't give up so easily," Mr. Jackman said. "This winter's trapping means too much. If Pe-tah-bo and I work out some arrangement, your own conscience would be quite clear?"

"Certainly! And I'd rejoice in your good fortune. But I can't offer any hope. Pe-tah-bo is a successful man and his large hunting territory represents a family fortune. Also he's very proud."

He went on to say that many hunters and their families had gathered at Blueberry Point down the lake to pick berries, fish, feast and dance. It was a summer celebration, with the men home from the fur brigade. Their wages as boatmen and the sale of the winter's catch had been spent. The drums would go all night. They'd eat and dance and use up their substance.

"When that's over, they'll all be broke until Treaty Day," he said. "Then each Indian gets 'treaty money,' which will be spent at once. Afterwards they scatter until time to get their fall debt."

"Don't they ever save?" Mrs. Jackman asked.

"The Indian lives in the present. You'd understand if you came to the treaty celebration. Why don't you come?" he urged. "I'd be delighted to have you as guests."

Treaty Day was several weeks off and when Mr. Jackman accepted he added, "That will show you how sure I am we will stay at Far Lake."

"I hope you do," Mr. Gillespie said with a cordiality which was convincing. "And why not take Michel as an interpreter when you go to talk to Pe-tah-bo? Michel is honest and he'll present your case fairly."

An hour later they were ready for the ten-mile paddle to Blueberry Point. Michel was jubilant at the prospect of a day's outing, but Ogema was crestfallen when he realized he wasn't to go. They had decided not to complicate the situation by risking a fight with dogs at the encampment. Mr. Gillespie, who had come to the shore to see them off, promised to take care of Ogema, and Ann knew he would. The dependability of the grizzled Scotsman was inescapable.

"Remember, Michel," the post manager cautioned, "to say just what white man say. This much important."

Michel, pleased to be entrusted with a mission, nodded reassuringly. Ann wished Mr. Gillespie would go on to say he believed her father would succeed. Her own faith was unshaken, but to express it would sound childish. So she stood beside the post manager and slipped a hand into his.

"I know Wah-be-goon will understand we just must stay at Far Lake," she said, and she couldn't keep a little fierceness from her tone.

Mr. Gillespie laughed and patted her shoulders.

"There's a daughter as resolute as the father," he said. "She looks ready to jump into a pow-wow. Michel will have quite a job between the two of you."

Mr. Gillespie and Ogema stood side by side and watched the Jackmans out of sight. The big Peterborough leaped with five blades swinging. Michel, in the bow, turned to grin and say it was like the big canoe of the company when the chief trader traveled.

"Only everybody work now," he said. "We get there quick."

It didn't seem that they had paddled ten miles when they heard the sound of a drum, a rhythmic beat which went on without cessation.

"Many blueberries," Michel said. "Now they happy and they dance."

It seemed a good omen for their mission. Mrs. Jackman suggested that they should not interrupt the party, lest they be considered a nuisance.

"We can wait at the shore until the dance is over," she said.

Michel stared in astonishment. "All time beat drums," he said. "One man get tired, he stop, another man beat drum. Maybe they beat drum all night. Someone see us, drum stop."

Michel knew the ways of celebrations for the beating ceased abruptly a few moments later. They pulled up before a quiet encampment. A short distance back a dozen wigwams stood in an old clearing. Smoke from smoldering fires curled skyward and drying racks heavy with fish and meat flanked the fires. A few dogs skulked in the bushes but not an Indian appeared.

"I get Pe-tah-bo," Michel said.

AN EVIL SPIRIT TO THE RESCUE

"Why don't we say 'B'jou'' to Wah-be-goon and Wen-dah-ban?" Mrs. Jackman suggested.

They made their way among the wigwams. Kettles of fish simmered over cooking fires and poles of the racks bent beneath strips of blackened meat and yellowed whitefish. Everywhere were birchbark baskets filled with blueberries.

No one was in sight. The blanket door of a wigwam would be pushed aside and a dark eye would look out for a moment.

"They're not overly sociable," Mr. Jackman said. "Which is Pe-tah-bo's camp?"

Michel stopped to ask and an old man came out of a wigwam and pointed to the end of the clearing. Pe-tah-bo's home stood by itself and Ann thought it was better made than the others. She would have liked to scratch politely on the bark as Es-quay had shown her, but Michel called and the family of three came out.

The Jackmans nodded and smiled and said, "B'jou'." The Indians said "B'jou'" and did not smile. They merely stood and waited, their faces blank.

These were not the people Ann knew. This was not the woman with the kindly smile who had touched her hair, or the boy who had cut the lobstick. Ann's vision of herself as the friendly ambas-

sador, one who would effect an understanding between two families, faded swiftly. It was her first
experience with the red race when it stands in
silence, watchful, unfriendly and withdrawn. She
was tongue-tied, and evidently her mother felt as
helpless.

"It's no use, Dave," Mrs. Jackman said. "We'll
wait until you've talked."

Mr. Jackman seated himself on the ground and
motioned the others to do so. Pe-tah-bo joined the
circle. Wah-be-goon sat in the doorway of the
wigwam, and the gravity of her manner made the
strong face of the Indian woman seem austere.
Wen-dah-ban moved about uncertainly until Pe-
tah-bo spoke to him at length. Then he sat down
beside his father.

"Wen-dah-ban is hunter too," Michel interpreted. "Pe-tah-bo say he get a hundred dollars'
fur last winter."

Mr. Jackman told the story of their coming to
Far Lake. He told it slowly, with many waits
while Michel interpreted. After each long speech
in Ojibwa, Pe-tah-bo nodded to show he understood. Mr. Jackman drew a map on the ground.

"You and the big company say you hunt here,"
he said.

Pe-tah-bo smiled for the first time. Ojibwa

184

flowed and crackled. Wah-be-goon relaxed and Wen-dah-ban looked less serious. Ann thought that suddenly they had become friends.

"He says good," Michel reported. "Everybody know it Pe-tah-bo's. Now you know. Everything is good."

Apparently the Indians thought the matter settled. Mr. Jackman had to wait until the excitement died before he could continue. But when he went on to ask that he be allowed to trap at Far Lake, Pe-tah-bo did not even wait to hear the arrangement Mr. Jackman had to offer.

"*Kah-win!*" he shouted, and sprang to his feet.

"He says, 'No,'" Michel repeated, faithfully fulfilling his duties as interpreter.

Ann knew what he had said. So did her father and her mother and Philip.

"But tell him to listen to me," Mr. Jackman pleaded.

Michel made an honest effort, but it was useless as Pe-tah-bo continued his swift flow of Ojibwa. When he had finished speaking, he turned and went into the wigwam. His family followed.

"He says long time he hunt there," Michel began. "His father and his—"

"Don't anyone tell me that again!" Mr. Jackman

185

snapped. "That's what everyone has said whenever I've tried to talk about this.

"It's no use," Mr. Jackman continued. "We've done everything we could."

"He says by-and-by he go Far Lake," Michel went on. "He says he hunt there this winter. He put up his wigwam. He says you no hunt there."

Ann felt almost sorry for Michel, trying so hard to be an interpreter. He almost ran to keep up with her father as he strode swiftly to the shore. Her father wasn't even listening.

All the Indians came to the doors of the wigwams to watch the white people depart.

"If Pe-tah-bo would only cool down," Mrs. Jackman said.

"I haven't given up yet," Mr. Jackman said. "I won't give up."

Ann looked at her father's face and knew that, despite the determination of his speech, he felt as sick as she did. Philip was full of war-like talk and plans until no one gave indication of joining him.

Ann paddled in silence. She knew she had not played the heroic role she had pictured, but no one could be heroic with a stubborn Indian who delivered an impassioned oration and then stalked off to his wigwam without giving the others a chance.

Michel tried to explain that Pe-tah-bo wouldn't

listen to his interpretation, and he wanted the post manager to know he had tried. Mr. and Mrs. Jackman said little, and finally there was only the sound of five dipping paddles as they finished the return journey.

Their faces told Mr. Gillespie the outcome of the visit. When they walked into the trade shop he looked sympathetic.

"Sorry I couldn't help," he said.

Mr. Jackman impulsively thrust out his hand and gripped one of the Scotch trader's.

"I understand," he said. "And—and I appreciate your position."

"And we admire you for it," Mrs. Jackman added. "No wonder your hunters have faith in you."

"But I haven't given up," Mr. Jackman said. "A man can do what he must do. It's that way with us now."

"Good for you," the post manager said. "I expected you'd feel that way. And I've been doing a little thinking—not unselfishly, for I'd like to have white neighbors."

"What do you mean?" Mr. Jackman demanded eagerly.

"Too long a story for the trade shop, where there are no chairs. And a spot of tea would be good for all of us. I'll be with you in a moment."

Ann was dazed as they walked to the dwelling house. Her face felt stiff and she wondered if she could ever smile again. Her father and mother didn't seem to have trouble. Their faces were beaming.

"He's found a way out for us!" Mrs. Jackman cried.

"He'll make that old Pe-tah-bo behave," Philip said.

Mr. Jackman didn't speak. He only grinned. Ann squeezed his hand.

"Isn't Mr. Gillespie nice?" she said. "But anyhow, I wouldn't have left Far Lake. Not for an old hunting territory that Wen-dah-ban is going to have some time."

"You're a fighter, Ann," her father said.

"Which is very strange indeed." And Mrs. Jackman laughed gaily.

Mr. Gillespie came a few moments later. He carried a map which he spread on the table.

"A predecessor at Fort Caribou had a hobby— cartography," he said. "Most of us have a hobby, maybe to keep from going crazy with no one but Indians to talk to. The former manager surveyed this district and drew this map. Afterwards he marked the hunting territories of all the post Indians. Here, for instance, is the one Pe-tah-bo inherited from his father, and adjoining it the one he got from an uncle."

The post manager's stubby finger followed the lines.

"Your cabin, unfortunately, is in the center of this territory," he said. "But down the lake is old Nah-sho-tah's."

"You mean I can get it from him?" Mr. Jackman demanded.

"Man! Man! You're impatient. Nah-sho-tah's territory is fifteen miles from your cabin. It's not large. Didn't have much fur at one time, but I imagine it's better now. Hasn't been hunted for many years."

"Where is Nah-sho-tah?"

"He's dead," Mr. Gillespie said. "The Indians believe he was a *win-di-go*, their worst evil spirit. His relatives would not claim the territory and no other hunter dared cross its boundaries."

"You're not suggesting that I'm afraid of an evil spirit?" Mr. Jackman said.

"No, but I want you to understand how little I'm offering. Fifteen miles from your place—you won't get home often. A bachelor shack for you.

You may not get much fur. And all the time you'll be worrying about your family, alone in the cabin."

Mr. Jackman looked at his wife. She smiled.

"Ann and Philip and I are woodsmen," she said.

"I know it isn't what you planned," Mr. Gillespie said, "but it will see you through the winter and retrieve some of your losses."

"What I planned and what I have to take are two different things," Mr. Jackman said. "And don't think, sir, that I fail to appreciate your offering this territory to me. It's just that—"

"You'll be too far from home."

"If it were fifty miles, I'd travel it," Mr. Jackman said. "I'm not thinking about myself but—"

"If you're worrying about Ann and Philip and me," his wife said, "we're not afraid. We want to stay. We'll get along splendidly."

Mr. Jackman frowned, and then suddenly he squared his shoulders.

"I'll take it," he said, "and I'm glad to have it."

"Good! You're a brave man, Jackman."

"No," and Ann's father drew her and Philip to him with one arm, his wife with the other. "These are the brave ones. I only try to keep up with them."

AN EVIL SPIRIT TO THE RESCUE

He loosened the grip on Ann and Philip and held out a hand to the post manager.

"And I thank you, sir," he said, "for doing a bit of thinking while I was only trying to force things through."

13 "WIN-DI-GO"

It was good to be home again. All four quickened their strokes as the Peterborough swept around the point into the bay. Ann looked proudly at the cabin.

"Quite a home we built," Mr. Jackman said.

The twinkle in his eyes made Ann suspect he was teasing.

"You told us we helped a lot when we pounded in all those bags of moss," she said.

"I meant it," he said. "I'll need a lot more help

too. Have to finish here and get started on my own cabin."

"We'll work on that too," Philip said.

"You'll be too busy taking care of the family," his father said.

"But you'll come home every week," Mrs. Jackman added quickly.

"I won't stay away longer than I have to." Mr. Jackman's tone was carefully casual, and then he added, "I know it's tough, Mary, especially after we planned on all being together this winter."

The Ottertails and Muckie were at the shore to greet them. John said nothing when he heard of Nah-sho-tah's hunting territory, but there was fear in his eyes.

"Do you believe Nah-sho-tah was a *win-di-go?*" Philip asked.

John stared blankly. He didn't care even to talk about the most dreaded of the Ojibwas' evil spirits, for Indians believe themselves powerless to combat it. A *win-di-go* might take possession of any man or woman and force him to eat human flesh.

Muckie was overjoyed to see Ann and Philip and greedily gobbled his present of a bag of hard candy in one mouthful. Then he spent a long time trying to free his jaws from the sticky mass. He was probably the only little bear in fur land that had ever had a whole bag of candy for his own.

Es-quay clucked about the waste, but she forgot that when she saw her own gift, somber woolen material for a dress. Her delighted *"me-gwetches"* were overwhelming and she made a speech through John.

"She say much warm this winter," he interpreted.

Mrs. Jackman had been distressed by Es-quay's only dress, which was disintegrating in twenty-four-hour service week after week. Es-quay carried the material to her wigwam, sewed industriously for two days and then made one of her rare calls at the cabin. She wore the new dress under the old and proudly pointed at the fresh material peeping through the holes.

John was equally ecstatic. On Treaty Day they planned to buy another dress and he carefully counted three on his fingers and said Es-quay would be "much warm in winter." Ann wondered how Es-quay would walk with a third layer of long skirts around her ankles. The whole family stopped work to admire Es-quay's clothes and Mr. Jackman suggested that she tear holes in the second garment so the third would show. The Ottertails went off laughing happily at the joke.

Ann was disappointed that Es-quay had not

admired the birchbark screen she was making to divide hers and Philip's room. She had sewed the bark with spruce roots as she'd seen Es-quay do. The Indian woman had only looked baffled by a strip of birchbark designed to keep out neither water nor weather.

"Es-quay's probably shaking her head and muttering, '*Shag-e-nash*,'" her father said. "You went one better on Ojibwa housekeeping."

"But she said, '*Nish-i-shin*' when I showed her how we'll make rope bedsprings," Philip boasted. "There's some use to them."

Philip had felt quite superior since his father had asked help in furniture manufacture. Now he questioned whether there was enough rope to make a close webbing.

"Been wondering about that myself," his father said.

Philip began to measure but soon found himself entangled in loops and snarls of rope.

"You needn't make all that mess," Ann said. "Find out how many crosswise and lengthwise lengths you need and figure it out."

Philip spent a long time with paper and pencil, and his facial contortions were as painful as had been Michel's. It was mental torment, but Philip

195

continued to do mathematics until he'd proved his answer twice.

"You figured it right," his father said when the three bedsprings were completed. "There's only ten feet of rope to spare."

That evening as they were preparing supper, Mrs. Jackman thanked Ann for helping with Philip's lesson. Ann was startled.

"We haven't opened a schoolbook all summer," she said.

"But this afternoon Philip used multiplication tables and struggled with some fractions," her mother said. "And he discovered arithmetic is useful."

"It would have been silly for Philip to go on measuring—" Ann began.

She stopped, thinking of evening chats around the campfire when they'd seemed to be talking only of strange lands and races and colorful heroes of the past. History and geography presented the same facts, only not in such an alive and interesting manner. And her letters written to girls in Bradford! Her father had carried dozens to the railroad. Might those have passed for compositions? And there was poetry, which she and Philip were always begging their mother to recite because they loved the ring and fire her warm voice gave to words. Could that possibly have been the dreadful subject, Required Reading?

"Mother, you've been cheating!" Ann cried. "We've been going to school all summer."

"And you didn't find it painful," her mother laughed. "Now perhaps you won't look so woe-be-gone every time you see a schoolbook."

Ann had dreaded home school hours and the everydayness of lessons and now suddenly she wondered if her mother had dreaded reluctant pupils. She and Philip had never acted the least bit glad that they would be taught at home. Teachers and mothers seemed such entirely different people that Ann could not imagine her mother in a schoolroom, nor had she understood why Mrs. Jackman's former pupils so often dropped in for visits. Ann never wanted to see her teachers. They seemed only interfering despots and she hadn't liked to admit her mother had ever been one. Now she flushed in quick contrition.

"You must have been a grand teacher, Mother," she said. "I'm glad I'm going to have you this winter instead of that mean Miss Ellery."

A few days later the cabin was complete. Mr. Jackman put away the tents while the others carried blankets and clothes to the new home. When Philip brought in the poplar hall tree, fixed now on a standard, Ann protested that it didn't belong in a house.

"I got a right to keep it on my side of the screen," he said. "It's fine to hang clothes on."

Mrs. Jackman had invited the Ottertails to a housewarming tea. They arrived promptly and ate plates of cake and cookies. Ogema was at the party and gravely inspected his blanket in a corner, and even Muckie was allowed to come because Esquay was there to make him behave.

Mr. Jackman asked John to go with him the next day to inspect the new trapping territory, but John shook his head.

"Maybe you shoot a moose," Mr. Jackman tempted.

"No moose there," John said.

"Maybe we see much fur sign," Mr. Jackman persisted.

Still John shook his head. He would give no reason except the need of working on the birchbark canoe. That had been in the making since the Jackmans had departed for Fort Caribou and John was still whittling cedar ribs and planking with his curved knife. Until now the canoe had been the least important task in his existence.

"You afraid of *win-di-go?*" Mr. Jackman asked. "I got white medicine."

John shrugged his shoulders and looked away. After a long time he spoke.

"White medicine only good for white man."

When the Ottertails had departed with many *"me-gwetches"* and *"nish-i-shins,"* Mrs. Jackman cleared away the dishes, swept up the crumbs and aired out the room.

"Dog, bear, Indians and children!" she said. "But I never had a better time. Doesn't the cabin look grand? No need to worry about our comfort this winter."

"And if every Indian feels as John does about Nah-sho-tah's trapping territory, I ought to get a lot of fur," Mr. Jackman said. "Are the rest of you afraid of *win-di-go?*"

All set out the next morning, taking a lunch and planning to be gone all day. As they paddled past the Ottertail camp, John and Es-quay came to the shore to watch them out of sight.

"They're not even sure white medicine will protect us," Mr. Jackman chuckled.

It was mid-forenoon when they reached the trapping territory. Mrs. Jackman suggested that they choose the cabin site at once and Ann found a level space facing the home bay.

"Only we never could see your cabin fifteen

miles away and past all those islands and points," she said.

"We'll decide about the cabin when I've laid out trapping lines," her father said. "Let's look for fur sign."

They tramped for an hour without finding a creek or large swamp. At last they came out on a small lake. On the shore was a dilapidated cubby, the stake enclosure leaning drunkenly. It was in dreary contrast to the neat little structures near Pe-tah-bo's camp. Mr. Jackman's face was bleak.

"Nah-sho-tah's line," he said.

"But there must be more than this!" Mrs. Jackman insisted.

"Got to be. I'll find rabbit runways and set for lynx. That spruce swamp should be good for fisher. But I haven't seen much sign."

Philip looked at the desolate low hills and asked fearfully, "Do you suppose there is a *win-di-go?*"

"Of course there isn't," Ann cried. "But this isn't half as nice as the country around our cabin."

"Darn that old Pe-tah-bo anyway," Philip said. "And that smarty, Wen-dah-ban, too."

"Now listen!" Mr. Jackman said sharply. "Pe-tah-bo is within fur land rights in keeping his territory for his son. They're going to be our neighbors and we don't want trouble."

Philip looked a bit abashed.

"And if Nah-sho-tah could make a living here," his father added, "I will too. Let's stop grouching and make a go of this."

Mr. Jackman climbed a ridge and returned to report a break in the trees which might indicate a small stream. That would give him a chance for mink, and if it didn't there was other fur to trap.

All felt more cheerful as they walked back to Far Lake. Even Ogema took an interest in the country when he caught a scent of game. His excited yelps as he dashed off were heartening until Mr. Jackman said he might be chasing a rabbit.

Late as it was when they reached home, John and Es-quay were on shore to verify that they were unharmed by a *win-di-go*. They shook their heads dolefully when John asked questions, and they made no effort to hide their misgivings a few days later when Mr. Jackman set off with a camping outfit to explore his new territory and lay out trapping lines.

14 MUCKIE GOES CALLING

John at last began to work industriously on the birchbark canoe, for he and Es-quay planned to return soon to Fort Caribou. Ann and Philip had long since tired of watching the interminable whittling of cedar ribs and planks, but now that the ribs were being shaped within a form of stakes driven into the ground, they spent every free moment with John. One afternoon as they neared his camp they heard strange voices.

"Who do you suppose it can be?" Ann cried, thinking that only one stranger had visited Far Lake since their arrival.

Two birchbark canoes were drawn up on the beach and Pe-tah-bo and Wen-dah-ban were squatting beside John. Everyone exchanged polite *"B'jou's"* and then gravely stared at one another. Philip tried to scowl and then forgot to as John began to fit cedar ribs between the gunwale strips. All five drew closer. Pe-tah-bo disapproved of John's method and a long conference followed. There was much head shaking, but when Pe-tah-bo proved his point by seizing the curved knife and demonstrating, all chorused *"Nish-i-shins."* After that they were friends. Ann smiled at Wen-dah-ban and he smiled in return.

Philip examined the Indian boy's canoe and the proud owner pointed out its merits.

"Gosh! He's got a birchbark of his own," Philip muttered to Ann. "I don't suppose it's his fault that Indian laws give him all this trapping country."

John constituted himself master of ceremonies and general interpreter. He told the two Indians more than he told Ann and Philip, but they learned that Pe-tah-bo's wigwam was in the next bay. Pe-tah-bo undoubtedly was told that Mr. Jackman had gone to Nah-sho-tah's hunting territory, for he looked at Ann and Philip and nodded with approval. Soon he put his canoe in the water and paddled away. But Wen-dah-ban remained.

"He say he help make canoe," John explained to Ann and Philip.

They had reached the same decision but John did not receive much help and had to stop often to exchange information. His command of English was often strained but Wen-dah-ban and Ann and Philip learned much about each other.

The Indian boy was Ann's age in years, although the exact difference in months remained in doubt. Ann knew she would be fifteen next May Day and Wen-dah-ban said he was born in new moon time when the poplars were in bud. Philip verified that Wen-dah-ban actually ran a trap line and had a two-dog team. Philip looked with new respect on the older boy.

Ogema was admired and Wen-dah-ban admitted him to be heavier and stronger than either of his dogs. All went for a paddle in Wen-dah-ban's canoe, and Wen-dah-ban was firm in taking the hunter's place in the bow. He promised to bring his bow and arrows when he came the next morning.

Ann and Philip returned late for supper. When their mother heard about Wen-dah-ban she not only forgave them, but extended the limits of "their woods" to include the new neighbor's wigwam.

"And you must bring Wen-dah-ban here," she said. "Your father will be relieved to know Petah-bo is friendly."

Before Mr. Jackman returned, the trio became inseparable. Soon they no longer needed John as interpreter. Ann and Philip learned more Ojibwa than from John and Es-quay, and Wen-dah-ban, unlike Es-quay, tried to speak English.

They were never at loss for occupation. There was always paddling, roaming the woods, or merely sitting on the shore and talking. John made bows and arrows for Ann and Philip and when Ann's marksmanship gave Wen-dah-ban competition she arranged a bargain. She would shoot with him only if he stopped killing birds and the little red squirrels. Wen-dah-ban could not understand why she felt keenly about this subject, but he indulgently conceded the point. They evolved a game of "trade shop," which was Philip's favorite because he always had the role of white trader. Ann preferred to enact an Indian woman who made unreasonable demands and drove hard bargains. Because Es-quay had an assortment of twine, bits of fur, strouds and beads, they usually played this game in her wigwam. Her fat sides would shake with laughter as Ann gathered up her pelts and departed from the trade shop in a rage. Wen-dah-ban thought this haughtiness broke the rules and protested in his mixture of Ojibwa and English.

"No sell fur, fur no good," he insisted.

"I can wear it!" Ann cried.

Wen-dah-ban usually appeared with Ann and Philip at the cabin for between-meal snacks. He devoured cake and cookies and brown sugar spread on bread as greedily as Muckie, but he never forgot to say "*Me-gwetch*" to Mrs. Jackman.

"I like the lad," she said to Mr. Jackman on one of his rare evenings at the cabin. "What a funny tangle it is! The inheritance of a boy no older than Ann is causing us a hard winter and keeping you from home. Yet he's our constant visitor."

"Owning a trapping district isn't Wen-dah-ban's fault," Philip said.

"Certainly not," Mr. Jackman agreed. "And I'm glad you'll have neighbors when I leave you alone in cold weather. How does Pe-tah-bo act?"

"He isn't home much," Ann said. "But Wah-be-goon smiles and calls me Wah-bo-sence, and her name for Philip is—"

"I know what it means," Philip interrupted. "It's Ojibwa for 'he-who-talks-much.' "

"Whoever would have imagined that!" his mother laughed.

"What do you think of a wigwam now?" Mr. Jackman asked. "Any improvement on a cabin?"

"It's terrible!" Ann said. "All three of them crowded into that one wigwam! And they sleep in their clothes. The other morning we were there when they were getting up. They looked so dirty, and Wah-be-goon had to lift the net before they could eat breakfast."

"And the fish went into the pot, head, eyes, fins, scales and all," her father guessed.

"They ate with their fingers out of the same kettle," Philip said. "But Wen-dah-ban can't help it if his family doesn't know any better."

"Honest, Mother," Ann said, "you ought to show Wah-be-goon some things. They haven't even got a basin for washing their hands and faces. Or a place to take a bath."

"Perhaps they bathe in the lake," her mother suggested.

"Even Wen-dah-ban is afraid of water," Philip said. "He can't swim a stroke."

"Few northern Indians can," Mr. Jackman said.

207

"And probably Pe-tah-bo's wigwam is finer than John and Es-quay's."

"It is," Ann said. "And Wah-be-goon keeps it better. Only—" she hesitated and wondered why they had noticed the crude methods in Wen-dah-ban's home—"only I guess it's because Wen-dah-ban is a friend of ours. It isn't fair that no one ever taught him things."

"I know what you mean," her mother said. "You want to share things with a chum. Perhaps I can help."

Afterwards Ann saw that her mother was especially nice to Wen-dah-ban. Often she invited him to stay for dinner and when Ann and Philip washed at the stand in the corner there was always a basin of water and clean towel for Wen-dah-ban. At the table he watched the others and began to use a fork as they did. If he arrived while they were at lessons, Mrs. Jackman invited him in and showed him how to write figures and print his name.

Mr. Jackman was delighted when he heard of this on his next visit home.

"You might teach him enough so he could get a job at the post," he said.

"What a good idea!" Mrs. Jackman exclaimed. "I'll show him different foods and then write the word. Ann and Philip have learned so much from

Wen-dah-ban, and it's only fair that we do something."

"And I'll stay home tomorrow and drop in for a visit with Pe-tah-bo," Mr. Jackman said. "Let him know I don't hold a grudge."

The call was planned for afternoon and all the family were going. They told Wen-dah-ban of it when he paddled around the point in the morning. His early appearance indicated a hope to share the study hour, and Mrs. Jackman suggested that they begin.

"I got to find that darned Muckie, first," Philip said. "He's slipped his collar again."

A limp circle of leather at the end of a chain lay on the ground but no little bear was in sight. They looked in his usual hiding places and even searched the cabin. Mrs. Jackman suggested that he'd run away to Es-quay's.

"She'll make him behave or send him home," Ann said.

"That cub is a nuisance," Mr. Jackman said.

For once no one contradicted as they separated for a search. Philip ran down the trail to the Otter-tails and Ann and Wen-dah-ban examined nearby trees, which Muckie loved to climb when they called him. It was his idea of an enchanting game of hide and seek. Philip reported that neither John

nor Es-quay had seen Muckie and the search began in earnest.

"Does he ever go as far as Wen-dah-ban's?"
Mrs. Jackman asked.

"Only with us, Mother," Ann said. "And then
we watch him every minute. Wah-be-goon doesn't
make him mind like Es-quay."

Mrs. Jackman looked troubled.

"You'd better run over—" Mr. Jackman began,
and then he stopped to stare at a birchbark canoe
rounding the point.

The lone paddler was swinging his blade with
vigor.

"There's Pe-tah-bo now!" Ann cried.

Mr. Jackman sent Philip to bring John Ottertail
for interpreter and the others walked to the shore.
Wen-dah-ban glanced anxiously at the approaching craft and even at a distance all were aware of
Pe-tah-bo's anger. As the canoe came closer a white
bundle in the bow moved suddenly.

"It's Muckie!" Ann cried. "What's happened to
him?"

It was Muckie, bedraggled, woe-begone, his
black coat looking as though it had been whitewashed. The canoe touched the beach and the
Jackmans gathered around their pet. Their concern
was only for the pitiful object which had once

been a frolicsome cub. Now his black eyes surveyed them dolefully from a white face. Ann had
heard that fright might blanch hair overnight,
but she had never heard of such a thing happening
to a bear.

"Is he hurt?" she demanded.

But Pe-tah-bo's wrathful Ojibwa sputtered and
crackled. At first he gave no opportunity for
John's halting English, but Wen-dah-ban's stricken
face and quick look of sympathy for Ann and
Philip told them it was disaster.

"Muckie get in Pe-tah-bo's flour," John said at
last.

"You mean Wah-be-goon's little sack!" Ann
cried. "Oh, Mother! She was saving it for bannock! For special treats!"

"Tell Pe-tah-bo we will pay him," Mr. Jackman
said.

Pe-tah-bo shook his head. He had bought the
last sack of flour the company would sell. There
would be no more until debt time, and in any event
the trade shop was two days' journey away. One
would have imagined that bannock was the staff
of life itself instead of only an occasional luxury
in Pe-tah-bo's wigwam.

"Tell him we will give him our flour and go
without," Mr. Jackman said.

Pe-tah-bo listened and nodded, but it was evident that he was still unsatisfied.

"He say bear make much trouble," John explained. "He say some day bear come to wigwam and eat everything. He say when bear live with people, bear get to be the boss. He say bad luck—kill him. What you going to do?"

Ann gasped. She had known that some day Muckie would cause damage she and Philip could not repair. Now he had enraged Pe-tah-bo and the Indian was not to be placated. She knew this from Wen-dah-ban's miserable face as he listened to his father. Wen-dah-ban felt sorry for her.

"Pe-tah-bo say he no live near bear," John said. "He say he hunt here this winter. What you do with bear?"

Mr. Jackman flushed with anger, but his tone was even.

"Tell Pe-tah-bo we get rid of little bear," he said.

15 SHADOWS OVER THE NORTH

Ann and Philip chained the miserable, contrite Muckie to his small house, long since outgrown. They were very stern with him and even Ogema stared disdainfully, as though he knew the cub was in disgrace.

Pe-tah-bo, somewhat mollified, departed with a sack of flour. Wen-dah-ban watched in embarrassed silence and a short time later he got into his own canoe and paddled away.

"But he stuck around long enough to show he was on our side," Philip said.

"Don't talk of taking sides," his father said sharply. "Trouble starts from that. I'm sorry Wendah-ban stayed. His father might resent it."

"Anyway, we gave Pe-tah-bo twice as much flour as Muckie spoiled," Ann said. "Wah-be-goon had only a few pounds left."

"And Muckie wore that home," her father said as he looked at the bedraggled cub huddling at the doorway of his log house.

"He looks like a paste brush," Mrs. Jackman said. "How could he have managed to make all that flour stick?"

"Probably his coat was wet with dew and he tried to crawl inside the sack," Mr. Jackman said. "He's a natural clown."

Ann and Philip washed off the flour and when Ann dried him, Muckie cuddled closely. His bright eyes were alight with the old glint of mischief. To the cub, attention was a sign of complete forgiveness.

"Do we really have to let Muckie go?" Ann asked soberly.

Her father hesitated.

"I know it's tough," he said, "but I can't see any other—"

"Your father wouldn't dare leave us alone this winter if we make enemies of our only neighbors," her mother said. "Flour could be replaced, but what if Muckie destroyed valuable fur?"

No one cared to discuss Muckie's fate. He was now far too dependent on human beings to be turned loose in the forest. Sending him out to starve or be killed by wolves was cruel. Yet no one in the Jackman family could have carried out Pe-tah-bo's sentence.

That night Ann lay awake a long time. Muckie did want to be the boss, and he wasn't just an enchanting baby thing any more. He was becoming a grown bear, and a spoiled bear at that. Suddenly she sat up in bed.

"I know what to do with Muckie," she said.

"What?" Philip asked, and his voice wasn't even drowsy.

"We'll have Es-quay adopt him. Then we'll know he's got someone to love him and to make him mind."

Immediately after breakfast next morning Ann and Philip went to Es-quay's camp. Wen-dah-ban was sitting before the wigwam and they were glad to have the Indian boy's fluent Ojibwa to overcome John's objections. They felt sure of Es-quay.

"All right," John said at last. "Es-quay boss little bear. By-and-by we go to Fort Caribou. We take him."

"Oh, thank you, John!" Ann cried. "You won't be sorry. He'll be good company for Es-quay and you know you like to box with him."

"And we'll see him when we go to the post on Treaty Day," Philip said.

Wen-dah-ban looked as relieved as Ann and Philip. He did not speak of his father's edict until he started to paddle home.

"My father be glad," he said. "He say bad medicine to kill bear."

Ann and Philip were embarrassed. They felt sorry for Wen-dah-ban having to apologize for his father.

"Ah, forget it," Philip said. "Grownups are always getting nutty ideas."

"Besides," Ann added, "Muckie was getting to be a lot of trouble."

She'd have liked to say that he was cute enough to make up for any trouble he caused. But she didn't, for she wanted Wen-dah-ban to feel comfortable about his father. Neither Ann nor Philip were restrained about their opinion of Pe-tah-bo when they talked about him that day at dinner.

"I'm glad Es-quay will take Muckie!" their mother said.

"And you two stop talking about Pe-tah-bo," their father added. "As Wen-dah-ban says, a bear is mixed up with native superstition. Probably that's what's bothering Pe-tah-bo. I've never seen that Indian when he wasn't mad, yet somehow I can't help but like him."

Muckie's last days at Far Lake were happy. He didn't realize he was to be banished, and if he noticed any change, it was only that he received unusual attention and extra tidbits. Mrs. Jackman made a batch of cookies for his going-away present. She knew the Ottertails would eat most of them, but Es-quay would not be deaf to the cub's pleadings.

When their neighbors' wigwam was dismantled and kettles, bundles and rolls of birchbark were being stowed in the canoe, the Jackmans went to see John and Es-quay off. There was as much confusion and delay as when they had left Fort Caribou, but at last everything was aboard. Muckie's crate and all the paraphernalia of wigwam housekeeping were heaped before Es-quay. She pointed to the crate and told the bear to get in.

Without a backward glance, Muckie leaped aboard. He had no sense of exile, was only delighted to be going somewhere, and Ann's expectation of a tearful and prolonged farewell faded swiftly. Everyone waved and called good-by and said they'd see each other soon on Treaty Day. The Jackmans watched the yellow birchbark canoe disappear around the point.

"We'll miss the little scamp more than he'll miss us," Mr. Jackman said.

Ann suspected her father was right. Muckie was absorbed in his own comfort and would be happy with anyone who fed him and gave him attention. A dog was different.

"We'll never let Pe-tah-bo send Ogema away," she said.

"Not a chance," her father said. "And that dog's got as much sense as you two."

Early the next morning Mr. Jackman departed for his trapping territory. Cabin, trails and cubbies were almost finished, and now that peace was restored in the home bay, he was anxious to complete preparations.

"Won't be back until my job is finished," he said as he paddled away.

"Don't forget you've promised to take your family to Fort Caribou for Treaty Day," Mrs. Jackman called.

Ann and Philip were looking forward to the

celebration fully as much as was Wen-dah-ban. The trio talked about it constantly. The Indian boy was now a daily visitor and often joined the morning study hour. Mrs. Jackman said that in their game of "trade shop" she learned more Ojibwa than Wen-dah-ban learned English. All could now count to twenty in either language, and when Wen-dah-ban at last managed to print his name and write figures legibly, Mrs. Jackman suggested that he show the page to Wah-be-goon.

The Indian boy's report that his mother had said "*Nish-i-shin*" so delighted his instructor that she straightway plunged into teaching "flour" and "tea." She put a little mound of each on a sheet of paper and printed the word below.

Wen-dah-ban sat down at the big table with his lesson before him. Ann was working on an Ojibwa-English dictionary in preparation for the visit to the post, and Philip was absorbed in map making. Mrs. Jackman shuttled between table and stove in her dual role of cook and instructor. The room was quiet and peaceful.

Suddenly the door was opened and Pe-tah-bo strode in. Startled, Ann looked up and wondered if they'd ever seen their neighbor when he wasn't angry. He was angry now, but Wen-dah-ban was the object of his wrath. He advanced to the table, snatched the pencil from his son's hand, and in his torrent of Ojibwa Ann distinguished the words for Indian and white man.

Ogema rushed out from under the table and growled warningly. Mrs. Jackman put a restraining hand on his collar and faced the visitor.

"Wen-dah-ban, what is the trouble?" she demanded.

"He say me hunter," Wen-dah-ban said. "He say no good to do this. He say me stay with Indians."

"You don't have to leave your people because you make a few marks on a paper," Mrs. Jackman said. "Tell him I was only trying to help you."

"He say half-breeds make mark on paper and work in trade shop," Wen-dah-ban said. "He say me hunter like him and his father."

Indignation faded from Mrs. Jackman's face and she looked with sudden understanding at Pe-tah-bo. He stood erect, uncompromising, and there was dignity in his bearing.

"*Om-beh,*" he said to Wen-dah-ban.

The Indian boy arose.

"Ann! Philip!" Mrs. Jackman cried. "Explain to Pe-tah-bo. Don't let him think we've been interfering."

But the door had closed. From a window the

Jackmans watched father and son walk down to the lake.

"Heavens!" Mrs. Jackman said. "Whenever we have trouble with Pe-tah-bo, you children forget every word of Ojibwa you know."

"Nobody can talk as fast as he does," Ann said. "And he never stops to listen."

"Gosh!" Philip said. "That Indian likes to make speeches."

"He does seem to be a natural orator," his mother said. "But we've got to explain to him somehow."

No one cared to argue with Pe-tah-bo in his present frame of mind. Ann and Philip suggested they let him cool off. Meanwhile they could discuss the matter with Wen-dah-ban.

"He'll tell us what to say," Ann said.

Mrs. Jackman agreed it might be wise to wait. "Next time Wen-dah-ban comes, I'll have a talk with him," she said.

The Indian boy did not appear that day, or the next. In late afternoon, when they felt certain Wen-dah-ban was not coming, Ann, Philip and their mother paddled beyond the point to see if their neighbors had departed early for the Treaty Day celebration. But smoke rose above the trees which hid Pe-tah-bo's wigwam.

"We can't let this misunderstanding go on any longer," Mrs. Jackman said. "I don't want your father coming home to find more trouble."

"Maybe Pe-tah-bo won't let Wen-dah-ban come," Philip said.

His mother sat staring at the spire of smoke rising above Pe-tah-bo's camp. When she spoke her tone was decided.

"We'll wait one more day," she said. "If Wen-dah-ban doesn't come, I'll go and see his father."

When they reached home Ann motioned Philip to stay with her at the canoe landing. Their mother started up the trail and they did not speak until she was out of hearing.

"Mother's worried," Ann began. "Let's go over and see Wen-dah-ban."

"I was thinking that, too," Philip said. "We'll tell her we're taking Ogema for a walk."

Ogema dashed ahead of them on the trail. Study hours, spent at the children's feet, had curtailed canine activity. Now he ranged on either side, treed a squirrel, barked news of a moose track and tried his best to change a mission into a ramble.

Wah-be-goon was sitting before her wigwam. When they asked for Wen-dah-ban she nodded to a trail leading to a small lake behind the camp.

"I hope Pe-tah-bo isn't there," Philip said as they hurried on.

Sounds of chopping at the lake shore made them fear he might be, but they found Wen-dah-ban alone. He seemed glad to see them and explained that he had been too busy to visit the cabin. It was time he prepared his trapping trail for winter and he had already started to build his cubbies.

Ann and Philip watched him pound stakes into the ground to form the enclosure, and soon all three were at work. They became absorbed in the project and when they had completed the stout roof of interlaced branches, Philip suggested they build another.

Philip loved to build things and apparently he had forgotten the purpose of their visit. Nothing had been said to Wen-dah-ban about the interrupted lesson and it was time they were starting home. Ann had intended to be tactful, but diplomacy was difficult with a boy who was absorbed by his work.

"Will you come to see us tomorrow?" she asked bluntly.

Wen-dah-ban shook his head. He was going to hunt with his father.

"Won't he let you come again?" Philip asked.

Wen-dah-ban's face became blank. "By-and-by I come," he said.

And with that they had to be content. Moreover, they would be late for supper and they had nothing reassuring to tell their mother. They talked it over as they hurried home.

"We couldn't do any more," Philip said.

"We should have told him Mother wants to see him," Ann said. "All you'd talk about was that fur cubby."

"He said he'd come, didn't he? Gosh, you can't make a boy talk about his father if he doesn't want to."

Ann had no answer for that. She never could argue with Philip when he retreated behind the mysterious barrier of how boys felt about things, but she was sure she could have managed better.

They walked along the trail in silence. Light frosts had edged poplar leaves with yellow. Autumn had come and already, as they hurried home for supper, the sun had set. Ann felt the chill of approaching night. Deep shadows lay in the forest and suddenly she became aware that Ogema was not with them.

"Where's Ogema?" she demanded.

When their calls and whistles did not bring

him, they tried to remember when they had last seen him.

"He was with us when we built that cubby," Philip said. "Maybe he got tired of waiting and went home."

Ogema had never deserted them, but they called hopefully as they neared the cabin. Mrs. Jackman came to the door. She'd not seen the dog since they went off together.

"We've got to find him," Ann said.

"It will be dark soon," her mother said. "Eat your supper. He's chasing game and he'll find his way home."

"But he's never left us before," Ann insisted.

Mrs. Jackman placed the meal on the table while she listened to their story. Wen-dah-ban's vague promise to come "by-and-by" disturbed her, but Ann and Philip could only wonder about Ogema's disappearance.

"If he isn't home soon, I'll help search," Mrs. Jackman said. "But nothing could happen to a dog in the woods."

Her tone was confident but she listened almost as alertly as did Ann and Philip for Ogema's familiar scratch at the door. Ann ate little and pushed away her favorite cake. It seemed impossible to swallow when Ogema might be in trouble.

225

"But nothing could happen to him," Mrs. Jackman had insisted for the twentieth time, when the latch clicked sharply.

The door swung open and Wen-dah-ban entered, carrying Ogema in his arms. He staggered under the heavy burden but he laid the dog tenderly on the floor. Ogema's eyes were dull. He tried feebly to lift his head and his whole body twitched convulsively.

"He's been poisoned!" Mrs. Jackman cried. "How could anyone be so cruel!"

She plunged into first-aid measures. Ann and Philip carried out crisp orders as she poured mustard and water down Ogema's throat, consulted a book on home remedies, rummaged through medicine locker and cupboards. Tea for tannic acid, bromides, hot-water bags, a warm bed were prepared in the hour they worked over the stricken dog.

Wen-dah-ban watched in silence. When Mrs. Jackman asked if strychnine was the only poison used in fur land, he could only shake his head.

Ann and Philip knelt beside their dog.

"Can you save him?" Ann implored. Never had she felt more dependent or more grateful for her mother's swift efficiency.

"Perhaps," Mrs. Jackman said tersely.

Wen-dah-ban arose. "I go now," he said.

His hand was on the latch when Ann looked up and saw the misery in his face. No matter what his father had done, Wen-dah-ban had carried Ogema home, and it must have taken courage to defy Pe-tah-bo. She hurried to Wen-dah-ban.

"It wasn't your fault," she said. "And we'll never forget you brought him. If he lives you've helped—"

Sobs choked her and she turned away as the door closed behind Wen-dah-ban. It was long past midnight when Mrs. Jackman said they'd done everything they could. Ann and Philip went to bed.

"Try to sleep," Mrs. Jackman said as she kissed them good night.

In the dark Ann heard Philip stirring and knew he was going to sit by Ogema, for that was what she had planned to do. She slipped out of bed and they bent over the dog together.

"Maybe we'd better keep him covered," Philip said.

Ann brought blankets and pillows. She was grateful that Philip shared the anxious vigil and she felt closer to her brother than she had ever been before. When they'd first come to Far Lake she hadn't really known Philip or realized how

227

stalwart and dependable he was. No longer was he merely a younger brother. Now he was a friend. She wanted to tell him so, although Philip always edged away when he was embarrassed.

"Philip!" she whispered. "Aren't you glad we really got to know each other at Far Lake? I am."

"Sure!" Philip said. "And if Ogema gets well, everything is fine."

It seemed only a moment later when Ann opened her eyes to see daylight. Her mother was standing beside them.

"Whoever heard of nurses sleeping!" she exclaimed. "But you've helped Ogema. He looks better."

Ogema did seem stronger and for the first time they held a real hope that he would live. As the day wore on they became more optimistic and in the evening when Mr. Jackman arrived even he thought that Ogema might recover.

"Getting him so soon has given him a chance," he said.

"Wen-dah-ban gave him that chance," Ann said. "Even if Pe-tah-bo did give him the poison."

Mr. Jackman looked grim.

"It's hard to believe it of Pe-tah-bo," he said. "But if he'd do that, where would he stop?"

"I've thought about this winter, too," Mrs.

Jackman exclaimed. "First the hunting rights, then Muckie, then his fury about Wen-dah-ban's lessons, and now Ogema and poison."

Mr. Jackman paced the cabin.

"I don't know, Mary," he said. "I didn't like the thought of you three alone here for weeks in bitter weather. I didn't want to work all winter with only a slim chance of getting fur. But I was willing to give the thing a try. Figured it was the only thing to do."

"And it still is, Dave! We can't give up now!"

Mr. Jackman smiled at her determination.

"I don't quit any easier than the next fellow," he said. "But there's some chances we've no right to take. If anything should happen when I am away, you couldn't reach me. And with a dangerous enemy in Pe-tah-bo, anything might happen."

16 THE JACKMANS STAND

ALONE

The next morning Ogema was much better and Mrs. Jackman said that in a few days he would be strong enough to travel to Fort Caribou. Ann and Philip, having given up all thought of Treaty Day, began once more to plan on the celebration when Mr. Jackman said they must go.

"More reason that ever now," he said. "And

don't mention this poison business to Wen-dah-ban until after I've talked to Mr. Gillespie."

Ann and Philip nodded. They knew the attitude of the post manager would determine their father's decision to risk a winter at Far Lake and they tried to be discreet when Wen-dah-ban came to the cabin. But it was difficult to avoid the subject, especially as Ogema struggled to his feet in joyful recognition of the Indian lad.

"Look!" Ann cried. "He's trying to thank you for bringing him—"

She stopped in confusion, for her words touched dangerously on a forbidden topic.

But Wen-dah-ban was much too excited even to notice the awkward pause. He and his family were leaving that afternoon for the fur post and he had come to tell this good news quite as much as to ask about the patient.

It was several days later before the Jackmans departed for Fort Caribou. Fall had come to the North. The shores of Far Lake were ablaze with color. Poplar and birch formed masses of yellow against the green of spruce, while here and there a shrub of maple or a vine made a splotch of crimson. As Ann stepped into the canoe her feet crunched into the sandy beach, frost-crystaled by the cold of a night in early September.

With fewer hours of daylight they could not reach the post in one day and it was the second noon before they arrived to find the great clearing bordered by an encampment of birchbark wigwams. Smoke rose from scores of cooking fires and the shore was lined with canoes.

"It's an Ojibwa Chautauqua!" Mrs. Jackman cried. "No wonder Pe-tah-bo's family came so early."

The presence of four hundred Indians had brought the post to life. Groups of women and children dotted the great clearing and smiling dark faces looked out from every clump of bushes. The men were clustered before the trade shop, and every hunter carried a trade gun and a powder horn. The scene would have seemed warlike except for an air of excited expectancy. It was evident they were awaiting a joyous occasion.

As the Jackman canoe touched shore, Mr. Gillespie beckoned them to join him inside the picket fence.

"Just in time to help with the salute," he said. "The official party is due any minute."

The manager was loading the post's lone cannon, but he was in considerable doubt as to its efficacy.

"Fire the thing only once a year," he muttered. "I'm never sure it will go off."

A hunter had been stationed on a point to signal when the government canoe came in sight down the lake. Everyone was awaiting the official who was bringing treaty money, and as Ann watched with the others she found herself as tense as were the Indians.

"Every man, woman, child, even babes in arms, gets five dollars," Mr. Gillespie said. "Tomorrow'll be a great day."

The trade guns were to supplement the cannon and Mr. Gillespie put the hunters in Mr. Jackman's charge. Philip was fascinated by the cannon and was dragged to a safe distance with difficulty. Ann and her mother prepared to hold their ears when the fusillade began.

Suddenly the man at the point shouted and waved his arms. The signal was intended only as a warning but every hunter raised his gun and fired despite Mr. Jackman's frenzied efforts to halt the premature salute. No one paid the slightest attention to his shouts, commands and pleas. Guns were reloaded and fired as fast as the men could ram charges into the barrels. Only an exhaustion of ammunition brought silence.

The hunters were highly satisfied with their part

in the welcome, but Mr. Jackman was crestfallen as the government canoe rounded the point after the last powder horn was empty.

"We've still got the cannon," Mr. Gillespie said comfortably as he lighted the fuse.

The dull plop and fizzle could not possibly have been heard in the approaching canoe. Ann considered the whole salute a fiasco and her father, chagrined by his failure to curb the exuberance of the hunters, continued to apologize for mismanagement. The manager laughed.

"We never do better than that," he said. "My dear fellow, you're not responsible because the natives haven't a gift for organization. Come and meet the guests."

The big government canoe was nearing shore. The three white men sitting amidships waved and shouted and the canoemen put on an extra burst of speed. It was evident that the priest, the doctor and the Indian agent, who made up the official party, were old friends of Mr. Gillespie. As Ann watched, cordial greetings, laughter, the excitement of arrival and introductions to the Jackmans all going on at once, she wondered if the post manager didn't look forward to Treaty Day as eagerly as did his hunters.

Mr. Haight, the Indian agent, made no polite pretense that he had heard the cannon. He expressed his doubt to Mr. Jackman.

"Every year Gillespie claims to have fired that salute," he said. "I've never heard it yet. Think he's too Scotch to use powder."

"I saw a small puff of smoke," Dr. Allen admitted. "He had to use a little powder to impress our fellow guests."

But the eyes of the two men smiled at the grizzled Scotsman as they bantered, and Ann noticed that even quiet Father Lemoin let his hand linger on the fur man's shoulder when he said, "It's good to be at Fort Caribou again."

If Mr. Gillespie's hunters lacked a gift for organization, the manager balanced their failure with a high degree of efficiency. In a remarkably short time he had seen the luggage despatched to the dwelling house on the shoulders of employees, sent the canoemen to their quarters, shown his guests their rooms and assembled the whole house party for tea.

There he outlined the next day's program. Treaty money and medical examination in the morning, a feast for the Indians at noon and canoe races and sports afterward.

"Wonderful fellow, our host," Dr. Allen's big voice boomed as he took his third tea cake. "He even reminded Louise that chocolate is my favorite frosting."

Louise giggled happily but Ann could see that gentle-faced Father Lemoin was the housekeeper's favorite. Louise was the only one at the post who had attended a mission school.

"Haven't many parishioners at Fort Caribou," the priest said. "But all the Indians are my friends. That's why I come each year."

Philip was fascinated by the worn black satchel Mr. Haight had dropped carelessly in a corner. Ann knew from her brother's facial contortions that he was doing mental arithmetic.

"It's the first time I've been in a room with two thousand dollars," Philip said at last. "Can I look at it?"

Mr. Haight laughed and opened the satchel. Ann and Philip stared in awe at the bundles of bills.

"Do you pay as much for a baby as a man?" Philip asked incredulously.

"We're not paying for people," Mr. Haight said. "When the Indians gave up their land, the government agreed to pay each one five dollars a

236

year, forever. This is the annual fulfillment of that promise."

"To which they have looked forward for months," Father Lemoin added.

"Yes," Mr. Haight said, "and two days from now not an Indian will have a cent. They'd spend it tomorrow if the trade shop was open."

"But your coming is the big event of their summer," Dr. Allen said. "The government only throws me in for good measure."

"I'm not so sure of that," Mr. Gillespie said. "There's nothing an Indian likes better than a chance to try white man's medicine."

"If they would only try it!" the doctor said.

"Do you mean they won't let you treat them?" Mrs. Jackman asked.

"They're perfectly willing, even anxious, to be examined," the doctor said. "They'll let me put on dressings and give medicines and even agree to go to hospitals. And when their one big day of medical orgy is over, how much do you think I've accomplished, Gillespie?"

The manager chuckled. "For one thing, you've pleased them because the government has sent a white medicine man. At least two hundred natives are thinking up symptoms for you now."

"Yes, and how about the dressings, the medicines and the ones who should be sent to hospitals?"

"They've given the white medicine man a try. And if you can't work magic in one day, you can't blame them if they go back to their own medicine man again."

"So you see the result of my visit lasts about as long as the five dollars Mr. Haight hands out," the doctor said. "I'm merely a part of the treaty celebration."

As they all laughed, Ann felt almost sorry for him. And she wondered why the post manager didn't compel his hunters to obey the doctor's orders or at least be polite enough to make him think they did. But Dr. Allen appeared to hold no resentment as he helped himself to another piece of cake and passed the plate to Philip. When Philip refused another piece, his father stared in astonishment.

"I've finished tea," Philip explained. "I want to find Wen-dah-ban and tell him I've seen his money."

Ann left the living room with Philip, for she was anxious to find Es-quay and Muckie. She had expected to search the clearing but she found the

Indian woman and the cub outside the picket fence. News of the Jackmans' coming had hurried the pair to the post.

Ann tried to lead them to the dwelling house, for she wanted to exhibit Muckie, but the Indian woman shook her head.

"*Shag-e-nash, shag-e-nash,*" she said.

For once, Ann rebelled at that word "white man." She thought that today racial boundaries might be ignored. It was a party and she urged that her mother would want to see them. Es-quay only smiled and shook her head, but the cub was easily convinced and started joyfully through the gate until stopped by a stern "*Kah-win.*"

So Ann had to bring the tea guests to see her former pet. Dr. Allen presented him with a cake, much to Louise's and Es-quay's horror. Neither approved of such waste of party food. And Muckie kept a wary eye on Es-quay as he sat on his haunches and crammed the sweet into his mouth. Even the excitement of Treaty Day had not broken down stern discipline.

Everyone agreed that Muckie was a captivating pet, but Mr. Gillespie did not sympathize so much over the sentence to exile as Ann had hoped.

"You're lucky to be rid of the cub," he said that

night at the dinner table. "He'd be a nuisance when he's grown."

"But Pe-tah-bo was just being mean," Philip said. "I bet he doesn't think a bear's bad medicine any more than Wen-dah-ban—"

"And you don't know what Wen-dah-ban really thinks," the manager interrupted. "Every Indian feels differently about a bear. Some won't risk killing one. Others do, but take a ceremonial bath at once. Not one will tell how he really feels. Probably doesn't know himself."

"But why should Pe-tah-bo resent my teaching his son English?" Mrs. Jackman asked. "Doesn't he want the lad to improve himself?"

Mr. Gillespie nodded at the Indian agent. "Ask him," he said. "He's the official representative of the red race."

Mr. Haight's eyes twinkled.

"You're making me explain to a very charitable and charming woman that her efforts to improve the Indian aren't appreciated," he said.

"But it would help Wen-dah-ban to be able to write his name and add and subtract," Mrs. Jackman insisted.

"From your point of view, an education is desirable," Mr. Haight agreed. "You consider the white race superior. But the Indian doesn't. Just turn your thinking around and try to look at it from his viewpoint. Like all Ojibwas, Pe-tah-bo considers himself superior to the white race. He can paddle, pack, travel, hunt and is competent in his environment, while Gillespie, here, has to have all these things done for him. Pe-tah-bo is a successful man among his fellows." He turned to the manager. "How much did Pe-tah-bo make last year?"

"About seventeen hundred dollars," the manager said.

"There's your answer," the agent said. "For seven months' work. And with fur prices going up he'll probably make two thousand this year. Do you know of any trade in which Wen-dah-ban could do as well? Why should Wen-dah-ban want to be anything but a hunter?"

"Oh, Wen-dah-ban just stuck around to be with Ann and me," Philip said. "He pretended to study to please Mother. But you ought to see him build a cubby! Gee! He works as fast and hard as anything."

"There you have it from your own son," Mr. Gillespie laughed. "Wen-dah-ban won't have time for lessons when fur is prime. He's going to be a hunter like his father."

"And with all this trouble as a background, you

still don't believe Pe-tah-bo poisoned Ogema?"
Mr. Jackman demanded.

Ann started. She did not know her father had
talked to the manager about Pe-tah-bo. Now Mr.
Gillespie shook his head.

"Your dog picked up a strychnine pellet put out
for foxes last winter," he said. "Pe-tah-bo would
not poison Ogema. I know my hunters."

The Scotsman's eyes were icy blue. Mr. Haight
glanced from him to Mr. Jackman, and his tone
was placating.

"Gillespie told me about your accusation," he
said. "I agree with him. If you respect Pe-tah-bo's
hunting rights, he'll give you no trouble. Let's look
at this reasonably."

Mr. Jackman's head came up and his face was
grim.

"I have been reasonable," he said. "But this is a
matter of safety for my family. If Pe-tah-bo is
trying to drive us out, and I believe he is, I can't
leave my wife and children alone. I can't earn a
living."

Ann's heart sank. She had been sure the manager and the agent would protect them against
Pe-tah-bo, but if they didn't believe him guilty
there was no hope of help. She stared at the post

manager and wondered why she had ever liked him.

Conversation was difficult through the remainder of the meal. There would have been little talk had it not been for the efforts of gentle Father Lemoin and Mrs. Jackman. Later, in the living room, she seated herself at the piano and began to play. The tension lessened and when Ann and Philip departed for bed the manager was humming old Scotch ballads.

"Darn him anyway," Philip muttered as they went upstairs. "A lot he cares what happens to us."

Ann started to agree and then she stopped as she remembered how pleased Mr. Gillespie had been the afternoon he had told them of Nah-sho-tah's hunting territory.

"I don't know," she said. "He's two different people. And Mother didn't like it the way you and I sat and scowled at dinner."

"If we could prove Pe-tah-bo poisoned Ogema, it would help," Philip said. "Then Mr. Gillespie would have to do something."

"We've got to think of how to make Pe-tah-bo admit he did it," Ann said. "Don't you see? Pe-tah-bo knows he can drive us out by making Dad afraid to leave us alone this winter."

Ann intended to think furiously as she waited

for sleep. She knew it was useless to ask Wen-dah-ban. He'd only look blank and shrug his shoulders. No one could get at the truth except the manager, and somehow he must be compelled to help them.

17 TREATY DAY

Ann and Philip were the last to leave the breakfast table the next morning. Their mother was in the kitchen helping Louise with a special company dinner and their father had departed early to supervise preparation of the Indians' feast. Since six o'clock fires had been burning under kettles in which food was being cooked for four hundred guests.

Members of the official party were as busy. Mr. Haight, his bulging black satchel beside him, sat at a table checking a long list of names. Father Lemoin's black-robed figure moved from wigwam to wigwam on a round of calls. Dr. Allen was established in a small cabin by the trade shop, and outside was a long queue of Indians eager to try the white man's medicine. Michel and a corps of assistants rushed about on errands. Hundreds of excited, beaming Indians milled around the trade shop, waiting for the great event of the summer to begin, and the clearing resounded with their shouts and happy laughter.

Ann and Philip stood at the gate and surveyed the scene.

"Did you figure how we could make Pe-tah-bo fess up?" Philip asked.

"Did you?" Ann countered, hating to admit she had nothing new to offer.

"We got to work it somehow," Philip said. "Today's our last chance."

Ann knew that as well as Philip. She knew also that Mr. Gillespie was their only hope. They met him on their way to the trade shop and his cheery greeting showed that he was again the genial host.

Also he was a very much occupied one. He was everywhere at once. Ann's half-hearted resolve to talk to him about Pe-tah-bo faded swiftly as she watched the manager rush from one project to another. A marquee was being erected by a crew of excited Indians, and chairs were being brought so that the official party could watch the day's proceedings in comfort. As the Indians struggled with such unfamiliar problems as the stretching of ropes and canvas, Ann doubted if the marquee would be ready for the afternoon canoe races. But the gay, colored awning gave the clearing a festive air, and no one seemed more pleased with its erection than was the manager.

His task of supervision was constantly interrupted. Mr. Haight called him to unravel the mystery of a family census. Dr. Allen asked him to interpret mysterious and vague symptoms of patients. Hunters besought aid in locating offspring as they rushed about collecting their families. Children who had been accustomed to play unwatched were not allowed to stray from sight. Treaty money would not be paid to absentees. Fathers rounded up their progeny, and ancient crones who had not visited the trade shop for a year hobbled into the line which was already forming.

Ann went to inspect her father's kitchen. This was camp cooking on a gigantic scale. Tubs of stewed prunes and apples were cooling for dessert, and huge kettles of fish and meat and beans were bubbling. Each was being stirred by an Indian helper armed with a long wooden paddle. Ann thought that four hundred people could not possibly eat so much food. Mr. Jackman rushed from one kettle to another, tasting, smelling, regulating fires and giving orders. He looked exhausted, but happy. Mr. Gillespie came up to see how things were going.

"My dear chap," he said, "don't take this job so seriously. Just keep 'em from letting the stuff burn and see that every Indian gets something."

He clapped Mr. Jackman on the shoulder and turned to the grinning assistants. "Good boss," he said, and was off on a half dozen errands.

Philip reported that the marquee was ready at last and the official party was expected to watch treaty payment. Father Lemoin and Dr. Allen and their mother were waiting for them.

"Better go, Ann," her father said. "Tell them I can't leave this job."

As Ann and Philip slid into their chairs she had a feeling of importance. They were witnesses that the white race was fulfilling its treaty pledges, and watched gravely as hunters appeared with their families, were identified by the manager, paid by the agent and checked off on the list. The recipients moved off with a chorus of "*me-gwetches*" to

make place for the next in line. It was all very serious until a new-born babe in its mother's arms
was greeted by congratulatory laughter that it had
arrived in time to win treaty money.

As the queue of natives moved slowly past the
table, Ann realized that treaty payment might go
on for hours. She looked at the long line of waiting
families and whispered to her mother that she was
going to watch the preparation of the feast. Her
mother frowned and shook her head.

"Mr. Gillespie has asked the white people to sit
here," she said.

"Then why doesn't he take sides with the white
race?" Ann muttered under her breath.

"Ann!" her mother whispered. "You're a
guest!"

When Mrs. Jackman used that tone, Ann and
Philip knew argument was useless. Further pro-
tests could be only yawns and fidgets. Ann and
Philip were free with both as Indians continued to
file by. At last the final payment was made. Mr.
Gillespie arose and gravely shook hands with the
Indian agent. The manager most evidently thought
a speech was in order for he cleared his throat and
looked around for his audience. But the Indians,
having secured the treaty money, had now moved
toward the kettles.

Dr. Allen covered the awkward pause by coming forward to shake Mr. Haight's hand. Father Lemoin, followed by Mrs. Jackman and then by Ann and Philip, took his cue from Dr. Allen. It seemed strange for the white race to have to thank the white man for having kept his word with the red race, but someone had to conclude the ceremony of treaty payment.

Philip nudged Ann. "Let's get over to the feast," he said.

They ran across the clearing. Mr. Jackman was giving last-minute orders. He had chosen an official server for each kettle, and these men, armed with ladles, stood at their posts.

"Later you and Philip can help pass dessert," their father said to Ann.

"How about it, Jackman?" Mr. Gillespie called.

"Come and get it," Mr. Jackman yelled.

The manager waved his arm and a solid mass of Indians rushed forward. Each carried something to hold food. Ann saw plates, kettles, cans, birchbark dishes, even frying pans. The invading ranks bore down on the kettles and swept the servers aside. Feasters splashed and spattered and screamed as each filled his dish at the nearest kettle. Fish, meat, beans or dried fruit—no one seemed to care.

Ann and Philip and their father were caught in a

back eddy. When at last four hundred Indians had scattered, each with a dish of food, the Jackmans returned to the campfires. The assistant cooks had disappeared. Every tub and kettle was scraped clean and already the dishes of the feasters were empty.

"Spent six hours cooking," Mr. Jackman said. "The steam roller took ten minutes."

He laughed apologetically as the white party arrived.

"Don't seem to have managed very well," he said. "I'd intended to serve this meal in courses."

"Couldn't have done it better myself," Mr. Gillespie said. "Everyone got something to eat, and that's all that counts."

The official party felt that Treaty Day had gone off very well and congratulated Mr. Gillespie as they sat down to the noonday meal. Even Louise was beaming because Mrs. Jackman had inducted her into the mystery of pudding.

"But Treaty Day isn't over, is it?" Philip asked.

"It is as far as the Indians are concerned," Mr. Haight said. "They've been given treaty money, have eaten a feast and talked to the medicine man. The sports-day feature is to please our host, who's a true Britisher."

Mr. Gillespie joined in the laughter, although he looked slightly bothered.

"But we can't have four hundred Indians doing nothing all afternoon!" he protested. "And competitive sports are good training."

"Isn't he wonderful?" Dr. Allen asked the table at large. "Each year we watch him cajole and plead and banter and command until he gets three races started. In the end he's more exhausted than the contestants, if you can call them that."

"But every year he persuades more Indians to enter," Father Lemoin said quickly. "And when you remember that the Indian paddles only for the practical reason of getting somewhere, these races are an achievement in organized effort."

"But don't they paddle just to win?" Ann asked.

"I'm afraid it's only the prize money that stirs 'em," Mr. Gillespie admitted. "Somehow they don't seem to have the sporting instinct. Perhaps I can convert the next generation, for in the candy scramble there certainly is competition."

With the feast as a warning, Ann and Philip determined not to miss the scramble. It began the afternoon festivities and they climbed onto the fur press to be able to look over the crowd. Wen-dah-ban joined them. The thought of pounds of candy being thrown into the air had aroused a competi-

tive spirit in Philip but Wen-dah-ban's lofty attitude quenched it.

"Women and children," he said. "A hunter
watches."

"Sure," Philip said, and looked thoughtful.

Mr. Gillespie appeared with a huge bag, directed
the audience to form a circle, and began to scatter
candies. The first few handfuls brought out the
younger children but as more candy was thrown,
excitement increased. Women and older children
joined the scramble and then a few abashed males.

"How about them?" Philip asked.

"No hunters," Wen-dah-ban said.

But when Muckie hurled himself into the melee,
Philip broke down.

"Got to help him," he said, and dashed into the
milling crowd.

Muckie did not need help. He was perfectly
constructed for this game. Not only could he take
possession of several prizes merely by squatting on
them but he could instantly settle any argument
of ownership by gobbling candy from under
grasping fingers.

Ann sensed Wen-dah-ban's growing excitement.
Occasionally he so far forgot himself as to make
an instinctive movement forward. Ann suspected
he wanted to scramble for candy as much as she

253

and was only waiting for her to suggest it. But if he had to comport himself as a hunter, she had to maintain the dignity of a guest in the dwelling house. But Ann knew a way out for both. That morning she and Philip had each been given a bag of candy by their father.

"I have some in my room," she said. "Let's go and get it."

Wen-dah-ban hesitated.

"Won't take but a second," she urged. "Come on."

At the front door of the dwelling house Wen-dah-ban refused to enter, although he agreed to wait for her. It took only a moment to run upstairs on her errand and she rejoined Wen-dah-ban on the porch as Mr. Gillespie hurried through the gate.

He scowled at the Indian boy and there was no mistaking the sternness of his tone when he said, "*Marchon.*"

Color flared in Ann's cheeks for she had brought this humiliation on Wen-dah-ban.

"But I invited him," she said.

"He knew better than to come inside the fence," the manager said. "And I thought you understood."

Wen-dah-ban started for the gate. Had there

been proud dignity in his bearing, Ann would have considered it a sufficient rebuke for Mr. Gillespie, but the apologetic droop of the Indian boy's shoulders aroused her anger. There was no understanding this uncompromising Scotsman, now on the side of red men, then on the side of white, never swayed by his emotions, guided only by strange rules.

"If he can't stay, I won't," she blazed out at the astonished manager. "When I have friends, I stick to them. And I'm going to paddle with Wen-dah-ban in the race this afternoon."

As they walked out together, Ann looked back defiantly. Wen-dah-ban did not seem to share her resentment nor did he seem pleased by her plan to paddle with him.

"We'll win the race and show him!" Ann said fiercely.

"Maybe first canoe get two dollars," Wen-dah-ban said.

"And you can have all the money," Ann said, hoping this would prod the competitive spirit of her bowman.

The Indians had gathered on the rocky point, preparing for the races. The first, the men's race, had progressed no farther than a discussion as to who would or would not compete. The arrival of

Mr. Gillespie with prize money stimulated interest. His banter got several men to their feet and
some even put their canoes in the water.

Then began interminable discussions as to how
competitors would team up. Partnerships formed,
dissolved, were finally cemented. Ann thought it
would be simpler if each man paddled singly.
Angry as she was with the manager, she felt almost sorry for him by the time he had persuaded
a dozen canoemen to enter.

Organizer, starter, judge, Mr. Gillespie worked
harder than any entrant. The Indians' natural
apathy was further dampened by a sudden shower.
Not enough rain fell to end the field day, but the
audience under the marquee looked thoroughly
miserable. Mr. Gillespie struggled on against dis-
couragement of the elements and reluctance of his
people until at last six canoes crossed the finish line
amid much splashing and shouting.

The women's race took even longer to get
underway. Es-quay consented to compete and
Ann tried to imbue her with a fighting spirit as the
canoes were lined up.

"Paddle hard, Es-quay," Ann called. "You can
win easy."

Es-quay laughed so hard she didn't take a stroke
when the starting gun was fired. The race was

finished with Es-quay trailing, and Wah-be-goon and a young Indian woman easy winners. When Wah-be-goon received her share of the prize and secreted it in her voluminous skirts, she smiled at Ann.

Ann was glad Wah-be-goon was her friend and she wondered if, when she and Wen-dah-ban won their race, his mother would help her make Pe-tah-bo confess. For now that Ann's anger had cooled she wondered how her flare-up had affected the Jackman fortunes. She watched Mr. Gillespie's face to see if he held resentment and decided he was ignoring her.

Her entry with Wen-dah-ban in the children's race caused much excitement and laughter among the natives. But it was friendly laughter, and Mr. Gillespie said Wen-dah-ban had a good paddler in the stern.

Ann waited tensely for the starting gun.

"Go!" she screamed to Wen-dah-ban, and paddled with all her might.

Her fire and driving force put them easily in the lead and Ann looked back at the other five canoes in triumph until two grinning boys began to overtake them. Ann dug in, but as the bow of the boys' canoe pulled ahead, Wen-dah-ban shrugged his shoulders and stopped paddling.

"Keep on!" Ann screamed. "We've got a chance."

But the loss from that momentary halt could not be retrieved after Wen-dah-ban thought he had no chance to win the money. His canoe was a poor second. When he grinned good naturedly, Ann could have shaken him. She watched the victors receive their prize money.

"Why didn't you keep paddling?" she demanded. "You're never beaten until a race is over."

"That's the true Jackman spirit," Mr. Gillespie chuckled.

As she watched the manager rejoin his guests under the marquee, Ann was grateful that at least he hadn't seemed angry with her. She knew this meant nothing when a man made his decisions on strange principles and was unmoved by friendships, and she realized the afternoon was almost over and she and Philip had accomplished nothing about Pe-tah-bo. The canoe race hadn't helped a bit. Wah-be-goon was admiring the winning boys' money and hadn't looked in the direction of Wen-dah-ban or Ann. She might even be angry that her son had paddled with a girl and lost.

Ann stood disconsolately among the Indians on the rocky point, although she knew she should join the party under the marquee. Philip had reported that her mother disapproved of the afternoon's absence and explanations must be forthcoming. She began to wonder if she had carried things too far in her loyalty to Wen-dah-ban.

Indians milled around her. Men and women were as ecstatic over the prize money as were the children. Dollar bills were passed about to be admired, although the owners never permitted them out of sight. Parents of the two brothers who had won the race were especially proud, for that prize money went to one family. The father held the bills aloft for everyone to see and as he returned them to his sons, one fluttered from his hand.

The boy made a quick dive to retrieve it. The lunge struck Wen-dah-ban and threw him off balance. His moccasins slid greasily on the wet rock and his feet went out from under him. Ann saw Wen-dah-ban's head strike hard as he fell. The next moment he had rolled off into deep water.

Instantly the point was in an uproar. Everyone shrieked and crowded onto the rock where they stood pointing into the water and uttering shrill Ojibwa ejaculations. Ann shoved through the crowd and looked down, waiting for Wen-dah-ban to come to the surface. But he did not appear.

"He'll drown!" she cried. "Get him out! He hit his head. He's unconscious! He'll never come up!"

259

Ann had forgotten that few Ojibwas knew how to swim. But as the moments passed and men and women only shouted commands and ran up and down the shore, she realized that she was probably the only person on the point who could save Wen-dah-ban. Precious seconds were slipping by and the surface of the lake remained terribly still.

Ann ripped off her dress, kicked off her shoe-pacs, poised an instant on the high rock and dived.

It was dark in the depths of the swamp-colored water. As she groped along the bottom she thought of many things. Helpless, Wen-dah-ban was lying there, and she must find him. If she didn't, she would never have strength or breath to dive a second time. And before her father or Mr. Gillespie could arrive to help, it would be too late.

Ann's lungs threatened to burst. She knew she could stay down only a few more seconds. But she would not, could not, give up the search. In a last desperate grasp, her hand touched the boy's clothing.

She struggled upward, blinded by pressure, fingers clutched in Wen-dah-ban's hair. It wasn't the good life-saving technique she had been taught, but at least she was bringing him inshore.

White men, cool and efficient, were there now. Mr. Gillespie drew Wen-dah-ban from the water.

Mr. Jackman lifted Ann, although she could have climbed out unassisted. Mrs. Jackman took her arm and helped her to the dwelling house. No one had ever worried about wet clothes before, but now she was toweled and rubbed.

Philip appeared while she was dressing. He reported that Dr. Allen had laid Wen-dah-ban on the lawn and was working on him.

"Resusi— you know what they call it," he said. "But anyway he brought him to."

"An Indian has to drown to get inside that precious picket fence!" Ann cried. "That was the way the whole trouble began when—"

"We won't talk about it now," her mother said. "Wen-dah-ban is alive, and that's all that matters."

Treaty Day's close approach to tragedy had sobered everyone. When Ann and her mother went downstairs they found the others talking in low tones as they waited for the women to join them for tea. Dr. Allen said that Wen-dah-ban had been taken home by his family. Groups of Indians still stood in the clearing. Mr. Jackman's eyes were very proud as his glance rested on Ann. Mr. Gillespie jumped to his feet and shook her hand.

"Young lady, I want to thank you," he said. "And you, too, sir," he added, turning to Dr. Allen. "We needed you both today."

"Ann didn't give me much to do," the doctor said. "She got the lad out so quickly."

"Good work, Ann," the Indian agent added.

Father Lemoin did not speak but there was an approving smile on his gentle face. Afterwards he called Ann "dear" and his hand rested often on her shoulder.

Ann had expected some approval, but as she drank her tea, and even Louise pressed the choicest tea cakes upon her, she found all this applause somewhat bewildering. When she had been moved by loyalty to Wen-dah-ban and had tried to help her family by paddling in the children's race, she had been aware of public disapproval. Now when she had merely behaved instinctively, had gone to Wen-dah-ban's rescue because she was the only one on the point who could do so, she suddenly found herself a heroine.

She was being praised for acting without thinking. But that, too, was reassuring, for Ann was beginning to suspect that she would always do things before she thought. However, she could hardly hope that the outcome would always be so gratifying.

Only Philip saw another side of the rescue.

"That old Pe-tah-bo ought to be ashamed of poisoning Ogema," he said.

262

Mr. Gillespie swung around to face Mr. Jackman. "Pe-tah-bo didn't poison Ogema," he said. "At least not by intention."

"Then you did go to Pe-tah-bo!" Mrs. Jackman cried. "I—I—I was sure you would do—" And her warm smile completed her thought.

"I didn't tell Pe-tah-bo of your accusation," the manager said. "But, sure as I am about my hunters, it was still my duty to investigate. The safety of everyone in this district, white or red, is in my charge. When I asked Pe-tah-bo this morning how much strychnine he had used last winter, he told me he put out ten pellets. One got a fox. He gathered eight in the spring, but could not find the tenth and thought a fox had managed to get away with it. That must have been the pellet your dog picked up."

"Then Pe-tah-bo isn't trying to drive us out!" Mrs. Jackman exclaimed.

"No. I talked with him this morning. He is still firm in his purpose not to permit you to hunt in his territory, but he will do nothing to harm you." The manager looked away, hesitated and then added with evident reluctance: "However, it is only fair to tell you that he said he wouldn't have to drive you out. Fur land will do that for him. He says there never has been much fur in Nah-sho-tah's territory, that you can't make a living and will not be able to stay through the winter."

No one spoke for a moment. Ann looked at her father and his face confirmed her fears.

"Dave!" Mrs. Jackman cried. "Do you believe that?"

"I've been suspecting it," Mr. Jackman admitted. "But I was willing to make a try."

"But see here," Mr. Haight said. "There ought to be some place in this country where—"

"But I've built my cabin at Far Lake," and Mr. Jackman's voice was bleak. "And fall is here."

Ann waited tensely. Surely someone would think of something they could do. Her glance searched Mr. Gillespie's face even while she wondered why she always looked to him for help. But it was evident that he was as distressed as were the others. He arose and walked to the window.

"My word!" he exclaimed. "It's after sundown and the Union Jack is still up. Perhaps we should have a little ceremony and let the heroine of the day bring down the flag."

Ann recognized the kindliness of his suggestion to end an unhappy discussion. All walked out together, a silent group. Ann looked at her father and her mother and was suddenly very proud. Their heads were up and their shoulders back.

That was the Jackman courage. And as she crossed the lawn and grasped the halliard she resolved no one should see her tears.

The flag fluttered down while Ann kept her eyes fastened on it. The others too seemed glad to have something on which to focus their attention. None saw Pe-tah-bo until he reached the picket fence. Tall and straight, he opened the forbidden gate without hesitation and walked toward them.

No one spoke as he approached. He stopped, looked calmly at the white people, and then began to speak to Mr. Jackman. Ann's pulses quickened as the words came with impressive dignity.

"He says that for many years his father and his grandfather have hunted in the territory at Far Lake," Mr. Gillespie interpreted when Pe-tah-bo paused. "He says that now all that country belongs to him. And some day it will belong to his son Wen-dah-ban."

Pe-tah-bo waited while this was said in English. Then he stooped, sketched a map on the ground, and with a sweep of his stick drew a line which divided the map. Then he spoke for a long time. The manager nodded, took the stick from Pe-tah-bo's hand and pointed to the map.

"On this side Pe-tah-bo will hunt," Mr. Gillespie said. "On the other side, the bay, the creeks, the swamps, all the lakes behind the cabin, the white man may hunt this winter and for two winters thereafter. The trails and cubbies he finds there are the white man's to use. So Pe-tah-bo pays his debt."

Pe-tah-bo listened. When the manager had finished, the Indian turned to the astounded group.

"*Nish-i-shin*," he said, and walked away.

No one spoke until Pe-tah-bo reached the gate.

"Call him back!" Mr. Jackman cried. "I've got to thank him."

Mr. Gillespie shook his head.

"Some other time," he said. "He's quite an orator, you know. Don't spoil his exit."

Tears were in Mrs. Jackman's eyes.

"But, Dave!" she cried. "We must thank him. Far Lake saved for us! How can we tell Pe-tah-bo how much he's done?"

Mr. Gillespie's eyes twinkled.

"Good Heavens!" he said. "You folks will be neighbors all winter and you can tell him in a hundred ways. But right now there's nothing to prevent your thanking the young lady who brought all this about."

Two days later in the warm sunshine of a September afternoon, a green Peterborough and a yellow birchbark approached the end of Far Lake together. At the point outside the Jackmans' home bay they parted. Pe-tah-bo and Wen-dah-ban waved their paddles and Wah-be-goon's kindly face broke into a warm smile as she looked at Ann.

"*B'jou*', Wah-bo-sense," she called. "*Keen git-che nish-i-shin.*"

The Jackmans waved and called "Good-by!" Philip shouted that Wen-dah-ban should come to the cabin the next day. Ogema sat up, thumped his tail and barked.

"What a happy homecoming for both families!" Mrs. Jackman said. "So different—"

She didn't finish it, and the Peterborough went on, four paddles swinging, until it was abreast the clearing and the cabin was in view. All looked at it, but no one spoke until the canoe touched the beach.

"Ann," Mr. Jackman said, "what did Wah-be-goon say to you?"

"I know!" Philip said. "She said Ann was 'heap big all right.'"

"There'll be no quarrel with the Pe-tah-bos about that," his father said. "Maybe I built the cabin, but Ann seems to have kept us in it."

Ann didn't speak. Pride and joy had brought a lump to her throat. She looked from the happy faces of the others to the cabin nestling against the dark green backdrop of the forest, and suddenly she remembered many scenes: the day she had learned from her mother they were going to the wilderness; the night after their terror in the spruce swamp when she and Philip had first realized all that fur land could mean to the family; and those dark weeks when they had feared they would be driven from their new home in the north. Now "Home Bay" and the cabin had been made more precious by the threat of danger.

They started up the slope, Mrs. Jackman on one side of Ann, her husband on the other. Their arms were around Ann's shoulders and Philip was close to his mother as they walked four abreast. Ann thought this was as they should walk. She squeezed her father's hand.

"Isn't this perfect!" she said. "All four together!"

THE END

268

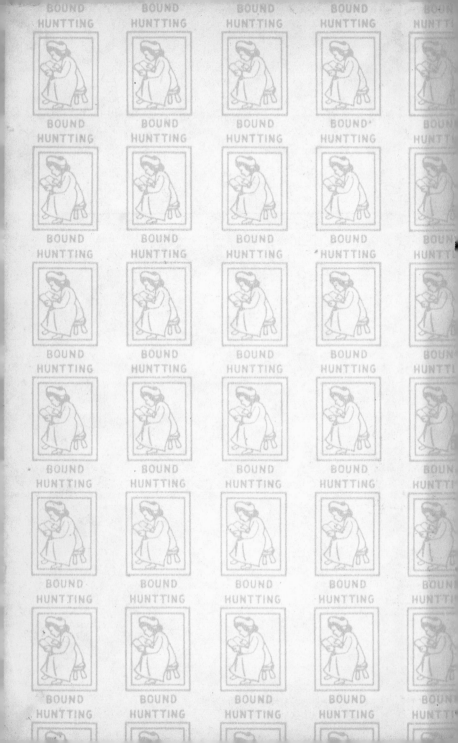

PREFACE

New Mexico is known as the Land of Enchantment. These words can be found on the state's
license plates and countless other places,
including books. For the non native New Mexican,
the three words may evoke an assortment of
thoughts or guesswork regarding what lurks behind
them. They may sound mystical and enticing, but
the allure of enchantment gradually captivates the
newcomer or visitor to our state once he or she
embarks on a tour of New Mexico. From the land-
scape to the people and its history, a mosaic of splen-
dor unveils before their eyes. But for us natives, the
words on the license plates are unmistakable. They
spell magic.

The stories in *Rattling Chains and Other Stories
for Children / Ruido de cadenas y otros cuentos para
niños* are typical of New Mexico's kaleidoscope of
enchantment. They can be enjoyed by grownups —
parents and grandparents — reading them to their
children or grandchildren or children reading them
on their own. I heard many tales like these at the
dinner table, around the potbelly stove on cold winter nights, at campfires during cattle roundups and
while working in the cornfields at our country ranch

where I spent the first nine years of my childhood before moving to Albuquerque.

I grew up in the Rio Puerco Valley in rural New Mexico, about forty-five miles northwest of Albuquerque. Ojo del Padre (Guadalupe in more modern times), today a ghost town, was the name of my village, although my family and I, along with my paternal grandparents and an aunt and uncle and their family, lived about two miles from the *placita* (town). My grandfather homesteaded near here during the latter part of the nineteenth century after migrating with his parents from the Rio Grande Valley.

It is said that Ojo del Padre was named in honor of a priest who discovered a spring not far from what was to become the hub of the village, now dating back more than 250 years. Water in that arid part of New Mexico is still a scarce commodity so the priest's discovery as he stumbled upon the spring in the middle of the desert was nothing less than a miracle in a state known for its magic.

When I was a small boy living on the farm there were no books at home, television, radio or record player (my mother did listen once a week to her favorite Mexican songs on a battery-operated radio that my father bought for her), but I was blessed with something more wonderful, precious and enduring. I had my parents and grandparents who could neither read nor write, but they were fabulous storytellers. Their tantalizing stories were the "real deal," the flesh and blood of narratives related to witches, the Wailing Woman, animals disguised as ghostly apparitions and a host of other supernatural creatures.

Rattling Chains and Other Stories for Children / Ruido de cadenas y otros cuentos para niños is a collection of stories lodged in New Mexican folklore whose appeal is universal in scope. The stories are my own creation. They embody a fundamental slice of my childhood world of fantasy and superstitions and were inspired by stories I heard or episodes I experienced firsthand at our ranch. Tales like these were appealing to kids like me when I was a small boy, and they are still just as engaging for children today. So come along and join Junie López, our narrator, on his journey of fun and fancy.

Nasario García, Ph.D.
Santa Fe, New Mexico
2008

THE MAGICAL *NICHO*

My name is Junie López. Junie is the nickname my parents gave me. It comes from Junior. Long ago I used to live in the Rio Puerco Valley in rural New Mexico, the Land of Enchantment. That's where I grew up. Now I live in the city. I was the first child in my family. That's important because I didn't have a brother or sister to look up to. Seven siblings came after me. Being the eldest of my brothers and sisters, each one sort of looked up to me perhaps more than I looked down at them.

The story you're about to read happened to me at our ranch when I was a little boy. Like most kids, I used to have all kinds of dreams. Some were exciting, others not so nice, including nightmares. But no dream equals what I now wish to share with you. The episode was both magical and real. I found it amazing, and so did my mother. But first things first.

Our *placita* was not far from our home. My parents, my little brother and I lived in a two-room house: one room was the kitchen and dining area while the second room was our bedroom. The rooms were both small and square in shape and adequate,

5

but, of course, things got crowded later on when my other siblings were born.

My parent's little house sat on top of a hill that overlooked the Rio Puerco and the Guadalupe Ruins across the river to the south. The cornfields and Black Mesa were situated to the east. To the west about two hundred feet from my house was a huge butte that protected us in the winter from the cold gusty winds. Not too far to the north one could see the famous Cabezón Peak, known for its gigantic size and majestic beauty, along with several other large, dark-blue peaks that rose like friendly giants ready to greet you at dawn.

As a kid I imagined I was sitting on top of the world with all the natural beauty that surrounded me. When I grew older and had a better sense of appreciation for nature, my feelings were confirmed. I was indeed lucky! For me these natural wonders were enchanting and thrilling. I entertained myself just by looking at them. At times I felt as though they even whispered to me from afar.

These wonders were also the sites where numerous stories of witches, magical donkeys, hooting owls and the Wailing Woman came from. I heard many tales about these superstitions or supernatural creatures from my parents, grandparents and other people in my village. But of all my childhood experiences, none tops "The Magical *Nicho*."

Let us go back in time. I was five years old going on six. My mother, who was a very religious person, had a *nicho* in our bedroom. A *nicho* is like a little alcove in the wall. This is where many devout people place their favorite religious saints. *Nichos* with carved wood or plaster saints can be found in many churches and chapels.

My mother's favorite *santo* was the Holy Child of Atocha, named in honor of the city of Atocha, Spain. The Holy Child, looked upon as the protector of the ill or imprisoned, is very popular among many New Mexican Hispanics. According to my mother, the Holy Child watched over us at night after we were asleep. He had a rosary draped around its neck that Mom would remove whenever she prayed at night before going to bed. The Holy Child of Atocha was her constant spiritual companion and friend. There was an unbreakable bond between them until one day when surprising things started to happen.

My father had been working for the federal government building roads and other projects. He didn't make much money, but he and Mom were able to save a few dollars. Because there were no banks where we lived (nobody out in the country used banks), they decided to put their savings in a safe place. I remember clearly to this day the argument they had at the dinner table about where to hide the money. Dad suggested putting it inside their mattress or a pillow. At first Mom thought the idea was good, but after thinking it over for a minute or two she decided against it. My father was quick to react.

"Well, where do you propose stashing away the money?" he asked Mom, a bit unhappy, if not disappointed, because his idea was rejected.

"Well, what do you think of placing it in the *nicho*?" she suggested. "Nobody would ever find it there."

"And how do you plan to do that? You can't just put the money in the *nicho* and leave it there!"

"Why not?" remarked Mom, leaving Dad to ponder what she had in mind. "Here's what we can do," she continued. "We'll use an empty jar for the money. Then—"

"Then what?" asked Dad, still a bit miffed.

"Wait, wait just a minute. Hold your horses!" exclaimed Mom. "After that we mud plaster the *nicho* with the jar and the money inside. Next we whitewash the wall and nobody will ever suspect that our life savings are in the bedroom wall."

Dad's sullen face suddenly turned to a smile. He was impressed with Mom's clever idea.

"And how did you come up with something like that? I could not have thought of anything like it in a thousand years," said Dad.

Mom had a smug look on her face as she went and got the empty jar. She was ready for the next step.

"How much should we put in it?" asked Dad.

The conversation went back and forth until he asked Mom how much money she had in her apron. That's where she kept their savings—in a pouch pinned to the inside of her apron pocket. It's a place many women kept the family's money.

"We can put away fifteen to twenty dollars," answered Mom.

That was a lot of money seventy years ago for a poor family on a tiny ranch like ours. And so an agreement was reached, and they placed a combination of bills and some coins inside the jar.

Sunday afternoon Dad made the necessary preparations to put the jar with the money in the *nicho*. After he mixed the mud, he asked Mom for a white cloth big enough to cover the opening of the *nicho*. She brought the cloth along with some *poleadas*, a paste made with white flour and water, to secure the material. But before putting the jar inside the *nicho*, Mom opened a little bottle of holy water that she kept on her dresser and sprinkled it inside. Next she placed the jar so that Dad could cover it with the cloth and mud. Afterward he whitewashed the wall. You couldn't tell that anything was "buried" inside. Mom and Dad's "piggy bank" was now in a secret and sacred place.

As for the Holy Child of Atocha, from that moment onward he had a new home, so to speak. He now found himself sitting right on top of Mom's dresser. Out of respect for the Holy Child, she made sure that hairbrushes, combs and other stuff did not clutter up the area around him. Dad, who was used to putting his leather coin purse on the dresser, now had to find another place for it. The only thing keeping the Holy Child company was Mom's rosary and the little bottle of holy water, which sat right behind him.

Over time Mom missed not seeing the Holy Child in his *nicho*, but she figured that he understood why he was moved. As for the jar with the money, it was to remain in the *nicho* until they needed money. When that would be was uncertain; they did not know. Maybe they would have to open up the *nicho* if they needed to put more money in the jar. Perhaps only the Holy Child knew when either decision would come to pass.

For the time being, Mom thought everything was settled, but she was in for a big surprise. And so was I! A few weeks after hiding the money I began having dreams. At times they were unpleasant, but I said nothing to Mom. First I dreamt that a thief had discovered my parents' secret and the money was stolen. I knew it was just a dream but I worried something like that could really happen. After all, Dad worked hard to earn his money, and Mom was equally conscientious in saving every penny possible for a rainy day.

The following night or soon thereafter, my dream was entirely different. I dreamt that the coins inside the jar had turned into gold, making the money much more valuable. *Could this really happen*? I asked myself.

One night, my aunt, who lived down the hill from us, came to visit Mom. Soon after I went to bed, they sat down to chat. Then I began to hear noises coming from the *nicho*. The whisper-like sounds were faint but audible although I couldn't quite put the words together to make any sense out of them. The noises occurred off and on at night for a period of two or three weeks, but I didn't reveal them to anyone.

One Saturday, smack in the middle of the night when my father was sound asleep and snoring, I clearly heard a voice that said to me, "Please tell your Mom that I belong in the *nicho*." Of course, I didn't know what to think or do after hearing what I heard. The voice certainly was not familiar to me. I decided to ignore it and did nothing.

A week later, more or less, I heard the same voice, once again in the middle of the night. "I, the Santo Niño de Atocha (he spoke in Spanish!), belong in the *nicho* like other saints. That is the home that your mother built for me. Could you please help me return to where I belong?"

His pleading words were clear and sincere. I got up the next morning and thought about them all day long. That evening I decided I'd better tell my mother while Dad was still away at work. At supper I built up enough courage to reveal to her the two incidents: the mysterious voice and the strange noises I had been hearing at night. In between bites we talked about ordinary things typical of a mother and child living on a ranch. At one point I simply came out and said, "Mom, I have something to tell you."

"What is it, son? You sound anxious."

"Last night for the second time I heard a voice coming from the Holy Child. He asked me to tell you something."

"And what is that?" she asked with a puzzled look on her face.

"He wants to return to his *nicho*. He says he belongs there."

"Oh, Junie! You've been dreaming again. You're just hearing things. That's very common when you're little like you."

"Little or not, I have been hearing things, and they're for real. You must trust me. They're not things that are in my head, buzzing in my ears or that I'm making up. They are real words coming from the Holy Child."

"Okay, *hijito*. Here's what we'll do. Next time you hear that voice, you wake me up immediately. Let me listen to the voice myself."

"Fair enough! But what if the voice doesn't show up? What do we do then?"

"Don't worry. If it's for real, the voice will come back. If not, then we can say that it was just a dream. How's that?"

"Okay," I answered, agreeing somewhat reluctantly.

For the next several days the voice did not return to talk to me. My mother did not mention it either. No doubt she thought the voice was nothing more than a fantasy of mine, so why bring it up again for discussion?

One night the most amazing things happened a few minutes after I went to bed. I suddenly saw a glow on the wall, right where the money was hidden. The white wall shone brightly. I couldn't believe my eyes. I was speechless! In a few fleeting seconds, a hundred thoughts and questions seemed to flash through my mind. I wanted to get up and tell Mom, who was in the kitchen playing a game of cards, but I held back. I decided not to bother her. I kept looking at the glowing light before it began to fade away, little by little. The light lasted no more than a few seconds, but it was real, unlike anything I had ever seen before at our ranch.

I pulled the covers over my head, not because I was scared, but because I was confused. First came the noises, next came the voices and now the light. I decided to go to sleep, but it was easier said than done. I tossed and turned, had a fight or two with the pillow, occasionally taking a peek from under the sheets. But the glow was there no more. I began to think that perhaps the light was a witch in disguise. After all, people were always talking about lights and witches being one and the same. Curious about the light and tired from the things that had happened to me, I guess I fell asleep.

As soon as I woke up in the morning I began to relive what had occurred to me that night. By breakfast time I had determined I would tell my mother. I wasn't going to wait until supper, as I did last time, and worry myself sick throughout the day. I came right out and told her.

"Mom, I have something else to tell you."

"What is it this time, more voices?" Mom's words spewed out with a wry smile.

"I saw a light in the bedroom last night after I went to bed. The light was coming from the *nicho*."

"Ah, Junie. There you go again. First it was voices. Now it's a light. What am I going to hear next?" she said with a skeptical look on her face.

"Those dreams are going to drive you and me crazy!" she warned.

I realized that Mom was not convinced of what I had seen, so I dropped the subject. In fact, the glow in the bedroom did not return for several nights. But when it did, a constant tapping accompanied the light. The tapping gave the impression that the glow made the wall expand and contract like Chopo's stomach when he breathed while he rested. The wall looked like it was about to explode, but nothing happened.

The last Sunday of the month was upon us, and the priest paid his monthly visit to our village to celebrate Mass. My parents, my little brother and I headed for church. A couple of hours later we were back home. The first thing Mom told me was to change into my playing clothes so as not to get my Sunday clothes dirty. As I went in the bedroom, I almost went into shock. I noticed the jar with the money lying on the floor. I looked up and saw the hole in the wall. The *nicho* was quite visible.

I didn't even finish changing clothes. I ran outside where Mom was talking to my aunt. Without hesitating to interrupt their conversation, I blurted out, "Mom, Mom! Come quickly!"

"Good-bye, Agapita. Junie needs you. I'll see you later," said my aunt.

Mom and I quickly dashed inside the house. I led the way. As we walked in she said to me, "Now, what's so important that you had to interrupt us?"

At that point, without saying a word, I pointed to the jar on the floor. The jar had popped right out of the *nicho* without breaking into little pieces.

"Look! It's not broken. It's a miracle!" shouted Mom, her eyes bulging like saucers.

"It's a magical *nicho*, Amá," I uttered in agreement.

"Well, I guess I should have paid more attention to you from the very beginning when you said you heard voices. The glow on the wall was also pretty incredible and hard to accept. Now I realize that the Holy Child of Atocha was trying to tell me something and he chose you as the messenger."

"And what are you going to do now with him?" I asked.

"He's going back to his *nicho* where he belongs, *hijito*."

At that point Mom picked the Holy Child of Atocha up in her arms like a baby, made the sign of the cross and gently stood him upright in his *nicho*.

"There he is," muttered Mom, proudly sporting a happy smile. "Now he's back in his little home," she added, letting out a short sigh as Dad walked in.

"What's going on here?" he asked with a curious look on his face, after he saw the uncovered *nicho*. Mom explained what had happened.

"And what are you going to do with the money now?" I asked Mom while Dad stood there with a bewildered look on his face.

"We're going to put it . . . "

"Put it where, Mom?" I said quickly before she could finish her sentence.

"We're going to hide it in our mattress for safekeeping," said Mother with a smile as she looked at Dad, whose puzzled look turned to a happy grin.

THE COQUIMBO OWL

My first year of school had just ended in Rincón del Cochino (Hog's Corner), where I lived. I was very excited because now I would spend the summer with my grandma in La Vega, a few miles from my home. My grandma's name was Lucinda, but I called her Cinda because it was shorter and easier to pronounce. She referred to me as *hijito* or Junie, and when she was mad at me, she called me Junio.

Grandma Cinda was a folk healer and really neat. Like many grandmas, she was very wise and always taught me new things. She loved to tell me stories about witchcraft, superstitions and spooky things. The mystery in her stories fascinated me. Her favorite stories were about animals, buried treasures, witches and ghosts. It didn't matter which stories she told, they were always scary and exciting.

With the excitement of finishing school and going to Grandma Cinda's, I hardly slept a wink. I was up before anyone that Saturday morning. Thankfully, the trip to grandma's by horse wagon was short. My parents, my dog Chopo and I arrived there before lunchtime.

"Good morning, *hijito*. How was school? Did you get good marks?" were Grandma Cinda's first questions. I only shrugged my shoulders, but she knew I had done well.

That evening after Mom and Dad had left, Grandma Cinda fixed us some stew with meat and potatoes. We ate it with bread that she had baked in the outdoor adobe oven. While we sat at the kitchen table, I heard a strange noise coming from the stovepipe. It sounded like a woodpecker. I felt into a stupor thinking of my cousins, Teodoro and Emilio, across the Rio Encantado and the good times we'd had together in past summers.

"*Hijito*, what's wrong? What are you daydreaming about?" she asked.

"Grandma Cinda, did you hear that strange noise on the roof? I wonder what it is. It sounded like a woodpecker."

"*Hijito*, that's the Coquimbo."

"The what?" I asked.

"The Coquimbo owl. In New Mexico it is known as a prairie-dog owl. He can be seen around prairie-dog mounds during the day but flies to higher places at night. The Coquimbo owl is the size of a large bird. It makes a playful, high-pitched, barking noise like a prairie dog. There are people who believe that at night the Coquimbo owl turns into a witch and then flies off to inflict bodily harm on its helpless victims."

"But, Grandma Cinda, if it's the Co . . . Co . . . "

"Coquimbo," she interrupted.

"Why do you suppose it has come here?"

"There could be many reasons, *hijito*. It's all part of the mystery of witchcraft."

"Grandma Cinda," I said, changing subjects, "after supper, can I go play with Emilio and Teodoro?"

"No, *hijito*. It will be dark before you know it. Besides, you'd have to cross the river."

"But, Grandma Cinda, there's no water in the river. I promise to be back before it gets too dark. I'm not afraid. I'm a big boy now. I'll be in second grade next year."

"No, *hijito*, tomorrow's Sunday and we have to get up early to go to church."

I went to my bedroom, pouting. A few minutes later my grandma came in, but she couldn't find me. I could see from under the bed—her feet were moving fast—that she was nervously looking for me. She finally found me.

"Junio! What are you doing under the bed? What's wrong?" her voice was shaking.

"I have a stomachache," I said, faking it.

She went to the kitchen and fixed me some blue corn gruel, a good remedy for a stomachache, and brought it to me. I didn't mind the taste of the corn gruel, but what I disliked were the tiny white-and-blue granules that felt like sand and got stuck between my teeth.

"Here, drink this. It will make you feel better," she said with some assurance.

A few minutes later, she came to see how I was feeling. I pretended to be asleep, so she kissed me on the forehead and said good night.

"Have a good night's sleep," she whispered softly.

All the while I was dreaming up an escape plan to sneak out to go see Emilio and Teodoro. They usually played games on Saturday night. This was my first chance to be with them in a while and I didn't want to miss the opportunity.

With my escape plan in place, I raised the window and propped it up with the stick that my grandma kept handy to let the cool air in during the summer. I was now ready to climb out the window, but before doing so, I grabbed one of my shoes from the closet. Next I carefully removed the screen and climbed out the window. Once outside, I removed the stick and propped up the window with my shoe so I could get back in when I returned.

Safely away from my grandma's house, I took off running until I reached El Jonuco before crossing the Rio Encantado. All of a sudden, the story Grandma Cinda had told me about the Wailing Woman and how she had drowned her children in the river popped into my head.

The thought didn't last long. I was too excited to see my cousins: I could hear all the kids having fun—yelling and screaming across the river. I reached La Loma, where Emilio and Teodoro lived. When I got to their house, everyone was playing hide-and-seek.

"Hey, Junie! What brings you here? We didn't know you were coming," shouted Emilio, somewhat surprised.

"Yeah, Grandma Cinda let me come over to play for a little while," I said even though it was a lie.

The longer we played, the darker the skies got, but I didn't pay much attention. I was having a lot of fun. The joyful sound of the hide-and-seek ditty we all bellowed aloud is all that mattered.

> *I am who I am,*
> *and here I come.*
> *I will find you,*
> *before you count to ten.*

When lightning started to streak across the skies and light up our hiding places I got scared. It was time for me to return to Grandma Cinda's house. I told Emilio and Teodoro I'd see them in church tomorrow morning, and took off running.

As I came close to the Rio Encantado, I heard thunder and roaring like a bellowing bull. Then I heard other noises, like hooting owls. I got goose bumps. The bull-like roaring sounded closer and closer. My hair stood on end.

I started crossing the river slowly and cautiously as I listened to the deafening sound of the flash flood, but then I picked up the pace. The louder the noise of the approaching flood, the faster I ran. Just as I reached the other side of the riverbed, the seething torrent wetted my shoes. I barely escaped being swept away by the sudden, deadly current.

As I started to go up the riverbank, almost out of breath, I thought I heard a woman's voice. Her wailing words were mournful and scary: "I'm looking for little boys who walk the dark nights alone. I'm the lady of the woeful night dressed in black who can be heard but not seen."

Scared out of my wits, I ran up the riverbank as fast as I could, slipping and sliding from the large raindrops that had begun to splatter the ground. I could feel them striking me. As I reached the top, I heard something like a prairie-dog owl. All at once it swooped down and aimed for my head but missed me. As lightning lit the sky, I saw that it was getting ready to fly toward me again. I was ready. I gave it a good whack in the face with a piece of driftwood I had picked up for anchoring my way up the river bed. The stubborn owl wouldn't leave me alone and it didn't miss its target on the third attempt. Its claws scratched the whole side of my face. I quickly felt the warm blood running down my face.

All kinds of thoughts ran through my head. *What was Grandma Cinda going to think or say? Was this the Coquimbo owl she had talked about? Was I going to die? Would I have a scar for the rest of my life?*

I approached Grandma Cinda's house carefully. Chopo must have heard me because he started barking. I whispered to him, and he calmed down when he recognized my voice. I was afraid my grandma would hear us. It was pretty dark. The moon was no longer visible, but I tiptoed to the bedroom window.

As I reached the window, I noticed that the shoe I had left was gone. I tried to open the window but couldn't. Suddenly I heard an eerie sound like the woman's voice I had heard down at the Rio Encantado.

"Who is the evil spirit who dares to come and scare my *hijito* in the middle of the night? Tell me, who?"

I tried to force the window open once more, and this time it went up like a rolling window shade, slamming at the top of the frame and making a horrible racket.

"Who is the disobedient child, the escape artist, who found an exit but now can't find his way back in?" echoed a voice from inside.

"It's me, Grandma Cinda! It's me!" I said, beside myself.

She lit the kerosene lamp next to my bed. When she saw me, she screamed, "Goodness gracious! What in the world happened to you, Junio? You're bleeding! Who did this to you?"

Scared to death and in shock, I managed to tell her where I had been, how an owl had scratched me and how I had whacked it a good one in the face with a piece of driftwood. She washed the scratches with cold water and rubbed cobwebs—one of her remedies—to stop the bleeding. She then tucked me into bed and said good night for the second time.

Next morning we attended Mass and then quickly headed back home. I didn't get a chance to see Emilio and Teodoro. A few moments after we got home, a strange-looking woman knocked at the kitchen door. She was looking for Grandma Cinda, who was changing clothes in her bedroom.

"Grandma Cinda, there's a strange-looking woman at the door. She's dressed in black and has one eye shut. She says she wants to see you."

Grandma Cinda finished dressing and went to the door to greet the woman, while I hid in the bedroom and listened to the conversation.

"Good morning, Doña Lucinda. I've come to have you treat an eye injury that I suffered last night. I bumped into the corner of the closet as I let my cat out."

After she left, I asked Grandma Cinda about the woman's eye and whether she was going to be all right.

"Listen," she said to me somewhat impatiently. "Never mind her eye. That's the woman who scratched you last night. I could tell by the splinters around the eye where you smacked her. She's Doña Brígida, the witch."

"But why would she want to hurt me?" I asked, more out of concern than curiosity.

"Because she knew you disobeyed me by going to your cousins' to play."

"But how did she know I disobeyed you?"

"Witches just know, *hijito*. It's the power of evil that motivates them, and that is part of their mystery."

NO MORE BOGEYMAN!

The sun had begun to set fast, but the kitchen where we finished eating supper was still hot as an oven from Mom cooking the beans and heating her flatirons on top of the stove all day long. Dad got up to feed the horses in the corral. Adancito and I stayed back to help Mom do the dishes. By the time Dad came back, the sun had already disappeared behind the stark-blue mountains not far from our little house. He sat down on the porch to rest. It didn't take long before Mom joined him. They were enjoying the cool evening breezes typical of the desert. Dad was rocking back and forth in his rocking chair. Mom sat down right next to him on her favorite wooden bench. While they talked, Adancito and I played different games. He pretended to be a cowboy on horseback and ran around slapping his hands on his butt hollering, "Git-up, git-up!" I ran right behind; imitating him.

After a short while, Mom told us to get ready for bed. We went inside the house, undressed and put our pants and shirts, neatly folded, on top of our shoes. We tucked everything under the bed. This was our routine every night.

Although the sun had disappeared, the July heat was unbearable. The mattress was hot, the pillow was hot and the bed sheet was hot. Everything was hot even with the window open. We tried to fall asleep but couldn't. Adancito started cutting up. I knew he was going to get us in trouble.

"Be still and go to sleep! Quit your horsing around!" came the first warning from Mom.

"Listen to what Mom says," shouted Dad from the porch in a gruff sort of voice. He was not as tolerant as Mom.

Dad had barely warned us when he headed for the kitchen because the mosquitoes were beginning to bite him. Mom followed him inside almost immediately.

Adancito continued his cutting up in bed. He liked jumping up and down on the mattress. The higher up he went the better. At times he even bumped his head on the ceiling. He was a real clown.

"Go to sleep or the Bogeyman is going to come and get you!" said Dad after he heard a thump.

The Bogeyman! Dad couldn't have mentioned anybody worse than the Bogeyman to scare me, but not even the devil scared Adancito. As if to show his courage — or how daring he was — he mockingly recited this short poem after imagining a knock on the door:

> Who is it?
> Old-man Inés.
> Who's with him?
> A tattered old man.

"Enough about old men. You're going to get it. The Bogeyman's going to come and grab you by your feet," Dad shouted from the kitchen.

"There's no such thing as the Bogeyman or anything like it. It's nothing but a lot of fuss and a bunch of lies! He only says that to scare us," remarked Adancito softly while I sneaked under the blankets, scared out of my wits.

"Enough is enough! You're trying our patience," echoed Mom.

Grandma Cinda had told me many stories about the Bogeyman and she wasn't one to lie or make up things, either. You had to believe what she said, and I for one believed her.

Adancito was sitting with his back up against the bed frame with a snicker on his face but covering his mouth in case Dad walked in. Dad could hear quite well. No one had better hearing than he did. It was incredible. Nothing got past him, not even whispers.

Instantly, I heard a chair scrape the wooden floor in the kitchen. I kept my head under the bed sheet. In just one swift movement, Dad was standing next to the bed. I could see from a tiny corner under the bed sheet that Adancito was face up, stiff as a corpse. Not from fear, but from his cutup nature. He faked being asleep. He didn't say "boo." Dad just stared at him without saying anything and went back to the kitchen.

"Dad already told you that the Bogeyman's going to come if you don't settle down. Go to sleep!" said Mom, but this time with a more forceful voice.

No sooner had she uttered her last words than Adancito and I heard some strange scratching on the window in the bedroom, "Hoooot! Hooot!". We were stone quiet. Listening. The noise was something new. We had never heard it before. We looked at each other. I shrugged my shoulders without knowing what to say or think. Then we heard the same noise all over again but this time there was a scratching on the window.

Adancito covered his head as if he were afraid and then poked me in the ribs and said, "Junie, did you hear that?"

"Come now, you clown! Don't be a chicken. It can't be anything!" I said to him, pretending to be the brave one.

The last word barely came out of my mouth when a terrible silence descended upon us. We got very scared. We could barely hear ourselves breathe. Then we heard the scratches on the window all over again. I uncovered one eye and took a peek. I saw a ghost. Something was moving from one side of the window to the other. I couldn't make out what it was. This time I poked Adancito in the ribs and whispered to him.

"Look! There's something in the window. I bet it's the Bogeyman."

"Me, look? What do you think I am, an idiot like you?" he said.

"Come now! Take a peek through the window if you don't believe me. You think you're such hot stuff."

Adancito raised the pillow and looked from under a tiny corner of the pillowcase. He didn't hear any scratching, but he did see something move slightly.

All at once he peeled off the bed sheet, because the heat was awful. He started laughing and he began jumping up and down again like a bouncing marionette. He couldn't stop laughing.

"Ha-ha, ha-ha do you know what it is?" asked Adancito, as his words came and went. "It's Uncle Samuel's donkey. It's loose. You know very well that it likes to peep through windows at night wherever there's a light."

"A donkey! Ha-ha, ha-ha! You're the donkey. The only things you're missing are the long ears. Besides, there's no light in here. The light's in the kitchen, dummy," I said to Adancito, trying to get even for calling me an idiot.

"Keep quiet! Do you want Dad to come in and warm up your butt with the belt?" warned Mom but Adancito and I knew it was just a bluff because Dad never spanked us.

At that very moment I heard the screen door to the kitchen, but I acted as if I had not heard it. Adancito didn't seem to hear anything. It wasn't long before the scraping began on the window once more. Adancito turned silent while I pretended to hide under the bed.

I then sneaked out of the bedroom and went outside. As dark as it was, I rounded the first corner of the house. Next I tiptoed carefully to the second corner. I held my breath and took a cautious look toward the window. At that point I heard the scratching and scraping. Little by little I began to see better with the light coming from the kerosene lamp in the kitchen.

I almost burst out laughing but I caught myself in time. The Bogeyman was none other than Dad! He was holding a broom with both hands. Whenever he didn't scratch the screen with the broom, he moved it gently from left to right, and right to left, like windshield wipers.

On about the third time that Dad touched the screen with the broom, I rounded the second corner of the house and quietly sneaked up on him on tiptoe, without him seeing me. I got directly behind him. Really close! He then bent at the waist and slowly buckled at the knees. He was facing the window and made the noise again, "Hoooot, hoot, hoooot!" Sounding more like a hooting owl than the Bogeyman. He scraped the screen with the broom once more.

At that very moment, I goosed him right in the butt. No sooner had I poked him than he gave out a holler, sprung forward and smacked himself right into the window frame.

I took off as quietly as I could and headed straight for bed.

"Did you see the Bogeyman? I heard a noise outside the window" asked Adancito as I got into bed.

Before I could answer him I heard the screen door in the kitchen.

"Goodness gracious! What happened? How did you get that goose egg?" Mom asked Dad as he sat at the kitchen table. Dad didn't say a word.

I peeked through a hole in the wooden partition separating the kitchen from the bedroom. Mom was holding her right hand up to her mouth. She could hardly keep from laughing.

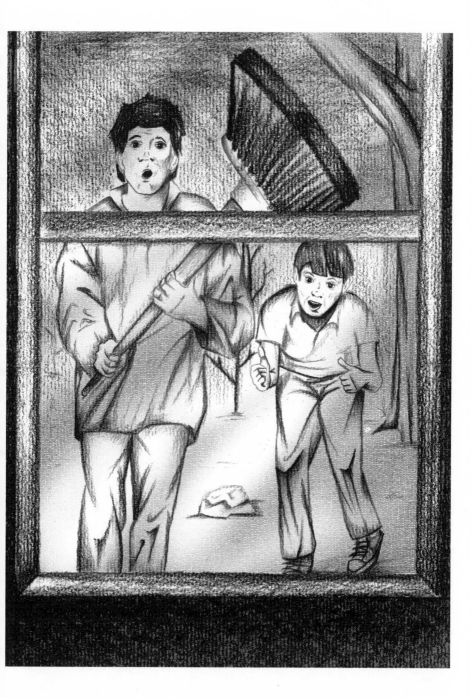

Dad sat down and applied the cold, wet cloth that Mom handed him so that the swelling would go down. He wasn't saying anything. He kept staring at the kitchen floor. It was hard to tell whether he was embarrassed, humiliated or both.

That same night, Dad put an end to the Bogeyman in our household and Adancito and I never again heard about it.

A BURIED TREASURE

Grandma Cinda and I had just finished eating lunch and were cleaning the table so that we could play games before my afternoon nap. We usually played cards, roulette with match sticks or I tried to solve her riddles.

I never knew what to expect from Grandma Cinda or what trick she had up her sleeve. One thing for sure, summers with her were never dull. She was full of surprises. She did many things to make me happy because she worried that I might get bored being away from my family. That was hardly the case. She was a lot of fun.

"Okay, *hijito*, are you ready?"

"Yes. What are we doing today?" I asked.

"Ah, I have a surprise for you! We're going to do something different."

I could hardly wait.

We both sat down at the table next to each other. I thought we were going to play a game, but I was wrong. Instead she handed me an empty pop bottle and a pair of my socks with holes in them. She was going to teach me how to mend socks using a pop bottle. First, she put the bottom side of the bottle all the way inside the sock. Next she pulled the sock over it and began mending the sock using the bottle for firmness. It worked like magic. I struggled at first, until she showed me how to hold the bottle between my legs. Before long it was easy to run the thread and needle in and out while sewing the sock without poking my fingers. As I sewed my socks, Grandma worked on a dishtowel that she was embroidering.

"Okay, *hijito*. It's time for your siesta," said Grandma Cinda after she saw me closing my eyes a couple of times.

I followed her into the little bedroom. At home Mom made me nap under the bed so I wouldn't mess it up. I could hear Mom's voice in my head, "Beds are to sleep in at night, not during the day." At Grandma Cinda's I was spoiled. She allowed me to take my nap on the bed, but I was always very careful to tidy it up after I got up.

"I changed my mind, *hijito*. Your nap can wait. How would you like to hear a story?" she asked with a sparkle in her eye. I was surprised. She had never told me a story at siesta time. At night, yes, but never in the afternoon.

"Of course I would," I said without blinking an eye.

"What kind of story would you like to hear?"

"I have no idea, Grandma," I said.

At bedtime she would tell me stories about witches and night creatures.

"Okay, I'll help you," she added. "How about the Bogeyman, the Weeping Woman or hooting owls?

No, no, no," she muttered, immediately answering her own question. "Those are nighttime stories. This is siesta storytelling. How about a story that has magical things or buried treasures?"

"Buried treasures!" I blurted out without even thinking.

"Okay, here we go. Listen carefully."

"Grandma Cinda, what's the name of the story?" I asked before she began.

"It's called 'A Buried Treasure.'"

Not long ago I had overheard a story from a group of old men at Grandpa's house. They talked about night lights at abandoned homes and how gold was buried in kitchen dirt floors or under a fireplace. So, I was anxious to hear Grandma Cinda's story.

I sat straight up. I wanted to make sure I didn't doze off. Grandma Cinda sat next to me. She had no book or anything. Besides, she didn't know how to read because she never went to school. Her stories were all in her head.

"A long time ago in a tiny village called San Miguel in the Sierra Nacimiento where your Mom was born, there was an old volcano. People called it El Copete (The Crest). Climbing to the top required strength even if you were young."

"Did you ever climb the volcano, Grandma Cinda?" I interrupted.

"Why, of course, *hijito*! But that was many, many years ago when my legs were strong and not wobbly like Jell-O. But I didn't go all the way to the top."

"Why not, Grandma Cinda?"

"Listen, that will come later, okay? Let's continue the story before I forget it," she said and winked at me.

"El Copete has been asleep for thousands, possibly millions of years. But you know what?"

"What's that, Grandma?" I said before she could finish her sentence.

"Boom!" she shouted and poked my tummy with her finger the way she poked her tortilla dough whenever she was in a playful mood. "You can be sure that whenever the volcano erupted it did so with such force that the earth shook and trembled and the frightened animals like deer, coyotes and jackrabbits ran for cover. Lava surely ran like red thick oil down the side of the volcano, lighting up the village night skies. It must have been scary but at the same time spectacular.

"San Miguel was tiny when your Mom and I lived there, with no more than twenty or thirty people. The stories about El Copete outnumbered its inhabitants. There were many, many and one of the most popular tales was that there was a buried treasure in the pit of the volcano. People believed that the crater would sometimes light up at night because there was gold in its pit. Yes, you heard me right, gold! Like what your grandpa has in his two front teeth.

"No one knew quite how or when the buried treasure story started, but one thing was certain: At different times many brave men from San Miguel tried climbing to the crest to find out if there was gold or not. But each time they hiked, as they got closer to the top, the louder it got. They couldn't stand the awful noise. Nor could they understand what caused it. So, one by one they gave up, unable to find out if gold was indeed buried at the bottom of El Copete. And for whatever reason, legend has it that you had to climb at night, not in broad daylight. Over time, the stories about the volcano continued and spread beyond our village.

"One day, a stranger showed up at dusk as the fading sun shone over the Sierra Nacimiento. No one had ever seen the man around those parts. The children, usually the ones to notice something new, ran to tell their parents about him. It wasn't long before the rest of the villagers knew why he was there. He had come after the buried treasure in El Copete! He was quite sure that he would be the first and last person to put his hands on the gold, if there was any. He was also determined to put an end to all the stories about the volcano. This surprised the San Miguel villagers. After all, the stories had been around forever.

"As the man walked down the middle of the only road in the village, he did so with lots of confidence. He pounded the dirt road with his feet and moved his arms back and forth as he headed for the volcano. The man was short and stocky and carried a knapsack over his right shoulder. He didn't utter a word. He just kept walking and looking straight ahead.

"'Not all that shines is gold, my friend,' came a raspy voice from an old-timer hiding behind a screen door who recognized the stranger and knew his name was León Lovato. He came from a tiny place called Azufre (Sulfur), a few miles from San Miguel.

"The longer he walked, the more people tagged along behind him like cows headed for water, especially the women and children. Even a few dogs joined in the parade."

"Grandma Cinda, what about the men?"

"The men were just as curious as anyone else. Most of them thought León Lovato was cuckoo in the head for wanting to climb to the top of the volcano, particularly when there was a full moon.

"By now the sun had disappeared behind the foothills and mountains, but people continued walking until they reached the bottom of El Copete along with León Lovato. That's where the villagers stopped.

"How do you like the story thus far, *hijito?*" asked Grandma, knowing full well that I was enjoying it.

"I like it. Can we continue?" I asked excitedly. I could hardly wait to find out what happened to León Lovato.

"Yes, let's continue, but first get me some water. My mouth is dry."

I hurried and almost stumbled over a rug as I got her a glass of water. I returned with the water and stood with my arms crossed in front of her until she drank the last swallow.

"Are you ready to continue or are you getting tired?" she asked.

"I'm ready," I said.

"At the bottom of El Copete, León Lovato paused for a moment as everyone watched, anxious to see what he was going to do next. He put his right hand in his pants' right pocket and took out a cotton ball. He tore off a couple of small pieces and put one in each ear. Then he reached in his knapsack and pulled out a scarf and tied it around his head to protect his ears and to muffle the noise from the volcano.

"Next, he started the slow climb. People wondered just how far he could climb before he gave up just like the many men before him. The full moon now was big and round and shining on the volcano. The higher León Lovato climbed, the louder the noise from El Copete, but he was a brave man. He was not about to give up. Besides, he had a small statue of St. Anthony, the saint that helps you find lost objects. There was only one problem."

"What was the problem, Grandma Cinda?"

"In León Lovato's case it was a hidden treasure he was after, not something he had lost. Just the same, he kept hiking the trail one step at a time. The noise was beginning to really bother him. The rumbling was deafening, and it roared like a thousand whirlwinds or dust devils in the middle of the desert. His ears felt like they were going to burst wide open, and he thought his head would split in half. His eyes even felt like they were bulging and ready to come out of their sockets. It was a horrible feeling, but he wasn't about to give up. He kept going and going as people down below looked in amazement. They thought he was either very brave or just plain crazy. No one had ever

climbed that far. He was somewhat exhausted, not so much from climbing, because he was in good physical shape, but from the horrible noise. He finally reached the summit of El Copete. He sat down, relieved to catch his breath.

"He removed his knapsack from his right shoulder and took out a kerosene lantern. He found a match in his pocket and lit the lantern, slowly turning up the flame as much as possible so the gentle mountain breeze would not blow it out. He tied a rope to the lantern's handle. Little by little, he lowered the lantern.

"By now the noise coming from the bottom of the pit was driving him nuts. He started shaking. He felt a weird sensation inside his ears, like worms tickling him. Suddenly he felt like the world was beginning to spin in circles. Then the volcano started spinning around him. A thought popped into his head. 'Could God be punishing me for having brought St. Anthony along?'

"When he could lower the lantern no more, he cautiously peeked again to see what he could see. He could not believe what he saw and heard. 'Do my eyes deceive me?!' he hollered, his voice trembled and his words echoed in the wind.

"The people down below heard the echo and right away suspected that something was horribly wrong. What he saw, much to his surprise, was not a buried treasure full of gold."

"What did he see, Grandma Cinda?"

"He saw a pit full of thousands of rattlesnakes crawling, curling and moving about one on top of the other. León Lovato was shocked! It was like a scene from Hell, ugly and frightening. Like something evil. That's where the noise came from, not from the gold that people suspected. 'This is the price I pay for yielding to temptation,' he mumbled and fell to the ground. He regained his composure after a few minutes and slowly started making his way back to the bottom of the volcano, where people stood with startled looks on their faces. They wondered what had happened? What had he seen?

"When León Lovato made it to the bottom, he was in a daze. His glassy eyes looked straight ahead and far into the distance. He didn't seem to notice the villagers who were staring at him. He walked away from San Miguel in silence."

"What happened to León Lovato, Grandma Cinda?" I asked.

"Story has it, *hijito*, that he went completely crazy. Some people speculate that León Lovato went nuts because of his greed or because of his disappointment at not finding the buried treasure. Or perhaps it was a combination of both. We'll never know for sure. Other people believe that he lost his mind as a result of the horrible noise from El Copete.

"One thing we know for sure, *hijito*, the words of the wise old villager who warned León Lovato that 'all that shines is not gold' turned out to be true."

"And how did the old villager know that, Grandma Cinda?"

"Ah, my dear child, funny you should ask. The old villager was a man named Don Faustino, who died a few years ago at the age of 109. When he was in his late twenties, he climbed to the very top of El Copete. Nobody saw him. He went up all alone and discovered the pit full of rattlesnakes. He kept it a secret for a long time until he shared it with only one person."

"With whom, Grandma Cinda?"

"With Grandpa Manuel! Don Faustino liked him very much and so he shared the secret with him on one condition: that Grandpa Manuel would not tell anyone, not even me, until after Don Faustino passed away. Grandpa was a young man at the time. And guess what?"

"What, Grandma Cinda?"

"Grandpa Manuel shared the secret with me before you were born. Listen, *hijito*, you're the first person I've told this to, so now it's your turn to keep it a secret, okay?"

"Okay, Grandma Cinda," I said and went to the bedroom for my nap.

RATTLING CHAINS

E l Coruco is said to be an enchanted place where chains rattled and witches and ghosts appeared at night. It was halfway between my village and my house so I often passed by there during the day — never at night!

One evening after supper I went next door to visit with Grandpa Lolo. He was alone because Grandma Lale had gone to Albuquerque. I knocked on the kitchen door and went in. He was eating supper.

"Come in, come in, Junie. I was just about to finish supper. Would you like a *bizcochito*? Grandma Lale baked them before she left for the city."

"Of course!" I answered. I loved Grandma Lale's cinnamon and anise cookies.

Grandpa Lolo handed me the tin can in which Grandma Lale kept the *bizcochito*s. I took one and started munching on it. Quickly I thought it was the perfect time to ask him about El Coruco. He was acquainted with the entire region like no one else. And if he knew something about El Coruco and rattling chains, I was sure he would tell me. That was his nature. He was always trying to teach his grandchildren something new.

"Here, have another *bizcochito*," said Grandpa Lolo, handing me the tin can as he spooned his last bite of lamb stew.

"Grandpa Lolo," I said to him, "is it true that you can hear rattling chains at El Coruco when you go by at night? Kids at school say that the place is enchanted and that ghosts and witches come out at night. Is that true? Do you know?"

"Well, let me tell you," answered Grandpa Lolo in a slow voice. "I've heard a bunch of stories over my lifetime regarding El Coruco. First of all, do you know what *coruco* means?"

I shook my head no.

"It means chicken louse. Why that place was named El Coruco is beyond me. But that's beside the point. As you know, there are no people living in El Coruco today. That's been true for many years now. It's kind of a ghost town. There weren't many people living there before it was abandoned. Next time you go by there, take a good look. The remains of about three, and no more than five, abandoned houses can still be seen. They're made of a mixture of rock and mud adobe. Two of the houses closest to the road sit right by a couple of pink-blossomed trees that miraculously bloom in the summer. Two more homes, I believe it's two, are a ways from the road, but in a little bit better shape. They're protected from the west winds by the hills. The walls are still standing. Of those two houses, one is close to the high waterfall toward the back of El Coruco.

"Bruja Maruja meets with other witches in that house at night. People claim to have seen lights inside after dark even though it was abandoned a long time ago."

"How do you know that, Grandpa Lolo?"

"As you know, the Rio Puerco runs only a short distance to the south of El Coruco. Across the river on top of a hill called La Loma is where several families lived once upon a time. Just about everyone there had a story to tell about El Coruco. All of them at one time or another had seen lights in that house after it was abandoned."

"Really, Grandpa Lolo?"

"Well, one night this man—Natividad was his name because he was born around Christmas—spotted a light and decided to go see for himself. He wanted to find out if witches really existed and lived in that house. He told several people, including his family at La Loma, what he was going to do. So he took off on his horse, Bole (Whiteface). Natividad went down to the Rio Puerco, crossed it near his house and caught the road alongside a string of cliffs that lead to El Coruco. He could see a light in the house not far off. The closer he got to the house, the brighter the light.

"Natividad began to feel a tingling sensation behind his neck and down his spine, but he kept going. He even thought he heard an owl hooting in one of the cliffs. Some people believed that owls were witches in disguise, but Natividad wasn't too sure about that. He was somewhat skeptical.

"Without warning he sensed that something was wrong because Bole started acting strange—sneezing, snorting and shaking its head. For one split second Natividad imagined that his horse had stopped breathing, but it was all in his head. In the meantime, he noticed the light had disappeared. When he reached El Coruco, Natividad tied Bole to one of the pink-blossomed trees and started walking toward the house.

"Things continued to feel increasingly spooky to Natividad. He got goose bumps, and his hair stood straight up. He was scared, but it was too late to turn back. As he got close to the house, he heard a woman's voice. 'What are you doing here at this time of the night?' she cried, while Natividad stood frozen in his tracks. 'Ah, silly man, how could you be so stupid to come here alone? Don't you know who I am? I'm a wandering spirit in search of souls like yours to carry back with me to purgatory. But I tell you what, I'll make you a deal.'

"'I make no deals with old hags like you, Bruja Maruja,' countered Natividad as he headed back to the trees where he had left his horse.

"'Ah, silly man. You uttered the magic words. I am Bruja Maruja!' said the voice and then it grew faint.

"Out of the blue, the light reappeared in the house. The light grew brighter and brighter. Gradually it began to emerge from one of the side windows. Unexpectedly the light started to move slowly on the ground. It was gaining momentum. Natividad kept looking back as he walked to his horse. The light was now getting larger and moving faster and faster. As it gained speed it began to turn into a round ball of fire aimed straight for Natividad and Bole.

"Scared out of his wits, Natividad ran and climbed on his horse, turned him around quicker than he could say let's go and off they went! At first the horse started at a fast trot but then it began running faster and faster. Natividad was so scared he dared not look back. Finally unable to resist temptation he took a peek over his shoulder. The ball of fire had grown larger and was now in the middle of the road moving rapidly, bouncing up and down, picking up more and more speed. It was gaining on Natividad and Bole so he dug his spurs into his horse.

"By now Bole was galloping at a pretty good pace. You could hear and feel his hooves dig into the ground. Although it was pretty dark, the ball of fire ironically helped Natividad see the road better. Before he knew it, bingo, the ball of fire had almost caught up with him, prompting the horse to whine and kick back. Natividad, who at this point was scared to death, kept spurring his horse and applying the whip at the same time. He had never been chased by a ball of fire.

"Natividad could hardly wait to get home, but first he had to cross the Rio Puerco. Since he had to go down a slope to reach the river bed before going across, he pulled on the reins to slow the horse down. He was afraid Bole might lose its balance going down and tumble over. Of course, slowing down would only give the ball of fire a chance to catch up to them. By now the ball of fire was really, really close, practically burning the horse's tail. When it caught up with them a few feet from the river, the ball of fire literally touched Bole's hind legs. At that very instant he launched forward like a rocket into the river's waters. Natividad held on for dear life. Bole hit and splashed the water with such force that the ball of fire went PUFF! The fire was gone! The river had saved Natividad!

"All at once Natividad heard a frantic voice coming from the rushing waters. Alas, the old witch-turned-ball-of-fire was still alive.

"'Help, help! I'm drowning!' begged the witch, swatting the water.

"'Drown, drown, Bruja Maruja! That'll teach you that the flames of hell are no match for the waters from heaven,' hollered Natividad as he rode away into the dark on his way home.

"Waiting at the front door for Natividad when he got home were not only his wife but also some of his neighbors. They had been witnessing the whole drama from La Loma. Natividad got off his horse, and he was still woozy from his narrow escape. All he could say was, 'A ball . . . fire . . . fire . . . !' and he fainted. His wife quickly fetched a tiny bottle of smelling salts that she kept around the house. A whiff of the strong stuff revived him. Although he was tired from the frightening experience, he proceeded to tell everyone what had happened.

"*Hijito*," Grandpa Lolo said, "I heard this story many years ago, but there are numerous others about El Coruco."

"But what about the rattling chains, Grandpa Lolo?"

"Ah, that's a story for another time, perhaps tomorrow night.

"But, Grandpa Lolo, tomorrow Grandma Lale's coming home."

"Ah, that's right. I tell you what."

"What?" I exclaimed, anxious to hear what he was going to propose.

"It's getting dark. Run home and ask your mother if you can stay a little longer. In the meantime, I'll think of a good story for you."

No sooner had Grandpa Lolo uttered the last word and I dashed out of the kitchen, slamming the screen door behind him. I was back before you could say "boo"!

"Junie, here, put those dishes in the cupboard while I make some coffee."

After Grandpa Lolo made the coffee and poured himself a cup, we sat at the table. I was ready to hear his story.

"Grandpa Lolo, what's the name of the story you're going to tell me?"

"Who knows?" he said with a smile. "This is the story about a man named Juan Algodones. That wasn't his real surname. People called him Algodones because he was born in a little place south of Santa Fe with that name. He moved to this valley where we now live, a long time ago with his family. He lived in a place called Santa Clara not far from Ojo del Padre.

"One night, on his way home from Los Altos, where he had gone to visit a friend, he and his burro Achaque . . ."

"Acha . . . what?" I asked.

"The word *achaque* means excuse. Juan Algodones named him that to show that his donkey always had an excuse for not moving swiftly. Anyway, it was already late at night, but not past midnight. The summer night was cool and crisp, and the stars were blinking and dancing in the sky. Juan could see the Big Dipper staring down at him as he looked up at the dark blue sky with thousands of sparkling stars. Juan was fascinated with nature. A full moon added to his joy.

"As he was approaching El Coruco, he noticed a star moving rapidly across the sky. At first he thought it was a shooting star. He had seen shooting stars before, but they moved much quicker and usually faded as they got close to the earth. This star was traveling at a much slower pace."

"You mean like a plane?" I asked.

"No, *hijito*. There were no planes back then. Anyway, Juan Algodones saw the light across the Rio Puerco where Don Natividad had lived. You remember Natividad, don't you?" asked Grandpa.

"Yes, he lived on top of a hill."

"That's right. Remember that Natividad crossed the river that night when the fireball was chasing him. Well, this is the same spot where the light crossed to this side of the Rio Puerco.

"Okay. Juan Algodones knew about El Coruco. He had heard countless stories concerning rattling chains, witches and that sort of stuff, but he had never had an encounter with anything like a light. So he became suspicious and kept a keen eye on the light as it moved through the sky after crossing the river. The light seemed to be slowing down as Juan continued on the only road home. The moon was peering down on El Coruco, lighting up the road for Juan. Right at that moment, he decided to take action."

"What was he going to do, Grandpa Lolo?"

"He was going to catch the light!"

"Catch the light? And how was he going to do that?"

"Ah, *hijito*. This is the fascinating and fun part of the story. Now, listen carefully. Perk up your ears like a donkey and don't miss a word I say so you can share the story with your schoolmates when school starts.

"You see, being a Juan or a Juana was special, and no single community was ever without a Juan or a Juana. They were born and blessed with unique powers that no one else possessed. One of their powers was the ability to catch witches, and that's what Juan Algodones intended to do. He had a strong feeling that the light was a witch in flight who was coming back home. Who knows? Maybe she had been away during the night causing mischief or inflicting harm on some innocent person.

"In any case, after the light crossed the Rio Puerco, and Juan Algodones saw that it was headed for El Coruco, he quickened his pace. When he approached El Coruco he heard a faint noise. He thought he heard rattling chains. However, it had rained the day before and what he heard in the distance was the water from the nearby waterfall.

"Juan promptly got off Achaque. The burro had become a bit skittish as though he knew something was wrong. After tying him to a fence post, Juan Algodones walked a few feet from the road. With the whip, he drew a large circle in the dirt. Next he proceeded to take off his shirt and T-shirt. He took the T-shirt, turned it inside out and tossed it in the middle of the circle. He went back to Achaque, and they both walked to the nearest abandoned home away from the circle. At once, the light reappeared in the sky behind some nearby hills and landed smack in the middle of the circle. Juan knew right then and there that he had caught himself a witch! The power of being a Juan had worked its magic. As the witch landed and her feet touched the ground, she made a horrible clatter. The noise indeed sounded like rattling chains, just like the stories he had heard."

"What happened next?" I said excitedly, wanting to know the outcome.

"When Juan Algodones walked over to the circle he found a woman sort of bending over as if scared and shivering. She was dressed in black with a black veil over her head. You could not see her face. But the strangest thing was that she had a chain strapped around her waist like a belt. It dangled down her side and rattled at the slightest movement.

Juan Algodones noticed, thanks to the bright moon, the most strange thing he had ever seen in his life."

"What was that, Grandpa Lolo?"

"The chain resembled a huge rosary. The links to the chain looked like the beads to a rosary, but each link had a grotesque human face. At that point Juan Algodones was more than convinced and satisfied that he had caught a witch."

"What did Juan Algodones do with the witch? Did he turn her loose?"

"You see, *hijito*, the witch was helpless. Juan Algodones, because of his magical powers, was able to trap her. She could go nowhere as long as she was inside that circle. She was Juan's prisoner. His power was too much for her. She begged, almost cried, for him to let her go.

"'Please, please, I ask you to turn me loose. I can pay you a ransom. Money is no problem for me. You name the amount and you've got it.'

"'That won't be necessary. I don't need your dirty money,' said Juan Algodones. 'I'll set you free if you promise to never come back to El Coruco.'

"The witch agreed and Juan Algodones broke the circle with his right foot."

"But, Grandpa Lolo, why the right foot?"

"Because the right foot in this case symbolized good, a triumph of sorts, whereas the left foot stood for evil. Juan Algodones was too smart. He wasn't about to fall victim to the witch. The moment he broke the circle, her chains made a rattling sound, like the fluttering of a flock of birds and off she flew into the sky. Juan then headed home to Santa Clara."

"Boy! That was a really neat story. I can't wait to tell it to my schoolmates when school starts."

"Okay, it's getting late. Go on home," gestured Grandpa Lolo with his right hand, "but watch out for the moving lights. They could be witches!" He added with a smile.

RUIDO DE CADENAS

y otros cuentos para niños

RUIDO DE CADENAS

y otros cuentos para niños

NASARIO GARCÍA

PIÑATA
BOOKS

PIÑATA BOOKS
ARTE PÚBLICO PRESS
HOUSTON, TEXAS

La publicación de *Ruido de cadenas y otros cuentos para niños* ha sido subvencionada por la Ciudad de Houston por medio del Houston Arts Alliance y por el Exemplar Program, un programa de Americans for the Arts en colaboración con LarsonAllen Public Services Group, un programa de la Fundación Ford.

¡Piñata Books están llenos de sorpresas!

Piñata Books
An imprint of
Arte Público Press
University of Houston
452 Cullen Performance Hall
Houston, Texas 77204-2004

Diseño de la portada de Mora Des!gn
Ilustraciones de Giovanni Mora

García, Nasario
    Rattling Chains and Other Stories for Children / by Nasario García; translated from the English by the author = Ruido de cadenas y otros cuentos para niños / por Nasario García.
        p. cm.
    Summary: A collection of scary stories based on the lore of New Mexico, in English and in Spanish.
    ISBN 978-1-55885-544-1 (alk. paper)
    1. Tales—New Mexico. [1. Folklore—New Mexico. 2. Spanish language materials—Bilingual.] I. Title. II. Title: Ruido de cadenas y otros cuentos para niños.
    PZ74.1.G365 2009
    [Fic]—dc22
                                                                2009003481
                                                                CIP

♾ El papel utilizado en esta publicación cumple con los requisitos del American National Standard for Information Sciences—Permanence of Paper for Printed Library Materials, ANSI Z39.48-1984.

9 0 1 2 3 4 5 6 7 8   10 9 8 7 6 5 4 3 2 1

ÍNDICE

PARA MIS QUERIDAS NIETECITAS
Ashley Cristina Morris-García
y Hannah Renée Morris-García

DOS FUTURAS LECTORAS

PREFACIO

Nuevo México se conoce como la Tierra del Encanto. Las palabras se pueden encontrar en las placas del estado y en un sinfín de otros lugares, incluso en libros. Para el que no es nativo de Nuevo México, las tres palabras pueden evocar un conjunto de pensamientos con respecto a lo que resta detrás de ellas. Es posible que también tengan un sonido místico y seductor, pero el encanto poco a poco va fascinando al recién llegado o al visitante cuando emprende un recorrido por el estado porque el paisaje, la gente y su historia le revelan un mosaico de esplendor. Pero para nosotros los nativos, las palabras en las placas son inconfundibles porque convocan algo mágico.

Los cuentos en *Rattling Chains and Other Stories for Children/Ruido de cadenas y otros cuentos para niños* son típicos de la multitud de imágenes encantadoras que se ven a través de Nuevo México. Dichos cuentos pueden ser apreciados por adultos, padres y abuelos cuando los lean a sus hijos o a sus nietos, o cuando los niños los lean por su propia cuenta. Yo escuché muchos de estos cuentos durante la cena, sentado alrededor de la estufa de leña en las

1

noches de invierno, en las fogatas de campamento durante la temporada de rodeos y mientras trabajaba en las milpas en el rancho de mis padres donde pasé los primeros nueve años de mi infancia antes de mudarnos a Albuquerque.

Me crié en el Valle del Río Puerco de Nuevo México, a unas cuarenta y cinco millas al noroeste de Albuquerque. Mi pueblito se llamaba Ojo del Padre (Guadalupe, en tiempos modernos); ahora está en ruinas. Yo y mi familia junto con mis abuelos paternos y unos tíos y sus hijos vivíamos como a dos millas de la placita. Mi abuelito se estableció cerca de allí a fines del siglo diez y nueve después de haber emigrado con sus padres desde el Valle del Río Grande.

Se dice que Ojo del Padre fue nombrado en honor de un cura que descubrió un manantial no muy lejos de lo que llegaría a formar el centro del pueblito que actualmente antedata más de doscientos cincuenta años. El agua en esa parte árida de Nuevo México sigue siendo un lujo, así que cuando el cura se tropezó con el ojito en medio del desierto fue realmente un milagro en un estado que tiene fama por su magia.

Cuando yo era niño y vivía en nuestro rancho, no había libros en casa, ni televisión, ni radio o tocadiscos (mi madre escuchaba una vez a la semana sus canciones favoritas mexicanas en un radio con pilas que le compró mi padre), pero yo tuve la buena fortuna de algo aún más precioso y duradero. Tenía a mis padres y a mis abuelitos. Ninguno sabía leer ni escribir, pero eran cuentistas fabulosos. Sus

fascinantes cuentos eran maravillosos —la carne y el hueso— de las narraciones sobre brujas, la llorona, animales disfrazados como fantasmas y un montón de otros seres sobrenaturales.

Rattling Chains and Other Stories for Children / Ruido de cadenas y otros cuentos para niños es una colección de cuentos del folclor de Nuevo México que le gustará a todo lector. Los cuentos son una creación mía y reflejan una parte fundamental de mi mundo infantil de fantasía y supersticiones. Algunos se basan el relatos que escuché de niño, mientras que otros se inspiran en mis propias experiencias. Cuentos como éstos encantaban a los niños de antes, y hoy en día, siguen cautivándolos. Así que los invito a que acompañen a Junie López, nuestro narrador, en su jornada de diversión y fantasía.

Nasario García, Ph.D.
Santa Fe, Nuevo México
2008

EL NICHO MÁGICO

Me llamo Junie López. Éste es el apodo que me dieron mis padres. Viene de *Junior*. Se pronuncia Yu-ni. Hace mucho tiempo yo vivía en el Valle del Río Puerco, una parte rural de Nuevo México, la Tierra del Encanto. Allí es donde me crié. Ahora vivo en la ciudad. Fui el primer hijo en mi familia. Esto es importante porque no tenía un hermano o hermana a quien admirar. Siete hermanitos y hermanitas nacieron después de mí. Como yo era el mayor, cada uno de ellos, me admiraba, más o menos, quizás más de lo que los admiraba yo a ellos.

El cuento que estás a punto de leer viene de algo que me pasó en nuestro rancho, cuando yo era un niño. Como le pasa a muchos niños, yo soñaba con todo tipo de cosas. Algunos sueños eran emocionantes, otros no eran muy bonitos, incluso tenía pesadillas. Pero ningún sueño se compara al que ahora quiero compartir contigo. El episodio fue tanto mágico como real. Yo lo veía fascinante, y también mi madre. Pero comencemos por el principio.

Nuestra placita no estaba lejos de nuestra casa. Mis padres, mi hermanito y yo vivíamos en una casa

5

de dos cuartos: un cuarto era la cocina y el comedor; el segundo cuarto era nuestra recámara. Eran habitaciones pequeñas, cuadradas y adecuadas, pero, claro, después de un tiempo, cuando el resto de mis hermanos nacieron, nos vimos un poco apretados.

La casita de mis padres estaba en una colina que daba al Río Puerco y a las Ruinas Guadalupe, hacia el sur, al otro lado del río; las milpas y la Mesa Prieta estaban situadas al este. Como a doscientos pies de nuestra casa, al oeste, se encontraba una meseta que nos protegía de los vientos y el frío del invierno. No muy lejos, al norte, se podía ver el famoso Cerro Cabezón, conocido por su gigantesco tamaño y su majestuosa belleza, a su lado había otros cerros grandes de color azul oscuro que se alzaban como gigantes amistosos, listos para darle a uno la bienvenida día tras día al amanecer.

De niño, pensaba que estaba por encima del mundo con toda aquella belleza que me rodeaba. Cuando crecí y llegué a apreciar mejor la naturaleza, mis sentimientos fueron confirmados. ¡Qué suerte la mía! Para mí estas maravillas naturales eran un encanto. Me entretenía con sólo verlas. A veces, hasta tenía la impresión que me hablaban silenciosamente desde lejos.

También eran los sitios de donde venían un sinfín de cuentos de brujas, burros mágicos, búhos y la Llorona. Escuché muchos cuentos que contaban mis padres, abuelos u otra gente en mi placita sobre estas supersticiones, o cosas sobrenaturales. Pero de todas

mis experiencias de la niñez, ninguna se compara a la de "El nicho mágico".

Volvamos al pasado. Tenía cinco años, casi seis. Mamá, una persona muy religiosa, tenía un nicho en nuestra recámara. Un nicho es como un hueco pequeño en la pared de adobe. Ahí, la gente devota coloca su santo favorito. Los nichos con santos de madera, o de yeso, también se encuentran en muchas iglesias y capillas.

El santo favorito de mi madre era el Santo Niño de Atocha, nombrado en honor a la ciudad de Atocha en España. El Santo Niño, protector de los enfermos y prisioneros, es muy popular entre muchos hispanos de Nuevo México. Según Mamá, el Santo Niño nos cuidaba por la noche después de que todos nos dormíamos. Tenía un rosario alrededor del cuello que Mamá le quitaba cuando rezaba por la noche antes de acostarse. El Santo Niño de Atocha era su fiel amigo y compañero espiritual. Existía un lazo inquebrantable entre ellos, pero un día empezaron a ocurrir cosas muy sorprendentes.

Mi padre había estado trabajando para el gobierno federal; construía caminos y otros proyectos. No ganaba mucho dinero, pero él y Mamá trataban de ahorrar algunos dólares. Como no había bancos donde vivíamos (nadie en el campo iba al banco), decidieron poner sus ahorros en un sitio seguro. Hasta hoy recuerdo claramente la discusión que tuvieron durante la cena sobre dónde poner el dinero. Papá sugirió ponerlo dentro del colchón o en una almohada. Al principio Mamá creyó que la idea era buena, pero después de

pensarlo por un minuto o dos decidió que no harían eso. Mi padre reaccionó muy pronto.

—Bueno, ¿dónde propones guardar el dinero? —le preguntó a Mamá, un tanto triste, y quizás hasta desilusionado porque su idea había sido rechazada.

—¿Qué tal si lo ponemos en el nicho? —sugirió ella—. Jamás lo encontrarían allí.

—¿Y cómo piensas hacer eso? ¡No puedes simplemente poner el dinero en el nicho y dejarlo allí!

—¿Por qué no? —dijo Mamá, lo cual dejó a Papá reflexionando en lo que ella tenía pensado—. Esto es lo que propongo —continuó ella—. Usaremos un frasco vacío para poner el dinero. Luego . . .

—¿Luego qué? —preguntó Papá, todavía un poco enojado.

—Espera, espera un momento. ¡Para el carro! —exclamó Mamá—. Después ponemos el frasco en el nicho y lo rellenamos con barro. Luego pintamos la pared de blanco y jamás sospecharán que nuestros ahorros están en la pared de la recámara.

La cara tristona de Papá en seguida se pintó con una sonrisa. Quedó impresionado con aquella ingeniosa idea de Mamá.

—¿Y de dónde sacaste esa idea? Yo no hubiera sido capaz de pensar algo así en mil años —dijo Papá.

Mamá fue por el frasco con una mirada de satisfacción. Estaba lista para el próximo paso.

—¿Cuánto ponemos en el frasco? —preguntó Papá.

La conversación fue de acá para allá hasta que Papá le preguntó a Mamá cuánto dinero tenía en su

delantal. Allí guardaba los ahorros, en una bolsita prendida dentro del bolsillo del delantal. Muchas mujeres guardaban el dinero de la familia así.

—Podemos guardar de quince a veinte dólares —contestó Mamá.

Eso era mucho dinero para una familia pobre en un rancho pequeño como el nuestro hace setenta años. Y así llegaron a un acuerdo; y pusieron una combinación de billetes y monedas en el frasco.

El domingo por la tarde Papá hizo las preparaciones necesarias para poner el frasco con el dinero en el nicho. Después de mezclar el barro, le pidió a Mamá un trapo blanco lo suficientemente grande para tapar el nicho. Ella trajo el trapo junto con unas poleadas, un pegamento hecho con harina y agua, para pegar el trapo. Pero antes de poner el frasco dentro del nicho, Mamá abrió una botellita de agua bendita que guardaba en su armario y salpicó una poca en el nicho. Luego puso el frasco con el dinero dentro del nicho, antes de que Papá lo tapara con el trapo y el barro. Después, Papá pintó la pared de blanco. No se notaba nada. La alcancía de Papá y Mamá ahora estaba en un lugar secreto.

En cuanto al Santo Niño de Atocha, desde aquel momento tendría un nuevo hogar, por decirlo así. Ahora se hallaba arriba del armario de Mamá. Por respeto al Santo Niño, ella se aseguró de que no hubiera cepillos, peines u otras cosas cerca de él. Papá, que estaba acostumbrado a poner su guarda monedas de piel sobre el armario, ahora tendría que buscar otro sitio en casa. Lo único que acompañaba

al Santo Niño era el rosario y la botellita de agua bendita que Mamá había colocado detrás de él.

Después de cierto tiempo, Mamá extrañaba no ver al Santo Niño en su nicho, pero creía que él entendía por qué lo habían cambiado de lugar. En cuanto al frasco con el dinero, se quedaría en el nicho hasta que lo necesitaran. ¿Cuándo sería eso? No estaban seguros. No sabían. Es posible que fuera necesario abrir el nicho en caso de que tuvieran que poner más dinero en el frasco. Tal vez el Santo Niño era el único que sabía cuándo tendría lugar una de estas dos decisiones.

Entretanto, Mamá creía que todo estaba en orden, pero a ella le aguardaba una gran sorpresa. ¡Y a mí también! Unas semanas después de esconder el dinero, empecé a tener sueños. A veces eran desagradables, pero no le dije nada a Mamá. Primero soñé que un ladrón había descubierto el secreto de mis padres, y que se había robado el dinero. Yo sabía que no era nada más que un sueño, pero me daba pena que algo así pudiera ocurrir. Después de todo, Papá trabajaba muy duro para ganar su dinero, y Mamá también era muy cuidadosa; ahorraba todos los centavos que podía para el futuro.

A la noche siguiente, o poco después, mi sueño fue totalmente diferente. Soñé que las monedas en el frasco se habían convertido en oro, dándole mucho más valor al dinero. *¿Podría pasar esto?* me pregunté.

Una noche, mi tía, que vivía al pie de la loma donde vivíamos nosotros, vino a visitar a Mamá. Poco después de que me acosté a dormir, ellas se

sentaron a charlar. Luego comencé a oír ruidos; venían del nicho. Los ruiditos, aunque se podían oír bien, no eran claros y no pude conectar las palabras para comprenderlas. Por dos o tres semanas los ruidos iban y venían durante la noche, pero no le dije nada a nadie.

Un sábado por la noche, cuando Papá estaba profundamente dormido y roncando, oí bien claro una voz que me dijo: "Por favor dile a tu mamá que pertenezco al nicho". Por supuesto que no supe qué pensar, o qué hacer, después de escuchar eso. La voz no me era familiar así que decidí ignorarla, y no hice nada.

Una semana más tarde, más o menos, volví a oír la misma voz durante la noche. "Yo, el Santo Niño de Atocha, como otros santos, pertenezco al nicho. Ésa es la casa que tu mamá me construyó. ¿Podrías tú ayudarme a regresar a ella?"

Sus ruegos fueron claros y sinceros. Me levanté a la mañana siguiente y pensé en ellos el día entero. Esa tarde decidí decirle todo a Mamá mientras Papá todavía estaba lejos de casa. Durante la cena me di valor para contarle los dos incidentes: la voz misteriosa y los ruidos raros que había oído por las noches. Entre bocados hablamos de cosas ordinarias, más bien típicas, que se discuten en un rancho entre madre e hijo. En un momento, cuando menos lo pensé, le dije: —Mamá, tengo algo que decirte.

—¿Qué, hijito? Te ves intranquilo.

—Anoche, por segunda vez oí una voz que venía del Santo Niño. Me pidió que te dijera algo.

—¿Y qué te dijo? —preguntó desconcertada.

—Quiere volver a su nicho. Dice que ése es su lugar.

—¡Oh, Junie! Has estado soñando otra vez. Estás oyendo cosas. Eso es muy común para un niño chiquito como tú.

—Chiquito o no, he estado escuchando cosas, pero lo que te digo es verdad. Tienes que creerme. No son cosas que tengo en la cabeza, zumbando en mis oídos o que me estoy inventando. Son las palabras del Santo Niño.

—Bueno, hijito. Esto es lo que haremos. La próxima vez que oigas esa voz, me despiertas inmediatamente. Deja que yo misma la escuche.

—¡Muy bien! ¿Pero qué pasa si no vuelvo a escuchar la voz? Entonces, ¿qué haremos?

—No te preocupes. Si es de verdad, volverá. Si no es, entonces podemos decir que no fue nada más que un sueño. ¿Te parece?

—Bueno—respondí, aunque no con mucho entusiasmo.

Durante los días siguientes la voz no regresó para hablarme. Mamá tampoco mencionó el asunto. Seguramente pensaba que la voz no era nada más que una fantasía mía, así que no merecía la pena discutir de nuevo.

Una noche, unos minutos después de acostarme, la cosa más sorprendente ocurrió. De repente vi una luz en la pared, justo donde estaba escondido el dinero. La pared blanca brillaba. No lo podía creer. ¡Me quedé sin poder decir ni una palabra! En unos cuantos momentos un centenar de pensamientos y

preguntas pasaron por mi cabeza. Quería levantarme y decirle a Mamá, que estaba en la cocina jugando a las cartas, pero no lo hice. Decidí no molestarla. Seguí viendo la luz que brillaba hasta que empezó a apagarse, poquito a poquito. La luz apenas duró unos cuantos segundos, pero era real, totalmente diferente a todo lo que había visto antes en nuestro rancho.

Me tapé la cabeza con las frazadas, no porque tuviera miedo, sino porque estaba confundido. Primero los ruidos, luego las voces y ahora la luz. Decidí dormirme, pero no fue fácil. Di muchas vueltas, luché una o dos veces con la almohada, dando un vistazo de vez en cuando por un huequito de la sábana, pero el brillo ya no se veía. Se me metió en la cabeza que tal vez la luz era una bruja disfrazada. Además, había gente que decía que las luces y las brujas eran una sola cosa. Pensando en la luz, y cansado por las cosas que me habían pasado, me quedé dormido.

Tan pronto como desperté, empecé a recordar lo que me había ocurrido esa noche. A la hora del desayuno, había decidido decirle a Mamá. No me iba a esperar hasta la cena, como lo hice la última vez, porque iba a estar preocupado el día entero. Le hablé a Mamá claramente.

—Mamá, tengo algo más que decirte.

—¿Qué tienes ahora, más voces?—las palabras le salieron con una sonrisita.

—Anoche vi una luz en la recámara después de acostarme. La luz brillaba en el nicho.

—Ay, Junie, ya empezaste. Primero eran voces. Ahora es una luz. ¿Qué más voy a tener que escuchar? —dijo con una mirada escéptica—. ¡Esos sueños nos van a volver locos a ti y a mí! —advirtió.

Sabía que Mamá no estaba convencida de lo que yo había visto, de manera que abandoné el asunto. De hecho, el brillo en la pared no regresó durante varias noches, pero cuando volvió, unos golpecitos constantes acompañaban a la luz. Los golpecitos daban la impresión de que el brillo hacía que la pared se ensanchara y se encogiera, como la panza de Chopo, mi perro, al respirar mientras descansaba. Parecía que la pared iba a explotar, pero no pasó nada.

Había llegado ya el último domingo del mes, y el cura vino como de costumbre a nuestra placita para celebrar la misa del mes. Mis padres, mi hermanito y yo nos fuimos a la iglesia. Después de dos horas estábamos de vuelta en casa. Lo primero que mandó Mamá fue que me quitara la ropa para que no la ensuciara, y que me pusiera la ropa de jugar. Al entrar en la recámara me pegué un susto. Vi que el frasco con el dinero estaba en el suelo. Di un vistazo hacia arriba y vi el hoyo en la pared. El nicho se veía bien claro.

Ni siquiera acabé de cambiarme de ropa. Corrí hacia donde estaba Mamá hablando con mi tía. Sin esperar, dije —¡Mamá, Mamá! ¡Ven pronto!

—Adiós, Agapita. Junie te necesita. Te veo más tarde —dijo mi tía.

Mamá y yo entramos corriendo a casa. Al cruzar la puerta, me dijo —Ahora bien, ¿qué era tan importante que tuviste que interrumpirnos?

En ese momento, sin decir una palabra, apunté al frasco. Había saltado del nicho sin hacerse pedacitos.

—¡Mira! No se quebró. ¡Es un milagro! —gritó Mamá, con sus ojos como platos.

—Es un nicho mágico, Mamá —dije apoyando su observación.

—Bueno, quizás te debí haber prestado más atención desde un principio cuando dijiste que habías oído voces. La luz en la pared también era bastante increíble y difícil de aceptar. Ahora me doy cuenta de que el Santo Niño de Atocha estaba tratando de decirme algo y te escogió a ti como su mensajero.

—¿Y qué vas a hacer ahora con el Santo Niño de Atocha?—le pregunté.

—Él va a regresar a su nicho, a donde pertenece, hijito.

En ese momento, Mamá lo levantó como a un bebé, hizo la señal de la cruz y con mucho cuidado lo puso en el nicho.

—Ahí está —murmuró Mamá orgullosamente, con una sonrisita de alegría—. Ahora ya está de vuelta en su casita —añadió, dando un breve suspiro al ver entrar a Papá.

—¿Qué pasa aquí?—preguntó Papá con una cara llena de curiosidad, viendo el nicho que estaba descubierto. Mamá le explicó lo que había ocurrido.

—¿Y ahora qué vas a hacer con el dinero?—le pregunté a Mamá, mientras que Papá se quedó allí parado un poco confundido.

—Lo vamos a poner . . .

—¿Dónde, Mamá? —dije en seguida, antes de que ella pudiera terminar la frase.

—Lo vamos a esconder en el colchón para que esté bien protegido —dijo Mamá con una sonrisa y volteó a ver a Papá, cuya mirada de confusión se convirtió en una sonrisita.

EL COQUIMBO

A cababa de terminar mi primer año de escuela en Rincón del Cochino y estaba muy emocionado porque ahora podría ir a pasarme el verano con mi abuelita en La Vega, a unas cuantas millas de mi casa. Mi abuelita se llamaba Lucinda, pero yo le decía Cinda porque era más corto y más facil de pronunciar. Ella me llamaba hijito o Junie, pero cuando se enfadaba conmigo me llamaba Junio.

Abuelita Cinda era una curandera muy interesante. Como muchas abuelitas, era muy sabia y siempre me enseñaba cosas nuevas. Le encantaba contarme cuentos de brujerías, supersticiones y cosas espantosas. Lo misterioso de sus cuentos me fascinaba. Sus cuentos favoritos eran sobre animales, tesoros enterrados y brujas y fantasmas. No importaba cuál de los cuentos contara, siempre eran espantosos y emocionantes.

Apenas pude dormir con la emoción de acabar la escuela para ir a quedarme con Abuelita Cinda. El sábado por la mañana que íbamos a viajar, fui el primero en levantarme. Menos mal que el viaje a casa de mi abuelita era corto. Mis padres, mi perro Chopo y yo llegamos antes del almuerzo.

—Buenos días, hijito. ¿Cómo te fue en la escuela? ¿Sacaste buenas notas? —fueron las primeras preguntas de Abuelita Cinda. Sólo me encogí de hombros, pero ella sabía que me había ido bien.

Esa tarde, después de haberse marchado Papá y Mamá, Abuelita Cinda nos hizo un caldito de carne y papas para comer con un pan que había hecho en el horno de adobe. Mientras comíamos en la cocina, oí un ruido extraño que venía desde el tubo de la estufa. Sonaba como un pájaro carpintero. Me quedé como en un estupor y me acordé de mis primos, Teodoro y Emilio, que vivían al otro lado del Río Encantado, y de los buenos ratos que habíamos pasado juntos en veranos pasados.

—Hijito, ¿qué pasa? Estás soñando despierto —dijo.

—Abuelita Cinda, ¿oyó ese ruido raro en la azotea? ¿Qué será? Es como un pájaro carpintero.

—Hijito, es el coquimbo.

—¿El qué?

—El coquimbo. En Nuevo México se conoce como una lechuza. Se puede ver cerca de los nidos donde viven las tuzas durante el día, pero de noche vuela a sitios más altos. El coquimbo es del tamaño de un pájaro grande, y hace un ladrido juguetón y agudo, semejante al de una tuza. Hay gente que cree que el coquimbo se transforma en una bruja y vuela de noche para atacar a sus desprevenidas víctimas.

—Pero, Abuelita Cinda, si es el co . . . co . . .

—Coquimbo —interrumpió ella.

—¿Por qué habrá venido acá?

—Puede haber muchas razones, hijito. Eso es parte de su misterio.

—Abuelita Cinda —dije, cambiando de tema— ¿puedo ir a jugar con Emilio y Teodoro después de la cena?

—No, hijito. Cuando menos lo pienses se oscurecerá. Además, tendrías que cruzar el río.

—Pero, Abuelita Cinda, el río no lleva agua. Prometo volver antes de que oscurezca. No tengo miedo. Ya soy un niño grande, pasé a segundo año.

—No, hijito, mañana es domingo y tenemos que levantarnos temprano para ir a misa.

Me fui a mi cuarto haciendo pucheros. Después de unos minutos, entró mi abuelita, pero no me halló. Yo podía ver desde abajo de la cama que movía los pies rápido porque me buscaba ansiosamente. Por fin me encontró.

—¡Junio! ¿Qué haces debajo de la cama? ¿Qué te pasa? —su voz temblaba.

—Me duele el estómago —dije fingiendo que estaba enfermo.

Se fue a la cocina y me preparó atole azul, un buen remedio para el dolor de estómago, y me lo trajo. No me molestaba el sabor del atole, pero lo que no me gustaban eran los granitos blancos y azules de maíz que se me metían entre los dientes, como arena.

—Aquí tienes, bébete esto. Te sentirás mejor —me aseguró.

Unos minutos más tarde vino a ver cómo me sentía. Me hice el dormido, así que me dio un besito en la frente y me dijo buenas noches.

—Duerme bien —murmuró en voz baja.

Mientras tanto, yo estaba planeando cómo escaparme para ir a ver a Emilio y a Teodoro. Ellos normalmente jugaban los sábados por la noche. Ésta era la primera vez que estaría con ellos desde hacía mucho tiempo, y no quería perderme la oportunidad. Con el plan de mi escape ya decidido, abrí la ventana y la detuve con un palo que mi abuelita guardaba para sostener la ventana abierta y dejar entrar el aire fresco del verano. Ya estaba listo para salir, pero antes cogí uno de mis zapatos del ropero. Luego quité la ventana de tela, y salí. Una vez que me vi afuera, quité el palo y coloqué mi zapato para que mantuviera la ventana abierta.

Lejos de la casa de mi abuelita, me eché a correr hasta llegar a El Jonuco, antes de cruzar el Río Encantado. De repente, aquel cuento que me había contado mi abuelita de la Llorona, sobre cómo había ahogado a sus hijos en el río, se me vino a la mente.

El pensamiento duró poco. Estaba emocionado porque iba a ver a mis primos, aunque ellos no sabían que iba a verlos. Podía oír a todos los niños divirtiéndose, dando gritos y chillidos al otro lado del río. Llegué a La Loma, donde vivían Emilio y Teodoro. Al llegar a su casa, vi que todos estaban jugando al escondite.

—¡Eh, Junie! ¿Qué haces por acá? No sabíamos que vendrías —gritó Emilio, algo sorprendido.

—Sí, Abuelita Cinda me dejó venir a jugar por un ratito —le respondí, aunque era una mentira.

Mientras más jugábamos, más nublado se ponía el cielo, pero yo no puse mucha atención. Me estaba divirtiendo mucho. Las palabras alegres de la

cancioncilla del escondite que cantábamos era lo único que importaba.

Yo soy quien soy,
y aquí les voy.
Los hallo,
porque soy buen gallo.

Cuando los relámpagos empezaron a verse en el cielo y a iluminar nuestros escondites, me dio miedo. Ya era hora de volver a la casa de Abuelita Cinda. Les dije a Emilio y Teodoro que los vería en misa al día siguiente, y salí corriendo.

Al acercarme al Río Encantado oí truenos y bramidos, como los de un toro. Luego oí otros ruidos, como el ulular de un tecolote. Se me pusieron los pelos de punta. Los bramidos se oían cada vez más cerquita. Se me puso la piel de gallina.

Empecé a cruzar el río despacito y con mucho cuidado, mientras escuchaba el sonido ensordecedor de la corriente, pero luego aceleré el paso. Cuanto más ruido hacía la corriente, más rápido corría. Justo en cuanto llegué a la otra orilla del río, el torrente agitado me mojó los zapatos. Por poco me lleva la inesperada y peligrosa corriente.

Río arriba, casi sin aliento, creí oír la voz de una mujer. Sus palabras eran espantosas: —Busco a muchachitos que andan solitos de noche en la oscuridad. Soy la mujer de la noche triste, vestida de negro, que se oye, pero nunca se ve.

Muerto de miedo, corrí cuesta arriba tan rápido como pude, resbalándome con las grandes gotas que empezaban a caer. Las sentía mojándome. Al llegar

arriba, oí algo como una tuza. De repente se me vino encima, contra la cabeza, pero no me pegó. Al alumbrarse el cielo con los relámpagos, vi que volaba otra vez hacia mí. Me preparé. Le di un buen porrazo en la cara con un palo que había recogido en el río para sostenerme al subir, pero aquella lechuza terca no me dejaba en paz. La tercera vez no falló; las garras me rasguñaron todo un lado de la cara. Pronto sentí que me corría la sangre caliente.

No sé cuántos pensamientos se me vinieron a la cabeza. *¿Qué iba a decir o pensar Abuelita Cinda? ¿Era éste el coquimbo del que me había hablado? ¿Me iba a morir? ¿Me iba a quedar una cicatriz para el resto de mi vida?*

Me acerqué con cuidadito a la casa de Abuelita Cinda. Chopo me oyó porque comenzó a ladrar. Le hablé en voz baja y, cuando reconoció mi voz, se calmó. Me dio miedo que nos oyera mi abuelita. Estaba bastante oscuro. Ya no se veía la luna, me fui de puntillas a la ventana de mi recámara.

Al llegar a la ventana, vi que el zapato que había dejado había desaparecido. Traté de abrir la ventana, pero no pude. De pronto, oí una voz misteriosa, como la voz de la mujer en Río Encantado.

—¿Quién es el espíritu malvado que se atreve a venir a espantar a mi hijito en la madrugada? ¿Quién es?

Intenté abrir la ventana una vez más, pero esta vez se elevó tan rápido que pegó contra el bastidor, haciendo un ruido horrible.

—¿Quién es el niño desobediente, el fugitivo que halló salida, pero que ahora no encuentra entrada? —retumbó una voz desde adentro.

—Soy yo, Abuelita Cinda. ¡Soy yo!—dije asustado.

Abuelita Cinda prendió la lámpara de aceite que estaba a un lado de mi cama. Me vio y pegó un grito —¡Válgame Dios! ¿Qué te pasó, Junio? Estás sangrando. ¿Quién te hizo esto?

Lleno de miedo y espantado, le conté dónde había estado, que un tecolote me había rasguñado la cara y que yo le había dado un buen porrazo con un palo. Abuelita Cinda me lavó los rasguños con agua fría, y me puso telarañas —uno de sus remedios— para que no sangrara más. Después me cobijó y, por segunda vez, me dio las buenas noches.

A la mañana siguiente fuimos a misa y regresamos a casa rápido. No alcancé a ver a Emilio o a Teodoro. Unos minutos después de que llegamos a casa, una mujer rara tocó a la puerta de la cocina. Buscaba a Abuelita Cinda, quien estaba cambiándose de ropa en su recámara.

—Abuelita Cinda, en la puerta está una mujer muy rara. Está vestida de negro y tiene un ojo cerrado. Dice que quiere verla.

Abuelita Cinda acabó de vestirse y fue a la puerta a saludar a la mujer de negro, mientras yo me escondí en la recámara para escuchar la conversación.

—Buenos días, doña Lucinda. Vine a que me cure el ojo que me lastimé anoche. Me di con el filo del ropero cuando eché al gato para fuera.

Después de que se fue la mujer, le pregunté a

Abuelita Cinda sobre el ojo de la mujer. Quería saber si iba a estar bien.

—Mira —dijo con cierta impaciencia—. Olvídate de su ojo. Esa mujer es la que te rasguñó anoche. Tenía astillas en el ojo, justo donde le diste el porrazo. Ella es doña Brígida, la bruja.

—¿Pero, por qué habrá querido lastimarme? —pregunté, más por preocupación que por curiosidad.

—Porque sabe que me desobedeciste cuando te fuiste a jugar con tus primos.

—Pero, ¿cómo supo que la desobedecí?

—Las brujas simplemente lo saben, hijito. El poder del mal es lo que las mueve y eso es parte de su misterio.

¡SE ACABÓ EL COCO!

El sol poco a poco iba desapareciendo, pero la cocina donde acabábamos de cenar todavía se sentía como un horno después de que Mamá había cocido frijoles y calentado sus planchas en la estufa el día entero. Papá se levantó de la mesa para darles de comer a los caballos en el corral, y Adancito y yo nos quedamos ayudándole a Mamá a lavar los platos. Cuando volvió Papá, el sol ya se había escondido detrás de las montañas azules, no muy lejos de nuestra casita. Papá se sentó en el portal a descansar y Mamá no tardó en acompañarlo. Estaban disfrutando de la brisa fresca que pega por la tarde en el desierto. Papá se mecía en su mecedora. Mamá se había sentado en su banco favorito a un ladito de él. Mientras platicaban, Adancito y yo jugábamos. Adancito pretendía ser un vaquero montado en un caballo de palo. Corría por aquí y por allá dándose manotazos en las nalgas gritando "¡Arre, arre!" Yo corría detrás de él, imitándolo.

Después de un rato, Mamá nos mandó a que nos preparáramos para la cama. Entramos, nos desvestimos y pusimos los pantalones y las camisas bien dobladitos encima de los zapatos. Pusimos todo

debajo de la cama. Hacíamos esto todas las noches antes de acostarnos.

Aunque ya no había sol, el calor de julio era horrible. El colchón estaba caliente, la almohada estaba caliente y la sábana estaba caliente. Todo estaba caliente, incluso con la ventana abierta. Tratamos de dormirnos, pero no pudimos. Adancito empezó con sus travesuras. Yo estaba seguro de que nos iba a meter en un lío.

—¡Quietos, ya duérmanse! ¡Dejen de brincar! —fue la primera advertencia de Mamá.

—Escuchen a Mamá —gritó Papá desde el portal con una voz más o menos fuerte. Él no era tan tolerante como Mamá.

Apenas dijo esto y entró en la cocina porque los mosquitos empezaban a picarle. Mamá lo siguió casi inmediatamente.

Adancito continuó con sus travesuras en la cama. Le gustaba saltar en el colchón. Cuanto más alto, mejor. A veces hasta se daba topes en el techo. Era un payaso.

—¡Duérmanse, o va a venir el Coco! —dijo Papá al oír el primer golpe en el techo.

¡El Coco! Papá no podría haber mencionado cosa peor para espantarme, pero ni siquiera el diablo espantaba a Adancito. Para demostrar su valor —o lo atrevido que era— recitó un poemita, fingiendo que había oído un golpe en la puerta.

¿Quién es?
El viejo Inés.

¿Quién es el otro?
El viejo roto.

—Ya basta de viejos. Les va a pesar. El Coco va a venir y los va a agarrar de las patas —gritó Papá desde la cocina.

—No hay Coco, ni nada parecido. ¡No son más que puros cuentos, puras mentiras! Solamente dice eso para meternos miedo —murmuró Adancito, mientras yo me escondía debajo de la sábana con un miedo espantoso.

—¡Ya basta! Se nos va a acabar la paciencia —declaró Mamá.

Abuelita Cinda me había contado muchos cuentos del Coco. Ella no mentía o inventaba cosas. Había que creer lo que decía, y yo le creía.

Adancito estaba sentado contra el respaldo de la cama y se reía bajito. Se tapaba la boca por si Papá entraba. Papá podía oír muy bien. No había persona con mejores oídos. Era increíble. No se la escapaba nada. Ni siquiera un cuchicheo.

De pronto oí que una silla se arrastró en el piso de madera en la cocina. Me quedé metido debajo de la sábana. De un salto, apareció Papá junto a la cama. Yo podía ver, por un huequito de la sábana, que Adancito ahora estaba boca arriba, tieso como un muerto. No del miedo, sino de lo travieso que era. Se hacía el dormido. No dijo ni pío. Papá se quedó mirándolo sin decir nada tampoco. Luego regresó a la cocina.

—Papá ya les dijo que va a venir el Coco si no se están quietos. ¡A dormir! —dijo Mamá, pero esta vez en un tono mucho más fuerte.

No acababa de decir sus últimas palabras cuando

Adancito y yo oímos algo extraño en la ventana de la recámara "¡Juuuut! ¡Juuut!". Nos quedamos quietecitos. Escuchando. El ruido era algo nuevo. Nunca lo habíamos oído. Nos miramos uno a otro. Yo me encogí de hombros sin saber qué decir o pensar. Después volvimos a oír el mismo ruido, pero esta vez parecía que algo arañaba la ventana.

Adancito se tapó la cabeza como si tuviera miedo, luego me picó una costilla y dijo —Junie, ¿oíste?

—¡Anda, payaso! No tengas miedo. ¡No es nada! —le dije haciéndome el valiente.

No acababa de pronunciar la última palabra cuando hubo un silencio terrible. Nos asustamos mucho. Apenas podíamos escuchar nuestra respiración. Pronto oímos los arañazos otra vez. Me destapé un ojo y eché una mirada hacia la ventana. Vi un fantasma. Algo se movía de un lado al otro. No sé qué sería. Esta vez yo le piqué las costillas a Adancito y le dije en voz baja.

—¡Mira! Se ve algo en la ventana. Te apuesto que es el Coco.

—¿Quieres que me asome? ¿Qué crees que soy tonto, como tú? —respondió él.

—¡Anda! Mira por la ventana si no me crees. Tú que te crees tan hombrote.

Adancito levantó la almohada y miró por un huequito de la funda. No oyó arañazos, pero sí vio que algo se movía despacito.

De repente, se quitó la sábana porque el calor no se aguantaba. Empezó a reír y a brincar en la cama como una marioneta. No paraba de reír.

—¡Ja, ja, ja, ja! ¿Sabes lo que es? —dijo Adancito mientras sus palabras iban y venían—. Es el burro de Tío Samuel. Anda suelto. Ya sabes que le gusta asomarse por las ventanas dondequiera que ve luz.

—¡Un burro! ¡Ja, ja, ja, ja! Tú eres el burro. Lo único que te falta son las orejas largas. Además, ¿qué luz hay aquí? La luz está en la cocina, tonto —le dije queriendo desquitarme por haberme insultado antes.

—¡Cállense! ¿Quieren que entre Papá y les caliente las nalgas con el cinturón? —advirtió Mamá, pero sabíamos que no era más que un truco, porque Papá nunca nos pegaba.

En ese momento oí que la puerta de alambre de la cocina rechinó, pero fingí no haberla oído. Parecía que Adancito no había oído nada tampoco. Los arañazos en la ventana se escucharon de nuevo. Adancito se quedó callado otra vez, mientras yo fingí esconderme debajo de la cama.

Me escabullí de la recámara y salí de la casa. En la oscuridad, doblé la primera esquina de la casa. Después me detuve en la segunda esquina y contuve la respiración. Miré con mucho cuidado hacia la ventana. Oí los arañazos y ruidos. Poco a poco pude ver con luz que venía de la lámpara de aceite en la cocina.

Estuve a punto de reírme, pero me detuve a tiempo. ¡El Coco era Papá! Rasguñaba la tela de la ventana con la escoba y después la movía suavecito de izquierda a derecha y de derecha a izquierda, como un limpiaparabrisas.

Como a la tercera vez que Papá rasguñó la ventana, doblé por completo la segunda esquina y

me paré detrás de él, sin que me viera o oyera. Me acerqué mucho. ¡Bien cerquita! Él se inclinó y dobló despacito las rodillas. Tenía la ventana frente a él, y una vez más hizo el ruido "¡Juuuut, juut, juuuut!" Volvió a rasguñar la ventana con la escoba.

En ese mismo instante le pegué en las nalgas. En cuanto lo toqué dio un grito, saltó para adelante y se dio un porrazo con el marco de la ventana.

Corrí lo más calladito que pude hacia la cocina y entré en silencio hasta la recámara.

—¿Viste al Coco? —preguntó Adancito cuando me sintió en la cama— Oí un ruido en la ventana.

Antes de que le pudiera contestar, escuché que se abrió la puerta de la cocina.

—¡Santo Dios! ¿Cómo te diste ese golpe? ¿Qué te pasó? —preguntó Mamá cuando Papá se sentó a la mesa. Papá no dijo ni pío.

Vi por un agujero en el tabique de madera que separaba la cocina del cuarto de dormir que Mamá se tapaba la boca con la mano derecha. No aguantaba la risa.

Papá se pasaba una toallita mojada por la frente para ver si se le bajaba el chichón. No decía nada, sólo miraba el suelo de la cocina. No se sabía si estaba avergonzado, humillado o las dos cosas. Esa misma noche Papá acabó con la historia del Coco y Adancito y yo jamás volvimos a oír de él.

UN TESORO ENTERRADO

Abuelita Cinda y yo acabamos de almorzar y nos pusimos a limpiar la mesa para jugar, antes de mi siesta. Normalmente jugábamos a las cartas, a la ruleta con palitos de fósforos o a las adivinanzas.

Yo nunca sabía cómo me iba a sorprender Abuelita Cinda, o si tenía algún truco bajo la manga. Los veranos con ella nunca eran aburridos, estaba llena de sorpresas. Además, hacía muchas cosas para mantenerme contento ya que le preocupaba que me aburriera lejos de mi familia. Todo lo contrario, ella era muy chistosa y bastante divertida.

—Bueno, hijito. ¿Estás listo?

—Sí. ¿Qué vamos a hacer hoy? —le pregunté.

—Ah, ¡te tengo una sorpresa! Vamos a hacer algo diferente.

Nos sentamos juntitos en la mesa, y yo creí que íbamos a jugar, pero me equivoqué. Me dio una botella de refresco vacía y un par de mis calcetines rotos. La idea era enseñarme a remendar calcetines. Primero puso el calcetín sobre el fondo de la botella. Después, apoyándose en la botella empezó a remendar el calcetín. Fue mágico. Al principio

batallé, pero Abuelita Cinda me enseñó a detener la botella entre las piernas. Entonces fue fácil meter y sacar la aguja y el hilo en el calcetín sin picarme los dedos. Mientras cosía mis calcetines, mi abuelita bordaba un trapo para los platos.

—Bueno, hijito. Ya es hora de tu siesta —dijo Abuelita Cinda después de verme cabecear un par de veces.

La seguí a la pequeña recámara. En casa, Mamá me hacía dormir la siesta debajo de la cama para no destenderla. Podía oír la voz de Mamá en mi cabeza: "La cama es para dormir de noche, no de día". En casa de Abuelita Cinda estaba mimado. Ella me permitía dormir la siesta en la cama, pero yo siempre tenía mucho cuidado y la arreglaba al levantarme.

—Cambié de idea, hijito. La siesta puede esperar. ¿Te gustaría escuchar un cuento? —preguntó con sus ojos brillantes. Me quedé sorprendido. Ella nunca me había contado un cuento antes de la siesta. Por la noche, sí, pero nunca por la tarde.

—Claro que sí —le dije sin pensarlo.

—¿Qué tipo de cuento te gustaría escuchar?

—No tengo la menor idea, Abuelita —le respondí.

Por la noche, me contaba cuentos de brujas y fantasmas.

—Bueno, te ayudo —añadió ella—. ¿Qué te parece uno del Coco, la Llorona o algo de tecolotes? No, no, no —murmuró, inmediatamente contestando su pregunta—. Esos son cuentos para la hora de acostarte. Ahora se trata de contar cuentos para antes

de la siesta. ¿Qué te parece un cuento de algo mágico, o de tesoros enterrados?

—¡Tesoros enterrados! —dije de buenas a primeras, sin pensar.

—Bueno, aquí va. Escucha bien.

—Abuelita Cinda, ¿cómo se llama el cuento? —pregunté antes de que ella empezara.

—Se llama: "Un tesoro enterrado".

Yo había escuchado, no hacía mucho tiempo, a un grupo de viejitos que estaban en casa de mi abuelito cuando hablaban de luces que aparecían en casas abandonadas y de que había oro enterrado en las cocinas o debajo de las chimeneas. Por eso estaba ansioso por escuchar el cuento de Abuelita Cinda.

Me senté bien derechito. No quería quedarme dormido. Abuelita Cinda se sentó a mi lado. No tenía un libro, ni nada. Además, no sabía leer porque nunca fue a la escuela. Tenía todos sus cuentos en la cabeza.

—Hace mucho tiempo en un pueblito que se llamaba San Miguel en la Sierra Nacimiento, donde nació tu mamá, había un volcán. La gente lo llamaba El Copete. Subir a la cumbre requería mucho esfuerzo, aunque fueras joven.

—¿Abuelita Cinda, alguna vez escaló el volcán? —dije interrumpiéndola.

—¡Claro que sí, hijito! Pero hace muchos, muchos años, cuando tenía piernas fuertes y no temblorosas como gelatina. Pero nunca subí hasta la cumbre.

—¿Por qué no, Abuelita Cinda?

—Eso viene más tarde, ¿de acuerdo? Vamos a continuar el cuento antes de que se me olvide —dijo guiñéndome un ojo.

—El Copete ha estado dormido por miles, posiblemente millones de años. Pero ¿sabes qué?

—¿Qué, Abuelita Cinda? —dije antes de que terminara la oración.

—¡Pum! —exclamó y me picó el estómago como picaba la masa de las tortillas cuando estaba de buen humor—. Te aseguro que cuando el volcán eruptaba, lo hacía con tanta fuerza que la tierra se estremecía, los venados, coyotes y las liebres se espantaban y salían corriendo para salvarse. Seguramente la lava corría como aceite rojo y espeso por el volcán, iluminando el cielo del pueblito por la noche. Tiene que haber sido algo muy espantoso y al mismo tiempo espectacular.

—San Miguel era chiquito cuando tu mamá y yo vivíamos allí; no había más de veinte o treinta personas. Los cuentos sobre El Copete eran más numerosos que la gente que vivía allí y a su alrededor. Uno de los más populares es que hay un tesoro escondido en el fondo del cráter. Dicen que en un tiempo el volcán echaba chispas por la noche y que la cumbre relumbraba a causa del oro que había al fondo. Sí, oíste bien, ¡oro! Como el oro que tiene tu abuelito en los dos dientes frontales.

—Nadie sabía exactamente cómo o cuándo empezó el cuento del tesoro enterrado, pero una cosa sí se sabía: Muchos hombres valientes de San Miguel, en diferentes ocasiones, habían tratado de subir a la cumbre del volcán para ver si había oro o no, pero cada vez, cuanto más se acercaban a la cumbre, se sentía un ruido muy intenso. No lo aguantaban. Tampoco sabían de dónde venía. Así

que, uno por uno, se rindieron, sin confirmar si había oro enterrado. Y quién sabe, pero se dice que había que subir de noche, no de día. Con el tiempo, los cuentos sobre El Copete continuaron y se extendieron más allá de nuestro pueblito.

—Un día llegó un desconocido a San Miguel por la tarde, cuando el sol se apagaba detrás de la Sierra Nacimiento. Los niños, que normalmente notaban algo nuevo, cuando vieron al desconocido salieron corriendo a avisarle a sus padres. En el pueblo, no tardaron en saber el motivo por el cual el hombre se encontraba ahí. ¡Había venido por el tesoro enterrado en El Copete! Aseguraba que sería la primera y última persona que pondría las manos en el oro, en caso de que lo hubiera. También había decidido acabar con todos los cuentos sobre el volcán. Esto sí que sorprendió a todo San Miguel porque ya hacía mucho tiempo que se escuchaban los cuentos.

—El hombre caminaba por el único camino que cruzaba el pueblito con mucha confianza. Daba pisotazos en la tierra, y movía los brazos hacia atrás y hacia adelante cuando se dirigía al volcán. El hombre era bajo y gordito, y cargaba una mochila sobre el hombro derecho. No decía ni una palabra. Seguía andando con una mirada de confianza en la cara.

—"No todo lo que relumbra es oro, amigo", se oyó la voz rasposa de un anciano que estaba detrás de una puerta de tela de alambre. El anciano reconoció al extraño, era León Lovato, y venía de un lugarcito que se llamaba El Azufre, a unas millas de San Miguel.

—Cuanto más caminaba, más crecía el número de gente que lo seguía como vacas que iban al agua, especialmente las mujeres y los niños. Hasta unos perros se unieron al desfile.

—Abuelita Cinda, ¿y los hombres?

—Los hombres tenían tanta curiosidad como los demás. La mayoría creía que León Lovato estaba chiflado porque quería subir a la cumbre del volcán de noche y más con luna llena.

—Ya el sol había desaparecido detrás de las colinas y las montañas, pero la gente siguió caminando hasta llegar al pie de El Copete, siguiendo a León Lovato. Allí pararon.

—¿Te gusta el cuento hasta ahora, hijito? —preguntó Abuelita Cinda aunque sabía que me gustaba.

—Sí, me gusta mucho. ¿Podemos continuar? —pregunté ansioso. Ya quería saber qué había pasado con León Lovato.

Antes de seguir, Abuelita Cinda me dijo —Ve a traerme agua de la cocina. Tengo la boca seca.

Me apuré, y por poco tropiezo con una jerga cuando le traía el vaso de agua. Regresé con el agua y me paré delante de ella con los brazos cruzados hasta que tomó el último trago.

—¿Estás listo para continuar, o ya te estás cansando? —preguntó ella.

—Estoy listo —respondí.

—Al pie de El Copete, León Lovato paró por un momento, mientras todo el mundo veía ansioso qué iba a hacer ahora. Metió la mano derecha en el

bolsillo derecho de los pantalones, y sacó una bola de algodón. Cortó dos motitas y se puso una en cada oído. Luego abrió la mochila, sacó una bufanda y se la amarró alrededor de la cabeza para protegerse los oídos y amortiguar el ruido del volcán.

—Entonces comenzó a subir despacio. La gente se preguntaba hasta dónde podría subir, y cuándo se daría por vencido, así como los otros hombres que habían intentado subir al volcán. La luna llena estaba grande y redonda, e iluminaba el volcán. Cuanto más alto subía, más era el ruido de El Copete, pero León Lovato era un hombre valiente. No se iba a rendir. Además, traía consigo una estatuilla de San Antonio, el santo que ayuda a encontrar cosas perdidas. Pero había un problema.

—¿Cuál era el problema, Abuelita Cinda?

—León Lovato buscaba un tesoro escondido, no algo que él había perdido. De todos modos, siguió escalando poco a poco. El ruido empezaba a molestarle. Se sentía el zumbido de mil remolinos o tormentas de polvo en medio del desierto. Parecía que se le iban a reventar los oídos y que la cabeza iba a partírsele a la mitad. Hasta parecía que los ojos se le iban a salir de las cuencas. Era una cosa horrible, pero Lovato no iba a parar. Subía y subía, mientras la gente veía todo desde abajo sorprendida. Creían que o era muy valiente, o estaba loco. Nunca había subido nadie tan alto. Estaba un tanto cansado, no tanto por la subida, ya que él tenía una buena condición física, sino por el horrible ruido. Por fin llegó a la cumbre de El Copete. Se sentó, contento de poder respirar un poco.

—Se quitó la mochila del hombro y sacó una lintera de aceite. Sacó un fósforo de su bolsillo y prendió la mecha de la lintera, avivando la llama lo más posible para que la brisa de la montaña no la apagara. Ató una cuerda al asa. Poco a poco, fue bajando la linterna con la cuerda.

—Ya en estos momentos el ruido que venía del fondo del pozo lo estaba volviendo loco. Empezó a temblar. Sintió algo raro en los oídos, como si le hicieran cosquillas unos gusanos. De pronto, sintió que el mundo daba vueltas. Sintió que el volcán daba vueltas a su alrededor, y pensó: "¿Será que Dios me está castigando por haberme traído a San Antonio?"

—Cuando ya no pudo bajar la linterna más, se asomó con mucho cuidado otra vez. No podía creer lo que veía y oía. "¡¡Me engañan estos ojos?!" gritó. Su voz temblaba, y las palabras hacían eco en el viento.

—La gente al pie del volcán oyó el eco, e inmediatamente sospechó que algo horrible había pasado. Lo que vio, no fue un tesoro enterrado lleno de oro.

—¿Qué vio, Abuela Cinda? ¿Qué vio?

—Era todo lo contrario, era un pozo lleno de miles de serpientes de cascabel, todas ellas arrastrándose, serpenteando y chocando unas contra otras. ¡León estaba asustadísimo! Era una escena espantosa, como del infierno. De allí venía el ruido y no del oro que imaginaba la gente. "Esto es lo que me gano por haber cedido a la tentación", dijo entre dientes, y se dejó caer. Se recuperó después de unos minutos y empezó a bajar del volcán. La gente estaba al pie de

El Copete. Todos se preguntaban, ¿qué habrá pasado? ¿qué habrá visto? León Lovato parecía atontado. Sus ojos, como de vidrio, veían hacia adelante y a la distancia. Ni se daba cuenta que lo observaban. León se marchó de San Miguel en silencio.

—Abuelita Cinda, ¿qué le pasó a León Lovato? —le pregunté.

—Se dice, hijito, que se volvió completamente loco. Hay gente que cree que León Lovato se volvió loco por su avaricia, o por el desconsuelo de no haber encontrado un tesoro enterrado. O tal vez fuera una combinación de avaricia y desconsuelo. Jamás sabremos. Otros dicen que perdió la cabeza a causa del ruidazo de El Copete.

—Una cosa sí sabemos, hijito. Las palabras del sabio anciano que le advirtió a León Lovato que "no todo lo que brilla es oro", resultaron siendo verdad.

—¿Y cómo sabía eso el anciano del pueblito, Abuelita Cinda?

—Ay, hijito mío, es curioso que me preguntes. El viejo era don Faustino. Murió hace unos años a la edad de 109. Cuando tenía veintitantos años subió una noche hasta la cumbre de El Copete. Nadie lo vio. Subió solo, y descubrió el pozo lleno de serpientes de cascabel. Pero guardó el secreto por mucho tiempo hasta que se lo contó a una persona, nada más.

—¿A quién, Abuelita Cinda?

—¡A tu abuelito Manuel! Don Faustino lo quería mucho, de manera que le dijo el secreto bajo una condición: Tu abuelito no debía decirle a nadie, ni

siquiera a mí, hasta que no muriera don Faustino. Abuelito en aquellos tiempos era joven. ¿Y sabes qué?

—¿Qué, Abuelita Cinda?

—Abuelito Manuel me dijo el secreto a mí antes de que tú nacieras. Mira, hijito, tú eres la primera persona a quien le he dicho este secreto, de manera que ahora te toca a ti guardar el secreto, ¿de acuerdo?

—De acuerdo, Abuelita Cinda—le dije y me fui a la recámara a dormir la siesta.

RUIDO DE CADENAS

Se dice que El Coruco es un lugar encantado donde se escuchaban cadenas y aparecían brujas y fantasmas por la noche. Aunque El Coruco está situado entre mi placita y mi casa, yo pasaba por ahí con frecuencia pero solamente de día. ¡Nunca de noche!

Una tarde, después de la cena, fui a platicar con Abuelito Lolo. Estaba solo porque Abuelita Lale se había ido a Alburquerque. Toqué a la puerta de la cocina y entré. Él estaba cenando.

—Entra, entra, Junie. Ya casi acabo de cenar. ¿Quieres un bizcochito que hizo Abuelita Lale antes de irse a la ciudad?

—¡Cómo no! —respondí. Me encantaban las galletas de anís y canela de mi abuelita.

Abuelito Lolo me pasó la lata en la que Abuelita Lale guardaba los bizcochitos. Tomé uno, y comencé a comérmelo. De pronto se me ocurrió preguntarle sobre El Coruco, era el momento perfecto. Después de todo, él conocía la región mejor que nadie. Y si sabía algo de El Coruco, seguramente me lo diría. Así era él. Siempre trataba de enseñarle algo nuevo a sus nietos.

—Ven, toma otro bizcochito —dijo Abuelito Lolo, entregándome la lata mientras él comía lo que quedaba de su guiso de cordero.

—Abuelito Lolo —le dije—, ¿es verdad que se puede oír ruido de cadenas en El Coruco cuando uno pasa por allí de noche? Mis compañeros en la escuela dicen que el lugar está embrujado, y que por la noche salen fantasmas y brujas. ¿Sabe si es cierto?

—Pues, te diré —contestó Abuelito Lolo con una voz lenta—. En mi vida he oído un montón de cuentos acerca de El Coruco. Primero, ¿sabes lo que quiere decir "coruco"?

Moví la cabeza, como diciendo que no.

—Es una chinche. Por qué fue que nombraron a El Coruco así no lo comprendo. Pero ése es otro cuento. Como tú bien sabes, hoy ya no vive gente en El Coruco. Es como un pueblo fantasma. No vivía mucha gente allí antes de que fuera abandonado. Cuando pases por allí, obsérvalo bien. Todavía se pueden ver las ruinas de tres o cinco casas, máximo. Son una mezcla de piedra y adobe. Dos de las casas que están casi completamente destruidas están a un lado del camino, junto a dos árboles que tienen flores color de rosa que milagrosamente florecen en el verano. Hay dos casas más, creo que sí son dos, están un poco retiradas del camino, pero están en mejores condiciones. Las colinas las protegen del viento del oeste. Las paredes todavía están paradas. De esas dos casas, una está cerca de la cascada, atrás de El Coruco.

—Se dice que en esa casa es donde Bruja Maruja se reúne con otras brujas por la noche. Hay gente que dice que ha visto luces después de que se

oscurece, aunque la casa fue abandonada hace ya mucho tiempo.

— ¿Cómo lo sabe, Abuelito?

— Como tú sabes, el Río Puerco corre a una corta distancia, al sur de El Coruco. Al otro lado del río, arriba de La Loma, vivían varias familias hace mucho tiempo. Casi todos allí tenían un cuento que contar sobre El Coruco. En alguna ocasión habían visto luces cerca de la cascada, mucho después de que la casa fue abandonada.

— ¿De verdad, Abuelito Lolo?

— Bueno, una noche un hombre, Natividad era su nombre porque había nacido durante la Navidad, vio una luz y decidió ir a ver qué pasaba. Quería saber si existían las brujas, y si se reunían en esa casa. Les dijo a varias personas, incluso a su familia en La Loma, lo que iba a hacer. De manera que se fue en su caballo, Bole. Natividad bajó por el Río Puerco y lo cruzó cerca de su casa. Tomó el camino que está al lado de un grupo de mesas que van a dar a El Coruco. No muy a lo lejos pudo ver una luz en la casa. Cuanto más se acercaba a la casa, más brillante la luz.

— Natividad empezó a sentir comezón detrás del cuello, y por toda la espina dorsal, pero siguió caminando. Hasta pensó haber oído una lechuza en una de las mesas. Algunas personas creían que las lechuzas eran brujas, pero Natividad no sabía si creerlo o no. Él tenía sus dudas.

— De repente sintió que algo malo pasaba, porque Bole comenzó a actuar extrañamente: estornuda, resoplaba y movía la cabeza. Por un momento breve, Natividad pensó que Bole había

dejado de respirar, pero eran tonterías que se le metieron en la cabeza. Entretanto, vio que la luz había desaparecido. Cuando llegó a El Coruco, amarró el caballo en uno de los árboles con flores color de rosa y caminó a la casa.

—Cada vez más, todo aquello le parecía espantoso. Se le puso la piel de gallina y el pelo de punta. Estaba espantado, pero ya era muy tarde para volver atrás. Al acercarse a la casa, oyó la voz de una mujer. "¿Qué haces por acá a estas horas?" gimió y Natividad se quedó tieso. "Ah, hombre tonto, ¿cómo puedes haber sido tan estúpido y venir acá solo? ¿Qué no sabes quién soy yo? Soy un espíritu andante en busca de almas como la tuya, para llevármelas al purgatorio. Pero, ¿sabes qué? estoy dispuesta a negociar contigo".

—"Yo no negocio con brujas como tú, Bruja Maruja", le respondió Natividad, mientras caminaba hacia los árboles, donde había dejado a su caballo.

—"Ah, tonto. Pronunciaste las palabras mágicas. ¡Yo soy la Bruja Maruja!" dijo y su voz se desvaneció.

—De buenas a primeras, la luz reapareció en la casa y brillaba más y más. Poco a poco empezó a salir por una de las ventanas de al lado. De repente, la luz comenzó a moverse despacio sobre el suelo. Empezaba a cobrar fuerza. Natividad seguía viendo hacia atrás mientras caminaba hacia su caballo. La luz estaba creciendo y se movía cada vez más rápido. Según iba tomando velocidad, se convertía en una bola de lumbre que se dirigía directamente a Natividad y Bole.

—Espantado, y fuera de sí, corrió y montó su caballo y adiós. ¡Se fueron! Al principio, el caballo iba con trote rápido, pero luego comenzó a trotar más y más de prisa. Natividad tenía tanto miedo que no se atrevía ni a voltear. Por fin, sin poder resistir más la tentación, echó un vistazo. La bola de lumbre había crecido e iba por medio del camino moviéndose con más rapidez, saltando de arriba hacia abajo. La lumbre casi alcanzaba a Natividad y Bole. Natividad le picó con las espuelas a su caballo.

—Bole ya iba galopando a buen paso. Se podían oír y sentir las pezuñas pegar en la tierra. Aunque estaba bastante oscuro, la bola de lumbre, irónicamente, le ayudaba ver mejor el camino a Natividad. Sin darse cuenta, ¡pum! la bola de lumbre casi los pesca, lo cual hizo al caballo relinchar y dar patadas. Natividad que ya se moría de espanto, picaba más al caballo con las espuelas y al mismo tiempo le daba con el látigo. A él nunca lo había perseguido una bola de lumbre.

—Natividad ansiaba llegar a casa, pero primero tenía que cruzar el Río Puerco. Como tenía que bajar para llegar al cauce del río antes de cruzar, jaló las riendas para que el caballo aminorara el paso. Le dio miedo de que Bole perdiera el equilibrio y se volcara. Claro que esto le dio una oportunidad a la bola de lumbre para alcanzarlos. Ya la bola de lumbre estaba bien, bien cerca; casi le quemaba la cola al caballo. Cuando la bola de lumbre los alcanzó, a unos pies del río, tocó las patas traseras de Bole. En ese instante, Bole brincó hacia adelante como un cohete y cayó en las aguas del río. Natividad se agarró bien fuerte. El caballo cayó en el

agua y salpicó con tal fuerza que la bola de lumbre se apagó. ¡No más fuego! ¡El río había salvado a Natividad!

—De pronto, Natividad oyó una desesperada voz que venía de las fuertes aguas. Desafortunadamente, la bruja todavía estaba viva.

—"¡Socorro, socorro! ¡Me estoy ahogando!" rogaba la bruja, dando manotazos en el agua.

—"¡Ahógate, ahógate, Bruja Maruja! Para que sepas que las llamas del infierno no se comparan con las aguas del cielo," gritó Natividad y desapareció en la oscuridad camino a su casa.

—La esposa de Natividad lo esperaba en casa así como algunos vecinos. Todos habían estado observando lo ocurrido desde La Loma. Natividad se apeó del caballo todavía un poco mareado. Lo único que podía decir era: "¡Una bola . . . lumbre . . . lumbre . . . !" y se desmayó. Pronto su esposa cogió una botellita de sales aromáticas que guardaba en casa. El fuerte olor lo despertó, y, aunque estaba cansado, les contó lo que había pasado.

—Hijito —dijo mi abuelo—, oí ese cuento hace muchos años, pero hay muchos otros que tratan de El Coruco.

—¿Y las cadenas, Abuelito Lolo?

—Ah, dejemos ese cuento para otra ocasión, tal vez para mañana.

—Pero, Abuelito Lolo, mañana regresa Abuelita Lale.

—Ah, es verdad. Está bien, haremos esto . . .

—¿Qué?—exclamé, ansioso de escuchar lo que iba a proponer.

—Se está oscureciendo. Ve a casa y pregúntale a tu mamá si puedes quedarte un rato más. Entretanto, yo pienso en un buen cuento.

No acababa de pronunciar la última palabra, cuando salí volando de la cocina, dándole un golpe a la puerta. Cuando menos pensé ya estaba de vuelta.

—Junie, pon esos platos en el trastero mientras preparo café.

Después de que Abuelito Lolo preparó el café y se sirvió una taza, nos sentamos a la mesa. Estaba listo para escuchar su cuento.

—Abuelito Lolo, ¿cómo se llama el cuento que me va a contar?

—¿Quién sabe? —dijo con una sonrisa—. Éste es el cuento de un hombre que se llamaba Juan Algodones. Ése no era su apellido verdadero. La gente lo llamaba así porque nació en un lugarcito al sur de Santa Fe que tenía el mismo nombre. Hace mucho tiempo que él se había mudado con su familia a este valle, donde vivimos ahora. Juan vivía en un lugar que se llamaba Santa Clara, no muy lejos de Ojo del Padre.

—Una noche, cuando Juan volvía a casa montado en su burro Achaque después de visitar a un amigo en los Altos . . .

—¿Acha . . . que? —pregunté

—"Achaque" quiere decir excusa. Para Juan Algodones era como decir que su burro siempre tenía una excusa para no moverse de prisa. De todos modos, ya era tarde, pero no pasaba de la medianoche. Era una noche fresca de verano, y las

estrellas parpadeaban y bailaban en el cielo. Juan podía ver que la Osa Mayor lo veía desde arriba del cielo oscuro lleno de miles de estrellas. Juan estaba fascinado con la naturaleza. La luna llena aumentaba su alegría.

—Al acercarse a El Coruco notó que una estrella se movía rápidamente atravesando el cielo. Al principio pensó que era una estrella fugaz. Él había visto estrellas fugaces antes que se movían mucho más rápido y normalmente se apagaban al acercarse a la tierra. Esta estrella se movía mucho más despacio.

—¿Cómo un avión? —pregunté.

—No, hijito. En aquel entonces no había aviones. Bueno, Juan Algodones vio la luz del otro lado del Río Puerco, donde había vivido don Natividad. Te acuerdas de él, ¿no?—preguntó Abuelito.

—Sí, vivía en una loma.

—Así es. ¿Recuerdas que Natividad cruzó el río cuando la bola de lumbre lo perseguía? Pues es el mismo lugar en donde la luz atravesó para este lado del Río Puerco.

—Bien. Juan Algodones sabía de El Coruco. Había oído un montón de cuentos acerca de las cadenas ruidosas, brujas y todo ese tipo de cosa pero nunca había visto algo así. Por lo que sospechó algo, y siguió observando la luz a medida que se movía por el aire después de haber cruzado el río. Parecía que la luz iba más despacio mientras Juan avanzaba por el único camino para llegar a su casa. La luna ya estaba encima de El Coruco, iluminando el camino de Juan. En ese momento, decidió hacer algo.

—¿Qué, Abuelito Lolo?

—¡Iba a atrapar la luz!

—¿Atrapar la luz? ¿Y cómo iba a hacer eso, Abuelito Lolo?

—Ah, hijito. Ésta es la parte fascinante y divertida del cuento. Pon mucha atención. Para las orejas como un burro y no pierdas ni una palabra para que puedas contarles el cuento a tus compañeros de clase cuando comience la escuela.

—Verás, llamarse Juan o Juana, era algo especial, y no había comunidad que no tuviera un Juan o una Juana. Los "Juanes" nacían dotados con poderes especiales, que nadie más tenía. Uno de los poderes era el de atrapar brujas, y eso es lo que Juan Algodones pensaba hacer. Estaba convencido que la luz era una bruja que iba de regreso a su casa. Quién sabe. Tal vez la bruja había estado lejos de casa durante la noche, haciendo sus maldades o causando daño a algún inocente.

—De cualquier manera, después que la luz pasó el Río Puerco, y Juan Algodones vio que se dirigía a El Coruco, se apuró. Al llegar a El Coruco, oyó un ruidito. Creyó que oía el ruido de cadenas que se arrastraban. Sin embargo, había llovido el día antes, y lo que oyó era el agua de la cascada cercana.

—Pronto se apeó de Achaque, que se había asustado un poco, como que sospechaba algo malo. Después de amarrarlo a un poste, Juan Algodones caminó unos cuantos pies al camino. Con el látigo hizo un círculo grande en la tierra. Luego se quitó la camisa y la camiseta. Agarró la camiseta, la volteó al revés y la echó en medio del círculo. Volvió hacia

donde estaba su burro, y los dos se fueron a la casa abandonada que estaba más cerca, pero lejos del círculo. De repente, la luz apareció de nuevo en el cielo, detrás de unas lomas y descendió en medio del círculo. ¡En ese momento Juan supo que había atrapado una bruja! Como buen Juan, había demostrado su poder mágico. Cuando la bruja descendió y sus pies tocaron la tierra, se escuchó un estrépito horrible. Era como el ruido de cadenas, tal como lo había escuchado en los cuentos.

—¿Y qué pasó?—pregunté ansioso por saber el resultado.

—Cuando Juan Algodones se acercó al círculo, se encontró a una mujer agachada, como si temblara de miedo. Iba vestida de negro, con un velo que le cubría la cabeza. No se le podía ver la cara. Pero la cosa más rara era una cadena que llevaba a la cintura. Parecía un cinturón. Le colgaba a un lado y cuando ella se movía, la cadena hacía un ruido. En ese momento, Juan Algodones notó, gracias a la brillante luna, la cosa más extraña que había visto en su vida.

—¿Qué, Abuelito Lolo?

—La cadena parecía un rosario grandote. Los eslabones de la cadena parecían las cuentas de un rosario, pero cada eslabón tenía una cara humana grotesca. Juan Algodones estaba convencido y bien seguro de que había atrapado auna bruja.

—¿Qué hizo con la bruja? ¿La soltó?

—Hijito, la bruja no era capaz de nada. Juan Algodones, gracias a sus poderes mágicos, pudo atraparla. Mientras ella estuviera dentro del círculo no podía escaparse. Era la prisionera de Juan, su

poder era demasiado para ella. La bruja le rogó, casi hasta lloró, implorando que la soltara.

— "Por favor, le ruego que me suelte. Le puedo pagar. El dinero para mí no es un problema. Dígame cuánto y se lo doy".

— "Eso no será necesario. Yo no necesito su dinero sucio", dijo Juan Algodones. "La dejo irse si promete no regresar jamás a El Coruco".

— La bruja aceptó, y Juan Algodones rompió el círculo con el pie derecho.

— Pero, Abuelito Lolo, ¿por qué con el pie derecho?

— Porque el pie derecho, en este caso, simbolizaba algo bueno, un tipo de triunfo, mientras que el pie izquierdo representaba algo malo. Juan Algodones era muy inteligente y no iba a ser víctima de aquella bruja. Cuando rompió el círculo, las cadenas hicieron un estrépito, como el batir de un montón de pájaros y la bruja desapareció en el cielo. Juan Algonodes se fue a su casa en Santa Clara.

— ¡Vaya! ¡Qué cuento más bueno! Ya quiero contárselo a mis compañeros de clase.

— Bueno, se está haciendo tarde. Anda a casa — me dijo Abuelito Lolo haciendo un gesto con la mano derecha —, pero cuidado con esas luces que se mueven. ¡A lo mejor son brujas! — añadió con una sonrisa.